DEAD
OF
SUMMER

ALSO BY JESSA MAXWELL

I Need You to Read This

The Golden Spoon

DEAD
OF
SUMMER

A Novel

JESSA MAXWELL

ATRIA BOOKS

New York Amsterdam/Antwerp London
Toronto Sydney/Melbourne New Delhi

ATRIA
BOOKS

An Imprint of Simon & Schuster, LLC
1230 Avenue of the Americas
New York, NY 10020

First Atria Books hardcover edition July 2025

ATRIA BOOKS and colophon are trademarks of Simon & Schuster, LLC

Simon & Schuster strongly believes in freedom of expression and stands against censorship in all its forms. For more information, visit BooksBelong.com.

For information about special discounts for bulk purchases, please contact Simon & Schuster Special Sales at 1-866-506-1949 or business@simonandschuster.com.

The Simon & Schuster Speakers Bureau can bring authors to your live event. For more information or to book an event, contact the Simon & Schuster Speakers Bureau at 1-866-248-3049 or visit our website at www.simonspeakers.com.

Interior design by Jill Putorti

Manufactured in the United States of America

1 3 5 7 9 10 8 6 4 2

Library of Congress Cataloging-in-Publication Data has been applied for.

ISBN 978-1-6680-7039-0
ISBN 978-1-6680-7041-3 (ebook)

To my island girls, Liz, Jess, and Lindsay

PROLOGUE

She hears a scream before she hits the water. Hers? Someone else's? It doesn't matter—it is quickly swallowed up in the roar of the waves. Even though it's July, the bay this far offshore is shockingly cold. And dark. Instinctively, she tries to paddle. She slips under.

She kicks herself back up, relieved to break the surface, gulping air while the waves crest and glow in the starlight.

She looks toward shore at the lights on that magnificent lawn. The party is in full swing now. The sounds large enough to carry across the surface. The thrum of conversation and the band playing a final raucous tune. She screams again, but her single voice is no match for the open ocean.

She turns as her whole body rises on a swell, looking for something, anything. But she only finds churning darkness. She is growing heavier with each passing second. Her kicks can't keep her head above the waves much longer. Panic crawls up her legs and she starts to thrash. Bad idea. Her lungs burn for more oxygen. She descends.

Up, gasping for breath. *Down*, heavy quiet. *Up*, now facing the other way she can see the outline of the Rock in the distance. The house is sinister in the dark, its stilts spindly like a spider's legs. A dim light shines from one of the windows. Could she make it there? She kicks harder but a wave rushes over her, hitting the back of her head and pushing her under.

Down, this time the water fills her nose. Her heart roars in the murky black. Then a light, suddenly wavering above her. She pushes toward it, breaks the surface, but it vanishes, leaving her alone in the dark again. She kicks and kicks no longer knowing which way is which. Her chest aches. A roar fills her eardrums.

She had so many plans.

But what good are plans when you're dead?

Part One

THE ROCK

FAITH

The ring box was hidden deep in his suitcase, in the folds of a light blue James Perse shirt. Faith Ellis's stomach twists as she picks up the little velvet dust bag stamped with curved gold font: Cartier.

The shower is going in the en suite and she tiptoes over to it, peeking around the bathroom door to be sure he can't see her. Through the fogged glass she can make out the tanned blur of David's back. She's safe for now. He'll stand like that for a while, his head bowed, letting the water pour over him. The shower is his "thinking time." Faith dashes back to the suitcase and slides the ring box out of the dust bag. It is red and angular with a little gold button on the front. She pushes on it, her heart thrumming, and the top flips open, revealing a massive marquise-cut diamond. She sucks in her breath and picks it up delicately between her fingers. The band is composed of a row of smaller diamonds so perfectly clear they look like tiny mirrors. A ring like this could probably pay for someone's college tuition. Faith resists the urge to try it on, imagining the horror of it getting stuck and having to fess up to David that she'd pawed through his things.

She peers down into the many glimmering facets of the stone, her face refracted in icy light. Even though she is pleasantly surprised, she isn't shocked. She'd had a feeling this was coming. David had eyed the suitcase the whole journey to the island.

"*I'll* get that," he'd said, snatching it away when the driver tried lifting it into the trunk of the Mercedes on the way to the airport, keeping it next to him in the back seat instead. It stayed with him on the Clarke private jet as well, as if someone could steal it there. Finally, Faith noted with growing anticipation that when they arrived at the house—though *house* is not really the proper way to describe David Clarke's childhood summer home; *Mansion? Villa? Estate?*—he made sure to bring the suitcase up to the bedroom himself, not allowing it to be taken up by the staff with the other luggage.

A little out of character for David, but Faith has had a premonition that he was going to propose for a while now. There had been something about the way he treated her the past few months, a shift in how he has been looking at her. It has been different from those very early days, when she could tell he was appreciating her mostly for her appearance. She hadn't been bothered by it. Attraction is important and she has never had any qualms about playing it up—a woman has to use every tool at her disposal, especially someone like Faith who came from so little. And she enjoys feeling pretty, relishes the attention and the rush of knowing someone is attracted to her. But these days David looks at her squarely in the eye, like they are partners. And she finds that she likes that even more.

The change is also evident in the way she's overheard him talking about her, on the phone casually turning down plans with the guys at work, the ones she knows he used to go out drinking with. These are finance guys, real boy's boys, and she enjoys hearing him reject them. "I can't. Faith and I have something that night." It is also the way he grabs her hand when they go out, walking through the West Village after dinner, like they are a pair.

But it was the invitation that sealed it for her.

They were in their usual seats at the Polo Bar and had already gone through half a bottle of Pouilly-Fumé when he turned to her, his face suddenly earnest, and said, "I was thinking you might want to come with me to the cottage this summer?"

His voice made it sound like a question, but they both knew that David Clarke was not used to having to ask.

The invite to Hadley Island was something she'd hoped for but never allowed herself to expect would happen so soon. *The cottage* was a cheeky reference to the ultraexclusive summer residence of David Clarke's famously wealthy family. It was someplace only their extreme inner circle was allowed to set foot. For Faith it would be a coup.

"For how long?" She had tried to keep her voice even, not wanting to sound overly eager, though inside she was absolutely squealing.

"The whole summer," he'd replied without missing a beat.

"But my job," she'd feebly started to say, a smile already starting in her cheeks. She didn't care much about her position as an underling to an elderly publicist and they both knew it. It was always meant to be just a stopgap, a layover between her old sad and desperate life and her new glamorous and exciting one. She'd been itchy about it lately, impatient for the next phase to begin. The job has lasted longer than she would have liked, stretching past the five-year mark soon. She hadn't looked elsewhere because she was lucky to have found it, grateful that someone took a chance on her even if the office smelled like tuna fish. Grateful for someone who didn't ask too many questions or do any sort of background check.

Faith didn't tell David much about her earlier days in New York, hiding the under-the-table gigs as a household assistant or bartending private parties way out in Bushwick. He wouldn't have known that her first taste of New York privilege didn't come from experience, but from the back of the house looking in and watching.

She had since learned to pass herself off as someone who belongs at the tables of impossible-to-get-into restaurants and on the inside of exclusive residences. She wanted to keep it that way. So she kept her past vague. And lucky for her, David didn't ask her much. The wine was warm in her veins as she gazed back at David. She twisted her leg around the barstool.

"You can come back if you need to. Dad has the jet." Ah yes, the private plane. Spoken of so casually because wealth was the only thing David knew.

"Maybe," Faith said, toying with him a little by drawing the acceptance out. Though she was sure that her dour-looking boss, with his sad tuna sandwiches for lunch every day, would absolutely not understand.

"Or how about you just quit," he'd said, taking a sip of wine. Being employed by his father for the last decade after a legacy stint at Yale, David had never struggled to find employment. *Look at him, so incredibly privileged, and somehow he doesn't even see it,* Faith had thought for one ungenerous moment before swallowing back her criticism with a gulp of expensive wine and reminding herself that this was an opportunity David was giving her. She had blinked at him trying to judge how serious he was being about the summer and about her no longer needing her job.

"We both know you don't like it." That was true. "And it's not like you need the money anyway." That part was less sure. She'd moved into David's place only a few months prior. And she'd met him only a few months before that. Was that really enough time to trust him so completely? It was all very tempting. And she was beginning to have an inkling that this trip was about more than just spending a fun summer holiday together. That it was the start of something far more serious.

"Come with me to the island, Faith," he'd pleaded one last time, taking her hand in both of his theatrically. "Or I'll—I'll have to bring someone else."

"You wouldn't dare," she'd said as she swatted his chest. He'd laughed and shrugged, putting a potato chip topped with caviar into his mouth. Of course, when it came down to it, there was never any real question that she'd go. She'd give up whatever was necessary, jump through whichever hoops were needed to go to the "cottage." Getting asked to spend the summer on Hadley Island was like winning the lottery. And Faith had the sense that if you are lucky enough to be invited it only happens once.

* * *

The shower water goes off and Faith quickly sticks the ring back into its slot.

"Faith?" David calls out from the bathroom.

"Just a sec!" she yells back. Fingers trembling, she slides the box back into its dust bag and reburies it under the blue shirt.

David stands next to the sink with a towel around his waist. Faith goes to him, leaning against the marble vanity and watching as he puts a layer of shaving foam onto his lower face. He's good-looking to the point she didn't even trust him when they first met. The swoop of hair, the perfect lips, the body maintained to its maximum potential.

"I can't wait to show you the island. This was the most important place to me growing up. I could be a regular kid here," he says. They'd gotten in late last night. When they arrived, David had taken her straight up to the bedroom, pulling her there eagerly, his hands all over her as they climbed the stairs two at a time.

"I can't wait to see it." Faith beams, trying to play it cool as she watches him expertly maneuver a gold razor around the contours of his chin. How did she get so lucky that David Clarke is her boyfriend? With a jolt she thinks of the ring. Not boyfriend for much longer, though. *Fiancé.* How surreal will it feel to call him that? Sometimes Faith's not even sure any of this new life of hers is real and she is not actually asleep in her childhood bedroom about to wake up to the palmetto bug problem and the drippy faucets, realizing she never made it out of there at all. She puts a hand to his chest, making sure.

"What?" he asks, leaning in to kiss her.

Faith studies him a moment before letting his lips touch hers. He pulls back and looks at her suspiciously. "Nothing! I'm just excited to be here." She dodges his face, still scattered with bits of shaving foam, worried now that she is going to give his secret away with the dumb smile plastered on her face. To hide it, she ducks out into the bedroom and puts on a pair of low-slung linen pants.

"Where would I find coffee if I were in the market for some?" she asks, pulling a white tank top over her head. He comes into the bedroom, the towel still slung around his waist.

"Why, in the kitchen, naturally, darling," he says in a pretend posh accent, slipping his hand around her waist and squeezing her in close to him. "Head downstairs and to your left. Someone will be there to make you whatever your heart desires."

"You're not coming?" she asks, surprised.

"I'll be down in a minute," he says with a wink. "Watch out for Pops. He's cranky in the morning."

Faith has yet to meet Geoffrey Clarke. She has only heard the rumors about the famously bullish financial titan of Park Avenue. That he is a charmer and a ruthless businessman who has never lost a deal, gobbling up companies and spitting them out, selling them for parts. And, less flatteringly, that he is a bully in the office, terrorizing his staff and pitting them against one another. The other more scandalous gossip Faith had found online while doing research on her new boyfriend right after they started dating. The stories in the *Post* alleging that he is a ladies' man who cheated on David's mother for years while she suffered from an addiction to pain pills. Faith had waited for David to fill her in on the details, but so far, he hasn't, mentioning his mother only in passing. It was strange, she thought, but Faith hasn't wanted to push, afraid of him asking for details of her own parents in return. Those were the sorts of things she wasn't ready to divulge. Not yet.

Faith wanders downstairs slowly, taking in the grandeur of the place in the daytime. The staircase is wide and marbled ostentatiously. A mahogany table in the very center of the landing holds a model of a ship on a brass stand. It looks old, probably some priceless antique, she thinks, leaning in to look at the miniature wooden hull brushed with gold leaf. Its sails, permanently caught in the wind, catch the sun, sending a shadow across the white floor.

Bright sunlight spills through the wall of tall windows at the back of the house where a large formal dining room has been updated with ceiling-height modern glass doors that open onto a sprawling veranda looking out at the water.

She twists the latch and steps outside, breathing in a rush of ocean-scented air. Below the veranda a long infinity pool fed by fountains on either side burbles, one end lined with inviting plush deck chairs in nautical stripes. The pool stands just above the edge of a crisp green lawn that continues all the way to the Clarkes' private beach with dock.

She continues around the side of the house where the veranda leads to an open-air spa. A white massage table stands inside a pristine white tent, its flaps drawn back to frame views of the ocean. Faith peers through a circular window into a sauna; its salt stone walls glow a welcoming pink. She'll have to come back later with a book, she thinks, excitement filling her chest. It was worth it to quit her job. Of course, she'd have followed David even if the perks weren't this good, she muses, looking out over a set of sparkling plunge pools tiled in Mediterranean blues. But they sure don't hurt.

She finds herself comforted by the somewhat hermetic environment of so much wealth. It's like being in an airport or the lobby of a skyscraper. It feels safe to her somehow, being somewhere so well kept and distant from the struggles of the real world and the life she used to have. The life she tries very hard not to think about.

She slips back into the house through a wide glass door that leads into a dining area. It has floor-to-ceiling windows with sleek golden hinges that must mean the entire wall can open away on a warm night. A large table stands at the center of the room. It seems to have been carved from a singular gigantic hunk of wood.

Through an archway she finds a sprawling kitchen with vast white marble countertops. A few people bustle around in chef whites cracking eggs into bowls and chopping vegetables. An Italian espresso machine, gleaming and statuesque, is being busily tended to in one corner. A loud hiss of steam comes off it when she walks into the room. No one looks up at Faith as she stands near the edge of the counter. She is trying to decide how best to ask for a coffee when she hears someone behind her.

"I didn't expect to find an unfamiliar woman wandering the house." The voice sounds like David's would if he'd been smoking cigars for many years. "Not that I'm complaining."

Faith turns to find Geoffrey Clarke standing behind her, a folded newspaper in one hand. Up until this moment Faith has only seen the elder Clarke in the pages of the *New York Post* and *Vanity Fair*, wearing dark slightly oversize suits with a young blond woman on his arm.

"Oh, hi. Lovely to meet you," she says, though there is something about his presence that makes her want to recoil. She steels herself and smiles winningly at him. "David said I should come down. I was just exploring the house. It's gorgeous."

"David said he was bringing someone," Geoffrey says, his tone impenetrable. His hard eyes scan Faith as though looking for defects. "Farrah, was it?"

"Faith." She tucks her hair behind her ear, trying to calm the sudden buzzing of nerves.

Geoffrey looks down at her with a slightly amused look on his face. Faith swallows and holds his gaze. He's shorter than she'd expected but no less intimidating with his boxy build and close-cropped salt-and-pepper beard. A series of hard angles, the wide head, the square shoulders. His face above the collar of his polo shirt is slightly pockmarked. She looks for signs of David in him. Maybe there is something around the eyes, the way the skin tugs ever so slightly downward in the outer corners. But even those seem duller, and they are definitely harder for her to read.

"Interesting name," he says finally, but he doesn't sound interested. His hand reaches past her and she flinches as he takes a coffee from the counter, giving a curt nod to one of the kitchen staff.

"It was my grandmother's," Faith starts to explain, but he is already moving away. As he passes, his body brushes so close to hers that she shrinks back to avoid it. He carries his coffee through the archway into the dining room where he sits heavily at the table and shakes open the paper without another word. Faith wavers in the kitchen, uncertain if she should follow. There is something familiar about his arrogance. She's met other men like Geoffrey Clarke in her life, though no one quite as rich. She trusts none of them.

"Oh, there you are, I've been looking for you." She sighs in relief as David's hand slips around her waist. His skin smells like aftershave and the bar of triple-milled soap from the walk-in shower.

"Finally awake I see," his father's gravelly voice chides David from the table, though his eyes never leave the pages of the *Post*. "I guess you never were much of an early riser. Preferred to leave that to the rest of us."

"Dad! I didn't see you there." David quickly pulls his hand away from Faith and gives his father a strained grin. "I see you've met Faith."

"What?" Geoffrey Clarke glances up, momentarily confused until his eyes land on Faith. "Oh, right. We've met, yes."

Faith ignores the slight and gives him a cool smile. She takes David's hand in hers, noticing the strange limp clasp of his fingers. "Should we go into town? I'll go grab my purse." She is eager to exit this uncomfortable breakfast and enter vacation mode.

"Town?" Geoffrey's voice reverberates through his newspaper. "Oh, no, my dear. I'm sorry but David is staying here—for the time being, anyway." He lowers the page and now she can see a small smile playing on his lips.

"Oh," Faith says, feeling the coolness at her back as David steps away from her.

"We have some things to discuss, don't we, David?"

"Sure, of course . . ." David falters.

"Right now?" Faith's stomach drops.

"Don't worry, it shouldn't be long," David says, not looking at her.

"Come on, son, don't have all day." Geoffrey stands abruptly. "Not like some people."

"I'll be done in no time," David whispers to Faith. "Have fun. Go to the pool. Explore the grounds. I'll text you as soon as I'm out." He smiles reassuringly. There is something about how quick he was to change course that makes her uncomfortable. David is not someone who generally flip-flops on things. His consistency is one of the things she loves about him. But she isn't going to make a big deal about it. She knows how counterproductive that would be.

Faith learned early on that if you want to make it in this world as a woman, you have to keep your hands on the dials at all times, turning them up and down as the situation calls for it. You can't ever let them see you lose your composure.

She keeps a placid smile on her face as she watches David follow his father down the hall. Faith has always been extraordinarily good at faking it. It is one of the main tools that has aided her in her rise from a literal nobody speeding toward a life of abuse and addiction in a tiny town to where she is today, in the house of a billionaire overlooking the ocean. To survive as someone like her, she knows that you must always remember who you were, and how easy it would be to fall back.

ORLA

The Hadley Island ferry backs away from the mainland, shuddering loudly. Orla O'Connor has stationed herself on the top deck, her suitcase wedged between her knees and the row of plastic seats in front of her. Their tops are cracked and bleached to the color of orange sherbet from the sun. She looks around at the other passengers, relieved to find that she recognizes none of them. They all seem to be tourists who, despite the relatively cool and windy conditions on the boat, are optimistically wearing shorts and T-shirts. They take pictures with their phones, calling loudly across the deck to one another. Orla feels like she is living on a completely different plane of existence than all of them.

Two women in their sixties settle into the row of chairs in front of Orla. They wear matching straw hats and lean back relaxed as they chatter on about where to get the best calamari on the island. Orla sinks deeper into her seat trying to bury her annoyance. What exactly is it that bothers her about these people? Happiness? The sound of their voices? Or is it that their lives seem so carefree, so different from her own?

The boat picks up speed as it cuts though the sound, and she looks nervously toward the bow where the swells undulate higher and higher, breaking into frothy whitecaps. Is it too soon for more Xanax? The last one she took was before she got on the bus in New York this morning, her throat sour with what she was about to do. She holds off for now. She'll certainly need another later.

After nearly twelve years Orla has almost managed to forget what it is like here, the briny vegetal smell of the water, the way the salt immediately tangles in your hair and makes it sticky. The rush of memory makes her stomach turn even before the front of the boat pitches up. It comes down hard, smashing into a wave. Her palms are damp as she braces herself, holding on to the bottom of her seat. It wobbles slightly as the boat collides with another wave, sending a giant spray up across the bow. A few of the people around her scream with delight. Orla wants to turn and glare at them, but she is too busy holding on as tightly as possible. She tries to focus on her breathing, to not let her nerves overtake her. Breathe in, one, two, three, four.

Orla hates the ocean. It is part of the reason she's avoided coming back to Hadley Island for so long. She cannot even bear to look at it, the way it is constantly moving, how staring down into the churning darkness you can hardly see a thing. The water can trap the light and play tricks on you. When you are out in it you have no idea how deep it is. You don't have any way to see the untold number of creatures waiting in the dark.

The boat cracks against a large swell, sending another blast of water up over the bow. Orla sinks farther into her seat, gripping the armrests as the tourists shriek with laughter. There are more of them than she expected so early in the season. It's only the first weekend in June.

The ferry rolls sideways against the waves as they move across the sound. Orla watches the horizon, holding her breath as the island comes into view. It starts as a thin strip of gray and green shimmering above the water. Without moving a muscle, she watches as it grows closer and crisper. The horizon tilts as anxiety grips at her chest.

Soon she can see Hadley Island clearly. Each rocky cove and out-cropping comes into focus, familiar as kin, followed by the ellipse of the town's main beach. A surprisingly large crowd of people are already out there, folding chairs and umbrellas claiming spots on the soft white-gray sand even though the water will still be too cold for swimming.

She's been trying to avoid it, craning her neck to look literally anywhere else, but now the ferry is moving directly past the inlet that holds the Clarke mansion. It's impossible to tear your eyes from the cliff-like marble exterior, blinding white in the sun. It's set on the back of a vast emerald lawn that slopes down to the private dock and crescent of meticulously combed beach. The only surviving Gilded Age summer home on the island stands in stark contrast to the cedar-shingled bungalows around it.

Orla's stomach sloshes as she sees a speck of a person step out onto the veranda, but before she can try to identify who, the ferry has pulled forward past a rocky outcropping obscuring her view.

They are almost to shore now, passing through a small city of yachts moored in the harbor. They tower above the little ferry, their multistoried facades stamped with tacky gold names. If engaging with the art world has revealed anything to Orla, it is that you can buy nearly anything in this world but taste.

The woman in front of her turns to her left, pointing at something away from shore. "Look at that house over there on its very own island," Orla hears her say to her friend. Orla's heart dips precariously as she follows her gaze to the tiny island. A lone single-story house is perched on stilts atop a gray pile of rock in the middle of the water.

"Like a fairy tale," the friend replies.

Or a nightmare, Orla thinks.

"Do you think someone lives there? Would it even be possible?"

If only she knew. She listens to them deliberate on the details. If Orla were in a different sort of mood, or maybe if she'd had a few drinks, she would have interjected to say that someone does live there. She may even have told the women what she knows about the strange, sad home of Marjorie and Henry Wright and the watery grave Henry made for her best friend Alice.

She turns her face away and pulls her hands farther into the sleeves of her sweatshirt as they chug through the harbor and approach a row of buildings painted in cheerful, if a bit weatherworn, colors hugging the water. The entire village of Port Mary. The ferry turns clumsily with a loud groan and the engine cuts. The awkward cries of seagulls pierce the sudden quiet; they swoop overhead, landing on the pilings as the ferry scrapes along the dock.

A teenage boy leaps from the deck, deftly twisting the lines and pulling the boat in. Back in high school Orla and Alice always knew the kids working the ferry. They were their peers; now she wonders how many of them have stayed on the island. Not many, she's sure. Very few people born on Hadley stay here for good. If you have the means, Hadley is the kind of place you return to in summers, not a place to live year-round. Not if you can afford not to. Winter on the island is desolate. Orla remembers it well.

Around her people gather their things. They have moved on from the novelty of the boat ride and are already chattering excitedly about trips to the beach and dinner reservations and where to buy the freshest lobsters. Orla feels conspicuously alone among them. She grabs her bag and adjusts her sunglasses and propels herself to the narrow staircase. The window of Mint Ship ice cream shop slides open to welcome the tourists clomping down the dock behind her, their faces pink from the wind. Orla dodges past them, yanking her suitcase behind her.

At the end of the dock, Orla turns to the left and walks quickly through the village. Harbor Street hugs the water in an arc of quaint shops and restaurants. She notes that not one has changed since she was last here. She rolls her suitcase past the Salty Crab, the seafood restaurant and dive bar where she spent many nights drinking with Alice before they were even legal. The sidewalk out front gives off a tang of spilled beer drying in the sun. But from the doorway, propped open slightly, wafts the smell of some deep-fried sea creature. Orla's stomach gurgles. An empty booth by the window catches the sunlight invitingly. She stops and presses her face to the glass.

A woman sits at the end of the bar below a collection of decorative ropes and anchors. She's wearing a half apron and has a pencil tucked

over her ear. Jean O'Malley has been a fixture at the Salty Crab as long
as Orla has been alive. Her curly hair is grayer now, her sturdy body just
a bit wider than Orla remembers her. She had always seemed so capable,
so resilient, that Orla never considered her life outside of the Crab. She'd
never left the island and never married. She had only her sister, Marjorie, and her brother-in-law, Henry Wright. Back when Orla was little,
she had seen the three of them occasionally wandering around town or
sharing dinner in the Crab. But after what happened with Alice, Marjorie and Henry stopped coming to the island altogether. Apart from her
shifts at the Crab, Jean was always on her own. Orla watches her wearily
begin to roll silverware into napkins, her wrists flicking with over thirty
years of muscle memory. Orla's sunglasses accidentally tap against the
glass. Jean looks up, startled.

Damn it.

Orla jerks back from the window and rushes the rest of the way up
Harbor Street. She passes the other restaurants, their awnings advertising lobster claws and scallop risottos, then walks past the liquor store
and the post office. She practically runs past the Clarke property, its
white marble facade looming down a drive accessible behind a sealed
metal gate. Orla doesn't so much as pause to catch her breath until the
road finally curves, and she can see the cedarwood shingles on the very
top of her childhood home poking up between the trees.

She approaches the house with an unexpected fluttering in her chest.
It's been kept up with the help of a caretaker and looks unchanged from
when she left. The lush green lawn is freshly mowed. Stands of indigo
hydrangeas in full bloom flank the lawn. The swing on the front porch
wavers invitingly in the breeze. She almost expects her dad to step outside holding a tray inviting her to try something he'd just finished cooking. She stops midway up the walk, turning her head to the right. She
had been trying not to look but she has to.

For nearly Orla's entire childhood Alice had lived right next door.
They were the same age, as luck would have it. A built-in best friend.
Alice, bold and smart with an adventurous streak that would have gotten

them into trouble more often were it not for Orla's more balanced and careful nature. The two of them were as close as any sisters could have been, spending every waking moment they could together, rushing back and forth between their houses from the time the sun came up until after dark when their parents called them back to their respective homes for bed.

Even their houses matched. Alice's house, once the slightly nicer of the two, is now so overgrown it is hardly visible even up close. Through the dense vegetation, Orla can find only a vague hint of the outline of what was once a beautiful and immaculately kept seaside home.

The wraparound porch where Orla and Alice once acted out a thousand made-up fairy tales with their dolls and stuffed animals is now almost completely obscured behind a dark mass of vines and hanging branches. The roof of the porch has caved in, the jagged edges of rotted boards peeking through the opening. The cedar siding, where it is visible through the overgrown brush, is curled back, with gaps in the shingles like a partly scaled fish. The glass in the picture windows is obscured by a thick layer of dirt. A shutter on one has come loose and hangs at an angle.

Orla hadn't known how bad it had gotten. She'd never dared to ask. But the extent of the neglect makes her realize how much time has passed. She turns away feeling sick and pulls her things up the steps to her house. As she crouches to dig for the house key in the pocket of her suitcase, a gust of wind blows over her bare legs. In the shadow of the front porch there is a chill in the air. It's the kind of cold that seemed impossible to imagine when she packed yesterday in her sweaty New York apartment. Her hands tremble a little.

The *feeling* is coming back. The pain of it twists in her chest, building and building like the pressure at the start of a scream.

She rushes to unlock the door.

HENRY

N ow that people are returning to the island for the season, Henry's days have become busy. There is so much to keep track of. Families are arriving on the ferry and people are congregating at the beach. The restaurants along the pier are open for the first time this year. They are all filling up, their back patios lively with people drinking martinis and eating oysters over the water. After a long and dreary spring, all the activity always fills him with a newfound sense of vitality and optimism. Soon all the summer residents will have arrived, along with a fresh boatload of tourists every day, and the island will be so active that Henry will have trouble keeping up with his logbooks. This is his favorite time of year. When his mind is occupied, and he can let himself get lost in the comings and goings, when he can, for a brief time, forget about the past.

"It's not nice to spy on people, Henry," Margie's voice comes from behind him, scolding.

His wife has never liked him watching through the telescope. Though she's never turned down a piece of gossip that was offered to her. Despite her disapproval, his passion for watching the people of Hadley has only grown over time, turning into more of an obsession. A need. So much so that he feels as though he personally knows each of the families whose homes he can see on the shoreline. He is invested in

all the lives he can see. It is what happens when you don't have much of
a family of your own, he supposes. It's natural he should want to connect. *No harm in it.* That's what he tells himself anyway. Even though
a part of him knows that it's wrong. Henry knows, for example, that
Marty Fredrick's wife has recently started going to sleep in a different
bedroom. And that Penny Gallagher spends most of her nights in her
bathrobe staring sadly into the glow of her computer screen. And he
knows that little Mary Elizabeth—well, not so little anymore, she must
be nearly sixteen—has a boyfriend. He's seen her duck out though her
bedroom window onto the porch roof and climb down the trellis to
meet him. He's watched the two of them kissing down by the water,
their bodies mashing together, arms groping in the dark, where they
think no one can see. He hears the newspaper rustling on Margie's lap.
She tuts disapprovingly.

They built the Rock on high stilts, which are anchored precariously
atop a craggy piece of shale that cleaves up through the sound. It had
been nearly a decade in the making for Henry, a retirement present
for the both of them, he'd said when at age fifty-five the house was
finally completed, and his pension had started. Once a local contractor,
Henry wanted to make something special for Margie. He'd planned it
all meticulously, even teaching himself to make rudimentary architec-
tural sketches.

The construction of it over nearly ten years had presented so many
challenges—electricity and plumbing and permits—that he nearly gave
up, but Margie always encouraged him to keep going. "It's a master-
piece, Henry," she'd said when it was finally done, and he'd brought her
to see it for the first time.

He beamed with pride as she took his arm and he walked her around
the house. He had carefully considered every detail, a galley kitchen
with tile the colors of sea glass that faced a wide, open living room with
enough space on one side for their large dining table. A bedroom off the
back had a skylight above the bed. The wood floor was reclaimed from
the old pier, taken down by a storm, sanded into imperfect strips that

he'd carefully arranged to match up. The ceiling also was crossed by two large beams that had once belonged to an old fishing vessel. An iron woodstove in one corner, a beast to bring up the narrow steps, would pump out enough heat to keep them snug in the winter. It was a space at once airy and cozy and when the windows were open it felt like being at sea. He'd designed the layout to be open so that no matter where the other was in the house they'd be together, able to banter back and forth, the way they liked.

Henry had watched with pride as Margie walked around the open floor plan, marveling at the view from the wall of wide-paned windows in the sitting area. She threw open the French doors and went out on the deck, leaning over the railing and closing her eyes as she felt the fine spray from the water on her face. "A sanctuary, truly. I never want to leave." Margie had turned to him and smiled. She didn't know that soon she wouldn't really have a choice.

Now the windows provide the perfect vantage point for watching the comings and goings of the houses on the western shore of Hadley Island. If anyone knew Henry was watching them, they'd probably put in window shades, which would be a shame. But no one has ever known about Henry's little hobby. Except Margie.

"You're going to have to go down there again soon and take care of things," Margie says.

"Yes, dear," he replies noncommittally, hoping she'll let it go. He is watching the ferry come in. The upper deck is nearly full today. He leans in, squinting to see if he can recognize any of them.

"The sediment's probably washing away after that last full moon tide. It'll become a liability soon." She presses. "Any boat that's passing could see if they looked hard enough."

"I heard you," he says impatiently and holds up a hand, trying to shush her. *A mistake.* Henry should know by now never to shush his wife.

"You know it's true. I'm just trying to take care of us." Margie's voice is clipped. He can tell he's hurt her feelings. And moreover, he knows she's right.

"I'm sorry. I'll go soon," he says quietly, a hard lump in his chest. He turns his attention back to the ferry, but he's missed it docking and the passengers have already scattered around the village.

"What do you see?" she finally asks.

"Well, the Clarkes are back for the summer," he says, knowing it will get her worked up enough to hopefully leave the other topic behind. She coughs, and it rattles like a warning in the back of her throat. Henry winces.

"Those monsters," she says. At one point he would have told her she was overreacting. But this time Henry doesn't correct her.

FAITH

Faith spends the entire morning lounging on the bed scrolling aimlessly on her phone, allowing herself to look at pictures of wedding dresses for longer than she'd ever admit. But by the afternoon David still hasn't emerged from Geoffrey's office. Slightly annoyed, she goes to the closet to put on one of her new bikinis. It took three suitcases to get all her clothes here. She unzips one of them and runs her hand across the carefully folded fabrics.

Her friend Elena squirmed with envy when she told her she was going to Hadley Island. "The whole summer? Jesus, Faith, that man must be really into you."

"You think?" she'd asked innocently. But she knew it was true.

"You have to buy all new clothes, you know. You can't be wearing this city stuff up there. Hadley Island is the real deal. Old money. These are people with yachts, Faith. Not boats. *Yachts.*" Faith had laughed but agreed to let Elena help her pick out a pile of new things at Bergdorf Goodman. She steered Faith around the floors of the store, stacking her arms with bright printed Ulla Johnson and Zimmermann sundresses, a Celine beach bag, preppy shorts, *two* pairs of Hermès Oran sandals, an embarrassing assortment of straw hats.

"You'll have to look the part if you want to stop people from asking too many questions. These people can smell someone who isn't like them; they love nothing more than to dig around in someone's past." Elena stopped at a display of handwoven beach bags and gave her a hard look. "And we don't want that."

No, Faith certainly did not. Elena was the only person in the city she had ever told about her life before and the tragedy that had shaped it. She was the only one Faith felt she could trust with her secrets.

At the register Faith had balked at the total, over six thousand dollars. Spending that kind of money felt straight-up irresponsible. The marketing firm paid her barely enough to live on, and unlike Elena, who seemed to have access to some free-flowing fountain of wealth, Faith had nothing to fall back on in terms of money. There was no aunt or uncle with a penthouse on the Upper East Side, no rich parents up in Westchester to ask for help if she ever needed it.

"It's an investment, trust me," Elena had said when Faith hesitated. And so, Faith had sucked it up and handed over her Amex card to the cashier, praying she was right.

Faith reaches into the suitcase and chooses a blue one-piece patterned with tiny yellow stars. She puts it on, swiveling to admire the scooped back and the high hips in the full-length mirror. She covers it with a loose white button-up and pads through the empty house and out to the pool with a book. She stations herself on one of the plush lounge chairs, her long legs angled to catch the sun. But she can't focus. Faith's mind keeps going to that ring, hidden away in its tufted box. Waiting for her.

She wonders when David is planning to propose. In their nearly one year together he's always been a thoughtful boyfriend, taking her out for dinners at five-star restaurants, on special outings to baseball games and museums, and even once on a surprise helicopter ride over the city. He probably has something magical in mind—by the water, no doubt. At sunset perhaps? Maybe a bottle of their favorite champagne to celebrate after. She holds her hand out and squints at it, trying to imagine the way the massive diamond will look on her delicate finger and what color nail polish would best complement it. A light pink, she thinks. Nothing too garish. Nothing that will take attention away from that diamond.

Where will the ceremony be? If they were getting married in the city, she could see it being at the Plaza Hotel. Faith allows herself to picture the dress she'd wear if it were there. A strapless column with a short train. Classic but still very feminine. Tailored within an inch of its life.

A ding comes from the inside of her straw Chloé bag and Faith pulls out her phone to find a text from Elena.

Hey girl! Are you on Hadley now? I'm so jealous of your glamorous summer while I'm toiling away in this cesspool of a city omfg. Meet anyone famous yet?

Faith's best friend is an amazingly adept social climber. She has no doubt that if Elena were here, she would already have finagled them both onto the invite list for every major event of the summer. Their lives in New York were orchestrated around her friend's social schedule.

She'd met Elena two years before at an event Faith had put together at the Whitney Museum. It was a cocktail hour for her boss, who was desperately trying to woo clients. It was Faith's first time arranging something like this, and it had been off to a great start. The wine was flowing. The way the tables were arranged made people turn and talk to one another. Even her dour boss looked happy.

In the midst of the event a woman strode up to her. She was wearing a black jumpsuit with a sheer V of lace cut down from her chest to her navel. "I'm looking for the host. Someone said it was you." Being in the woman's presence made Faith's face go hot and the words dry up in her throat.

"No, I, um, I just helped organize it. My boss is over there. The one in the gray jacket," she'd said nervously, gesturing into the crowd of gray-toned jackets. Not knowing how else to identify him, she'd whispered, "The one who smells like tuna fish."

Elena gave her a big laugh. Then she looked at her again and this time Faith felt that Elena could see right into her. She had leaned in conspiratorially. "Are you happy with him? Because *I* have a strong suspicion you are being underutilized. Let's connect." She'd said it with the kind of confidence that made Faith immediately agree and give out her phone number. Then she'd watched Elena swish back toward the group, folding into the crowd with a sense of belonging that made Faith's throat catch. What she wouldn't give to no longer be watching from the periphery.

True to her word, Elena called her the next day, inviting her to an intimate dinner for young businesswomen in Manhattan. Faith had instantly been intimidated by the group. The glossy hair and fitted trousers, the bottles of wine and sparkling water being passed back and forth. A chasm opened in her chest.

"What do you think, Faith?"

"Faith is in event planning," Elena had said, stretching the truth. "I met her at the Whitney." The smile she gave Faith from across the table made her feel both seen and important. As Elena launched into a story about the event, for the first time Faith felt she might actually deserve to feel that way.

Ha! I wish. Faith writes back, quickly, happy for the distraction. *We haven't even left the house yet.*

Elena, bless her, misreads the situation entirely.

Oooh sexy. I love it. So, what have you two been doing? Besides the obvious.

Faith pauses but doesn't correct her. She almost starts to tell her about the ring but stops herself. As much as she loves her friend, Elena is well connected and can't resist sharing a juicy piece of gossip. A fatal combination for a secret. There is a good chance that anything Faith says will make its way through her own social circles and beyond. And Faith can't have all Manhattan knowing that she snooped through her boyfriend's bag. Plus, she thinks, looking down at her bare hand, it'll be better when she can show it to Elena on her actual finger. More impactful.

Instead, she types, *At the pool currently. It's so pretty here.* And then as though to prove it, she takes a photo looking out from the porch. But the picture doesn't do the place justice at all. The vast yard shrinks and dulls in her phone's lens. She stands up and walks to the other side of the pool where a broad set of stairs spills onto the sprawling green lawn. A wide slate stone path picks up at the bottom and leads straight toward the shimmering blue water. Faith follows it, stopping every so often to raise her phone and snap a photo. Up close the private beach is bigger than it looked from afar, fringed with cultivated clumps of seagrass and several clusters of wooden Adirondack chairs.

She takes off her slides and steps down into the sand. It is surprisingly soft, a light gray powder that has been recently raked. She walks out to the shoreline and lets the waves run up over her feet. When the water hits her, she yelps with cold but doesn't move away. Instead, she forces herself out another step, staying in the water until her legs begin to get used to it. She takes another picture. This one is better than the first, a crescent of beach, a dappling of clear water with a few sailboats in the distance. She sends this one to Elena.

Seconds later her phone dings.

So pretty there! Where are the yachts?

But there are no yachts. At least none that Faith can see when she shades her eyes and looks out to the horizon. There is only a tiny island offshore with a small single-story house balanced on top of stilts. So odd, she'll have to ask David about it.

Faith turns back to the house with its sparkling swimming pool and imposing marble exterior. Maybe they could get married right here? Faith imagines the pathway is the aisle. She steps lightly across the stones back toward the veranda. There could be rows of chairs on either side and an archway down at the end made from flowers, all in white, of course, with the water glimmering in the background.

Faith sees her mother suddenly and stops. She is sitting in the front row on one of the white chairs. She is frozen the way she exists in Faith's memory, her skin overly tan and her hair damaged from boxed dye bought at the grocery store, the fin from a faded tattoo of a dolphin poking up from the bust of a dress she got from Marshalls. Too tight and glittery, of course, but she thinks that's what makes it fancy, her impression of wealth pieced together from whatever Bravo show she is currently watching. Her eyes are red-rimmed.

"Hey, Peanut," her mom's voice says in her imagination, hoarse as usual from smoking and self-neglect. The rest of Faith's fantasy dries up and floats away and she is left standing alone on the lawn with her mom. "Look at you," her mom says a little sadly, a smile flickering across her thin lips.

A guilty lump forms in Faith's throat. She looks away from the lawn, her eyes blurring. She wouldn't invite anyone from her family to the wedding, of course. It was too risky.

To rid herself of the icky taste that has crawled up into her mouth, she takes out her phone and texts Elena. *You'd love it here.*

Faith wouldn't have even met David if it wasn't for one of those benefits Elena was always dragging Faith to. A thousand dollars a plate for cystic fibrosis or an auction to raise money for glaucoma research. These things were always filled with the kind of people who made Faith feel especially shy and introverted. She could never quite figure out where she belonged among them, what she was supposed to say, who she was meant to be. She'd said no at first but Elena, always eager to network and in the market for her own rich boyfriend, had been relentless this time.

"It's for Atlantic Ocean animal habitat restoration, Fay," she'd said. "Why do you hate ocean animals?" She'd pulled up a photograph of a manatee on her phone and turned her lips down into a pout.

"Okay, fine." Faith had laughed. "I can't say no to a manatee." And she also couldn't turn down a cocktail hour underneath the belly of the giant blue whale sculpture in the museum's Hall of Ocean Life, where she was assured the who's who of New York would be in attendance.

It was one of those perfect New York days in late September when the air has a hint of crispness to it and the city feels like it has woken up after the slumber of summer. Faith had felt a rare surge of optimism as she and Elena had arrived at the Museum of Natural History, laughing and tapping up the steps in their high-heeled sandals.

Elena had dragged her around the room, introducing her to people along the way. They were mostly WASPs with names like Chip and Birdy, a subset of the population that felt foreign and exotic to Faith. She took it all in, downing her drink quickly.

"Come meet Lauren Stamford. She's the queen of Park Avenue," Elena had said, grasping her elbow and pulling her into a darkened exhibit room where a woman with a blond bob and rigid posture was holding court.

"Ah, Elena, good to see you." The woman had kissed Elena's smooth cheek. Faith was always impressed by how well her friend blended in, how she always knew what to do while Faith had to work at it like she was learning another language.

"This is Faith. She's up-and-coming in the PR world," Elena had introduced her generously, giving Faith a little nudge forward.

"What's your last name, dear?" the woman had said, peering down her aquiline nose at Faith. The rest of the group stopped chattering and turned their eyes on Faith, waiting to see if she was someone they should care about.

"Ellis," Faith stammered, feeling her cheeks growing hot. The woman had given a little sniff.

"I haven't heard of you," she'd said simply, and she turned toward a man to her right wearing an ascot, icing Faith out.

"She seems nice," Elena had said dryly as they retreated to one edge of the room where a diorama of ocean animals glowed from the wall.

"I don't fit in with these people," Faith had moaned, wanting to leave.

"Don't take it personally. If anything, she's just jealous," Elena said, brushing it off.

"Of me?" Faith said in disbelief.

"She's from that generation that hates any woman younger than them. She's a nightmare to work for apparently. And totally insecure after that facelift. But her husband's business is on the verge of collapse. Her reign won't last much longer," Elena said, her eyes twinkling.

"How do you know so much about people?"

"It's a hobby," Elena said. "My version of sports."

Faith had smiled at her friend, grateful not to have to navigate the Mitzis and Tads of the world on her own. She tilted the last of her drink into her mouth as Elena used the new vantage point to scan the room. There was something in the way she would look for the richest and most influential person in the room that reminded Faith of the old version of herself, the one she'd been trying to escape.

Faith turned away from the party and pushed her face close to the glass of the diorama. When she was growing up, the ocean always felt mystical to Faith; with its rainbow of corals and shimmering fish, it was a magical place that felt as mysterious and otherworldly as a fairy-tale kingdom populated with unicorns. This diorama showed a giant squid attacking a whale. Its tentacles were wrapped around the whale's belly, ready to pull it into the deep. "I think I dated that one," she joked to Elena.

"The squid or the whale?" a surprisingly resonant voice had replied. She'd backed up, startled. Elena must have wandered off and left her, and now a man stood in her place. A very handsome man. He held a glass of wine in one hand, the other was on the waist of his jacket. He peered through the glass.

"Oh, I don't know, probably both of them at one time or another," Faith said, turning to face him. Just past his shoulder she saw Elena deep in conversation with a tall, serious-looking woman in black-rimmed glasses.

"Oh, I wonder which one I'd be if any of my exes were here to speak," he replied, amused by her reaction. She'd tapped her chin, gazing around the room.

"Probably the anglerfish," she said. "Something about the eyes."

His laugh was genuine. "I'm David," he said, adding, "Clarke," a moment later and pausing as though the name should mean something to her. She would have to ask Elena later.

"Faith," she replied, letting him take her hand and shake it. He raised his eyebrows presumably at her name or perhaps the very slight twang left over in her voice, a sound she's since managed to nearly eradicate.

"Can I get you another drink?"

"Sure," she'd agreed quickly, liking the way they looked together in the reflection of the exhibit. *Perhaps too quickly*, she thought, glancing up at him. He was handsome, sure, but there was something else about him. A certain kind of vulnerability that showed in his face. It made her feel an immediate connection with him.

"What were you having?" He nodded down at the bright pink remnants of her martini glass.

"I think it was the Axolotl Punch," Faith said, smiling at the silly name. "But I'm up for a new adventure."

He'd looked at her for a beat, infusing her words with more meaning than she'd intended. "Excellent."

As he left to get her a drink, she saw Elena was now watching their exchange. Faith raised her eyebrows at her friend and gave a little shrug, like *we'll see*.

But Faith hadn't needed to wait long for her and David to slip into the rhythm of a relationship together.

From the very start their dates were weekly events, but these quickly turned into every other night sleepovers until she was practically living at his West Village apartment. It was all more than fine with her. Faith preferred the comfort of his apartment, spacious and sparsely furnished, with its chrome espresso machine and bank of windows looking out over a street full of tasteful brownstones. *It's the sort of place a thirty-one-year-old woman should live*, she thought. And it was refreshingly far from the chaotic roommate situations she'd found herself in the last ten years, the only thing she was able to afford in the city.

Sometimes they went out with other couples from his work, but more often just the two of them. She noticed that he never seemed to have much use for other people. His friends blurred together, and Faith felt sometimes as though they were only there as props, dull to make their own relationship sparkle and shine in the foreground. She never minded much, enjoying the way she and David got along, the relaxed back-and-forth, the easy laughter. She started to feel more confident with him and then with herself. She didn't need anything else.

In those nights spent over at David's, she'd started to allow herself to imagine a life of comfort and stability. She began to crave the feeling she got every time she woke up there—the peacefulness she found with him amid the clean Scandinavian furniture and the still, open space. It was what she had always longed for.

"Move in with me," David had begged Faith one unseasonably warm spring evening while they were out having oysters at one of their favorite neighborhood restaurants.

Her head had snapped toward him.

"So soon?" she asked.

But David, whose entire life existed in this space of beauty and privilege, didn't seem to have any worry about moving things along. "Just think, we could have this every night. No more of you rushing back and forth to your apartment to get things."

Faith had been watching a parade of people pass by on Christopher Street. The neighborhood was so lovely it made her insides hurt. She'd have been lying if she said it wasn't a relief to slip into the warm feeling of not having to worry day in and day out like she had growing up. To order whatever she wanted off a menu, without thinking about the bill at the end. It shouldn't have felt crass to say it, not when she came from so little.

"You really think you have enough closet space for me?" she'd finally said slyly, not wanting to give him a full answer right away.

"Sure. And if I don't, I'll get rid of my stuff." He'd tossed a hand in the air.

"Oh, is that right? Just toss it?" The wine was kicking in and her words floated from her lips into the hazy summer evening.

"Why not? You can throw it into the street for all I care. I want your things displacing mine." His eyes shone in the last of the late-evening sun. He gave her that disarming smile of his, the one that was somehow both boyishly earnest and a little mischievous below the surface.

They'd clinked glasses, and she'd leaned back in her chair, letting her body relax. So, this was how it was going to go, she thought, watching appreciatively as he ordered another bottle of wine and a plate of frites.

Later, in the restaurant's cramped bathroom she'd washed her hands and smiled at her reflection in the speckled glass mirror. Faith marveled at this unlikely cozy cocoon of belonging she'd found with the son of a billionaire. She'd never had anything like it before. And if in the process the relationship, as her friend Elena so delicately put it—"changed her financial situation" for the better—what was the harm in that?

There was a brief moment, a rush of nerves, as she put her hand to the door to leave, when she'd imagined her mother's face in the shadow behind her.

"Be careful with that one, baby doll," her mom said to her reflection, her fingers twitching nervously as she raised a Virginia Slim to her lips and inhaled deeply. "We don't want you getting hurt."

ORLA

Orla spends the afternoon opening up the house, shaking out linens and yanking up storm windows, swollen with age and humidity, slowly replacing the stale damp air with a fresh ocean breeze. Her childhood home is still furnished with the kind of oversize decor you'd never fit into a cramped New York apartment. In the living room there are several large stuffed chairs, an ottoman, and a long davenport all facing the soot-stained stone fireplace. An antique sailing flag hangs above it. The faintly musty smell of it all brings on a wave of nostalgia so strong it makes her dizzy. She puts a hand to the wall to steady herself. It's funny how everything else kind of just disappears when you return to the place you grew up, like the rest of your life has been some sort of hallucination and the childhood you, the one from all those years ago, is the only version that is real. Being back on Hadley, Orla can almost pretend that New York never happened at all. Would things have been better that way?

She walks out to the screened-in porch at the back of the house. The evening sun has only just snuffed out behind the trees. The remnants of it cast a bluish light across the wooden floorboards. A shadowy tower of chipped wooden oars and nets leans against one corner. She gulps in the humid salt-tinged air and looks out on a lawn. It's hemmed in on both sides by thick stands of trees framing what her dad hopes is a multimillion-dollar view of water. *If the buyers can ignore the abandoned house next door, that is,* Orla thinks, glancing into the dark woods separating her property from the Gallos'.

During the summer Alice and Orla had spent their evenings out here lounging on rattan chairs, eating ice cream bars, and drawing pictures on paper spread across the floor. Art Club they called it, until they got a bit older and more serious.

Their last summer together, she remembers Alice had them working on pieces for their portfolios for their applications to the School of Visual Arts. They had two years to go before college still, but Alice said they needed practice. She was right. Orla was struggling. The sailboat she'd been drawing looked out of balance. The perspective was skewed and the paper had become smeared with frustrated eraser marks. Alice had leaned over to look, but before she could properly see it, Orla snatched up the page and balled it up, tossing it into the corner. "Let's do something else," she'd said. Ignoring her, Alice had gone to retrieve it, smoothing it out on the coffee table in front of her.

"Stop, Orla. It's so lovely. I think it's one of your best." She always had a special way of looking at things, turning the flawed and mundane into something magic.

Orla had tried to hide a shy smile. "Stop! It's terrible."

"No. Look at the waves, the way you've done it, with all those lines, they're almost moving. It's like a Van Gogh." Alice said it with such conviction that Orla almost believed her, even if she would never admit it.

"No, it's not! And even if it was, no one is going to like it. Besides, he wasn't even successful until he was dead."

There's a loud snap of a branch to Orla's right, followed by the rush of something moving through the woods beside the house. Orla clutches her chest as a rabbit runs out from the brush and hops across the lawn.

She laughs out loud, but it comes out strangled and nervous. She goes back inside, twisting the lock behind her.

Orla pauses at the staircase, looking up into the darkness of the second floor, before full-on exhaustion propels her toward her childhood bedroom. Her fingers glide along the banister, remembering the familiar knots and dips in the wood. The upstairs of the house is narrow, holding two bedrooms and a small bathroom at the end of the hall. She stops at the door to her parents' room. Its double windows look out through the trees at the water. Her throat goes tight at the sight of an old quilt folded neatly at the foot of the bed. Being alone in the house fills her with a strange heaviness she hasn't anticipated. The silence here catches her off guard.

Orla turns back and crosses the hall to her old room. It has been cleaned up since she left for college, stripped of all her old band posters and toys for the one time her parents half-heartedly tried to rent it out. Orla takes in the white beadboard walls with a strange ache in her chest.

She pulls back the edge of a cotton curtain printed with tiny blue and red sailboats. In the near dark, the dust-caked upper windows of Alice's room stare back vacantly at her. When they were kids, Alice and Orla played games with flashlights at these windows. "Morse code" they called it, but they'd never had any interest in learning how to do the real thing. Instead, they invented their own made-up language of flashes and pauses that only the two of them could decipher.

Two flashes in quick succession meant *hello*.

Two short, one long meant *come over now*.

One long, two short, one long was to be used only in an emergency.

They were only fifteen when Alice disappeared. Drowned presumably. Her mother had left Hadley Island a few months later. She'd never said why to anyone, just silently packed up a few suitcases and left it all behind to rot. Orla assumed that it was too painful to carry on looking out to sea and wondering what had become of her daughter. Speculation about why she'd never sold what had to be a valuable piece of property was rampant on the island, but Orla had always had a feeling it was superstitious, in case Alice ever returned. Maybe her mother didn't want her to find another family living there instead. Either way, the vines started to claim the house soon after.

Her old twin bed sags when Orla lies down on it, the springs creaking like they are ready to give up. She pulls her grandmother's afghan blanket from the foot of the bed up over herself, willing herself to sleep. She reaches for the switch on the bedside lamp, and the room is submerged in darkness. Orla lies still trying to shut it all out. She wants nothing more than to escape into a delicious oblivion but her mind spins on the periphery of sleep replaying the last few miserable months in New York.

After a yearslong hiatus it was meant to be her big return, a solo show at the prestigious Ornament Gallery in Chelsea. Orla was so confident in its success that she'd shown up to the opening in a gown by Alaïa, a shimmering black number with one sleeve. She had learned how to dress the part by now, taught herself to carry herself like a real artist. She'd learned in New York that to be given a chance, half the battle is to take yourself seriously. Even though she didn't feel like herself, Orla had gotten the cool shaggy haircut with curtain bangs and made sure to stand with her shoulders down and back instead of up by her ears. But this time, none of her posturing was enough to bring in a crowd. This time, the reviews had already spoken.

"A dearth of imagination," *Artforum* pronounced, rather gleefully it felt to Orla, in their review of her paintings, which were not portraits like her earlier work, but images of boxes, stacked on top of one another.

Before she could recover from that blow, a write-up in *The Times* agreed. "This transparently eager attempt has none of the confidence of her earlier work."

The boxes, shadowy cubes, some open, some closed on a stark white background, were meant to be symbolic. "Of what?" the writer was quick to ask. "It is hard to be sure."

"Of solitude and hidden trauma," her agent assured the gallerists, who'd grown nervous about the reviews. "They just don't understand," he'd scoffed dismissively at the time. But even Orla could hear the doubt creeping into his voice. She saw the flicker of worry as it passed over his eyes that he might have bet on the wrong horse after all. The show was the one that was meant to resuscitate her stagnating career, and Orla put everything she had into it, working methodically on the cubes, their sharp edges and geometric sides imprinting into her brain late into the night. Somewhere in that time she'd convinced herself that it was going to work, that the feeling she had while painting them was inspiration, not exhaustion, but even Orla had grown skeptical by the time she'd dropped them off at the gallery.

At the opening, her agent had been solemn and frantic on his phone in the corner while Orla wandered around the empty room. She hadn't put in the effort to get anyone to come. So she drifted around in her dress feeling increasingly ridiculous in a room full of boxes she'd made for herself. In the bright lights they looked less impressive than they had in her studio. Amateurish. Empty vessels with no purpose. The same could be said of her, she'd thought then.

After the fiasco, the intimate dinners and party invitations had slowed to a pathetic trickle. Not that Orla wanted to go to them anyway. She hardly had the stomach to show her face outside her apartment building by that point, let alone to posture inside the snobby museum atriums and at the self-conscious dinner parties of the elite art world. She didn't need her agent dumping her to tell her that her career was over. She had lost something in her work. Something as an artist that is necessary to survive.

And then, her dad called with an escape plan. "Think about it, Orla. You'd be doing us a huge favor," he'd said. Pressing the phone to her ear, Orla had regarded the congealing take-out noodles sitting in front of her on her coffee table. She could barely afford the rent on her apartment even before the gallery flop. The art that people once clamored for sat stacked against the walls, unviewed, gathering a layer of dust. She'd stopped painting months ago, paralyzed by the strong suspicion that no one would like it even if she did finish a piece. But Orla knew that if she didn't do something drastic, soon, she was going to start having to make portraits of people's dogs to make ends meet.

And so, she'd agreed to come back to Hadley Island. Partly as a favor to her parents, who so clearly would rather keep drinking cocktails on their Miami patio than return to Hadley, but mostly because Orla knew that to survive, she had to do *something*. And right then she had no strength to come up with anything else.

Orla's mind finally starts to drift, and her thoughts blur toward the edge of sleep, when the sound of a voice jolts her back into her childhood bedroom. It is familiar and close, a whisper into her ear like the rush of a wave. *You lie you lie you lie,* it says.

Her eyes fly open. She sits up, pulling the scratchy blanket to her chest, her ears pricking. Orla scrambles to switch on the bedside lamp, which casts a dim yellow light across the bed. She looks around the room, dark in all the corners. Her heart roars in her ears. The curtains blow out on a strong breeze revealing the black tangle of trees, and just through them the window to Alice's old room. She imagines her friend coming to the window. The way the light would flash on and off sending a beam of light across the ceiling.

The breeze stops abruptly, and the curtains go slack. Orla yanks the covers off and flees the room, scrambling downstairs, not stopping until she is under the bright kitchen light trying to catch her breath. Her fingers are clammy as they paw at the bottle of Xanax, pulling out a single pill. She gulps it down at the kitchen sink, cupping her palm under the running water. The glass rattles in the window above the sink. Startled, she raises her eyes. As she peers through her own reflection out at the darkness a strange prickling starts in her neck and radiates up through her hair and down her spine. It is the strong sensation that someone is watching her.

HENRY

There is someone moving around inside the O'Connors' house. Henry points his telescope across the bay, panning through the trees and focusing on the O'Connors' living room window. For years the family has stayed away from Hadley, using a caretaker to check in on the place, but someone is there now. Henry searches for Mary or Ed but finds no sign of them. A light goes on in the upstairs bedroom and he is startled by the flash of red hair backlit in the window. His heart thuds. *The daughter.*

It's been twelve summers since Orla O'Connor left the island. Henry knows this for certain because he made note of it, diligently writing it down in his logbooks. The same way he records everything that happens on Hadley Island. Everything he can see anyway. And based on years of observation, he'd long since concluded that the O'Connors, much like the Gallos before them, had left for good. But Orla is back.

Henry spins away from the window toward his own living room and claps his hands together. "Margie, you wouldn't believe it," he starts to say. His eyes land on the twin armchairs facing the windows and he trails off. They are lit by a floor lamp; a cup of tea has been recently abandoned, left steaming on a stack of books piled on the side table. He can hear her soft snores coming through the open bedroom door. The words catch in his throat, and he turns back to the window feeling heavy.

When he finds the O'Connors' house again, another light has come on, this time in the kitchen. The last time he saw Orla she was a surly eighteen-year-old heading off to college in the big city, her face creased into a permanent look of regret. Now in shadow he can only make out the shapes and planes of it, the broad forehead and tapered chin, the slight frown she wore even as a child. She raises her hands to her face. When she lowers them, a scowl forms on her brow. The glass disappears from view and her head tilts up to the window and she looks right at him. His heart bangs and the telescope jerks in his hands as he steps back. *No, no, that is silly, there's no way she can see me hundreds of yards into the darkness.* But still, he feels exposed. He goes to the lamp and turns it off to better hide himself.

When he returns, Orla has gone deeper into the house. The kitchen light goes off and a warmer, dimmer living room lamp comes on. He can see the edge of a blanket and the bottoms of her bare feet poking out from the side of the sofa. He wonders what has brought her back. From the brief glimpse he got of her face it didn't seem like she was here on vacation. Certainly not if she's come alone. Henry goes to his cluttered dining table and quickly pulls his most recent logbook from a pile of tidal charts and maps. He retrieves his pen from behind his ear and marks it.

6/14/23, 9:14pm. Orla O'Connor has returned.

He hurries back to the window, steadying the telescope once again on the island. He carries on, running the lens up the shore the length of the O'Connors' property, moving the telescope on its familiar path along the coastline to the Gallos' house next door. In the moonlight Henry can barely make out the shape of their old dock jutting into the water. He follows it back through the tangle of foliage to the sagging front steps.

It seems like only yesterday those two little girls would play together there. He can see them clearly in his mind even after all these years, the one with red hair and one with brown, picking their way barefoot across the strip of rocky beach at low tide, carrying toys and chattering in that delighted, open way children do. When they were young their families would meet up some evenings. He'd watch them carrying food to eat at one house or the other for Sunday dinner. Until that terrible event with Alice. He feels guilty about it still.

Henry moves the telescope up the front of the house. Now he can only see the outline of the top floor, the peak of the roof jutting up through the overgrowth like some long-buried temple. All of it left to rot. His telescope catches the glint of something. Startled, he braces himself and focuses on an upstairs window.

A light!

He sucks in a breath as a blur of something passes the window. A shadow climbs along an interior wall and tapers off. Someone is inside. He loses his grip on the telescope, sending it careening up and then down.

He fumbles to right it, his insides churning violently until once again he finds the dark outline of the roof poking up through the trees and follows it down to the second-floor window. It is dark now. Still.

He turns to a fresh page in the logbook, the pen trembling in his fingers.

FAITH

Faith has dressed herself for a night out. She's wearing black linen pants and a matching strapless top, which she's paired with gold sandals and flat round abalone earrings that glint iridescently when they catch the light. Trying to pass the time while David was away, she took forever putting on makeup, doing her lids in deep bronze, applying perfume to her wrists. She'd kept an ear attuned to the door, expecting David to show up at any moment.

But evening stretched into night with no sign of him and now Faith is beginning to feel anxious. She slips out into the hall and goes downstairs. The house is painfully quiet. And empty.

She remembers what Elena recently told her about rich people. They'd been out to dinner at a hip new omakase restaurant. A man with a Rolex had given the young women a smile, sending the two of them a round of drinks. "Looks rich," Faith had whispered.

But Elena wasn't sold. "The Rolex is too try-hard. The way you can really gauge how wealthy someone is, is by how much space they take up," she'd instructed, delicately picking up a piece of sashimi. "A truly rich person will have endless amounts of space, homes, land, cars. And it will mostly be empty and unused."

"Isn't that a little pointless?" Faith had laughed. Elena had looked at her in mock seriousness, but it was clear who was the student and who the pupil.

"I thought you wanted to learn their ways before your big vacay on Hadley next week."

"Yes, sorry. I do. Can I have more sake first?"

"Only if you listen to me." She'd laughed as Faith tipped her cup to catch sake from a small earthenware pot. "Kanpai."

The lights of Midtown Manhattan sparkled out the window behind her. "I know what I'm talking about. They aren't like normal people. Especially billionaires like the Clarkes. You can't just waltz in and be accepted. It's going to be rough at first. You have to expect them to act like they don't like you. Not just don't like you, like they hate you."

"But why would anyone hate me?" Faith asked, her eyes twinkling. "I'm so charming."

"That's exactly why. They won't trust you. They don't trust anyone."

Faith passes though the open doors out onto the veranda. The sun has already slid past the horizon. The waves are bigger now, capped with frothy white. She can hear them rushing in along the beach.

"There you are! You've made yourself at home, I hope?" David says from behind her. Faith smiles into the darkness and turns to him. *Finally.*

"I'm so sorry. I didn't mean to be gone all day. Dad had some things he wanted me to look at." She waits for him to elaborate but he doesn't. He puts his chin on her shoulder, peering out at the water. She is relieved to feel the weight of it there. All day she's felt strangely untethered.

"What have you been up to?"

"Lazing about mostly. I went to the pool."

"Sounds glorious. I wish I could have joined you."

"Tomorrow," Faith says. He murmurs a noncommittal agreement. Out in the distance, a light glints off the waves. Faith can barely make out the house on stilts she saw earlier. A dim light shines from one of its windows then blinks out. She points to it. "Does someone live out there?"

David's body tenses behind her. "Ah, yes, the Rock. Home to our island's famous recluses." He snorts derisively.

"They never leave?" The idea of it fills Faith with questions. It's like something out of a fairy tale.

"Not in years, as far as I know. But I don't pay much attention. They're total oddballs. And Henry doesn't exactly have the best reputation."

Faith continues to stare. The idea of a couple living out there with no contact to the outside world intrigues her. "In what way?"

But David is no longer paying attention. His face is illuminated by the screen of his phone.

"David!" she chides him.

"Sorry, what did you say?"

"I said, what happened to give him a bad reputation?" Faith says, irritation creeping into her chest. Bad enough that he's left her alone all day but now he's ignoring her. David must sense her frustration because he slips his phone into his pocket and takes her hand in his.

"Well, if you must know, he killed a young girl named Alice Gallo. Took her out in his boat and did god knows what to her."

Faith's heart jerks in her chest. "When was this?"

"Long time ago now." His voice is gruff, and Faith can tell the conversation is hitting close to the bone. He is looking out at the Rock now, scowling. "He was never convicted, though he should have been. There was plenty of evidence though they never found the body."

"You knew her, didn't you?" Faith asks gently.

"Just a bit, I used to see her around Hadley in the summers. Poor thing. You can never account for what people will do when they are allowed to just follow their impulses."

"I'm so sorry. That's awful," Faith says, feeling selfish. She shouldn't have pressed it. She's brought up something sad and traumatic on what was meant to be a relaxing night.

"Enough about them," David says. "Leave the past in the past, isn't that what they say?" He lifts her arm up and twirls her away from the water. "You look incredible. What is this, another of your stunning new vacation outfits? Well done." Faith smiles, giving in.

"Never mind. Where are you thinking for dinner? I'm starving," she says, eager for a reset. One day alone is nothing a glass of wine and a platter full of oysters won't fix. "Elena says that the Oyster Room is incredible."

David's smile falters. "Actually, would you be okay with eating here on the patio tonight? Dad has asked the staff to make lobster. He has his heart set on it, I think."

"Oh, okay." Faith tries not to look disappointed. She has trouble imagining Geoffrey Clarke's feelings being hurt.

"Just for tonight." David puts his hands on her shoulders to reassure her. "Says he has something important to tell us. I'll take you out tomorrow and show you off to the whole island."

"Intriguing." Faith raises her eyebrows, buoyed by the promise of being included in some interesting information.

"Come on then, let's go dine with the most terrifying man on Wall Street. Just don't tease him about his lobster bib."

David holds out his arm to her and without hesitation she takes it.

Across the table, Geoffrey cracks a lobster shell in a pair of silver pliers. He peels it apart with his fingers and slurps the head from the shell. Faith finds her stomach turning as she looks down at her plate. The lobsters came out on absurdly large platters, one for each of them. She's never liked the idea of lobsters. The boiling water, the tanks of them with their claws rubber-banded together, waiting for their time in the pot, has always made her queasy. It tugs at her conscience as she delicately pulls a claw apart, but she can't bring herself to eat it.

Geoffrey clearly has no compunction about any of it. "Got to get in there, get your fingers dirty," he booms at David. He hasn't touched his lobster yet, either, Faith notices. She catches his eye, and he gives her a tired smile.

"So, David." Geoffrey leans back in his chair. His fingers and mouth glisten with melted butter.

"So, Dad," David replies, trying to act casual, but Faith catches the strain in his voice.

"You know I had something I wanted to tell you." Geoffrey looks at him for a beat, drawing out the information. His eyes glitter in the candlelight. A small smirk plays on his lips; he's enjoying keeping them guessing.

"I'm all ears," David says.

Faith finds that she is holding her breath.

"I'm bringing back the Fourth of July party this year," he pronounces.

Faith exhales, *a party*. Elena will be so jealous. She smiles, relieved, and looks to David. But he is staring at his father, his face white with shock.

"Are you sure?"

"Damn straight," Geoffrey says.

"But why? It's been so long, what reason would you possibly have to bring it back?" Faith looks between the two of them, confused by the panic in David's voice.

"Can't the Clarkes host their annual Fourth of July celebration?"

"What reason could you possibly want to have it now after fifteen years?" His face has gone red, and pinpricks of sweat have started to form on his forehead.

"You see that dock you love so much, well it needs a real fucking mooring, okay?" Geoffrey growls. "I need the town council to grant me the fucking mooring for the yacht, but they are a bunch of morons. Size restrictions blah blah blah. Fucking idiots."

Faith reaches for David's hand, but he jerks it away and brings it clenched to the top of the table. When she looks to Geoffrey, she sees that he is watching them, amused. He takes a lobster claw and slurps from it, the matter sorted.

"This is for a boat?" David asks, incredulous. "Can't you just pay someone?"

"I would. Believe me. That would certainly be easier than this dog and pony show. But they're on about corruption. They want a celebration. And my dear old father loved that party."

"I won't go," David says, his face settling into an expression that reminds Faith of a belligerent teenager.

"You will." Geoffrey's face is getting red now.

"Do you think they'll even want to come?" Between the lines there is another conversation happening that Faith is not privy to.

"*That* had nothing to do with us." His father shuts him down. Faith waits for David to explain but she may as well not even be there. They are ignoring her completely, locked in whatever power struggle is playing out in front of her.

"You don't think they'll remember that the last time we hosted a party someone died?" David snaps. Faith's head whips up toward David.

"Alice?" she says in quiet disbelief.

Now Geoffrey turns his furious eyes on her. With a startling jolt of velocity his fist beats the table, rattling the plates. "What that man out there in his little hideaway did to that girl had nothing to do with us. And it was years ago. Enough. It's done. About damn time the rest of them realize that too. He's the one who is hiding. We don't need to."

Faith blinks and draws back from the table.

"It's not about hiding, Dad. It's respect." Faith looks out toward the water. The house on its stilts no longer looks quaint. Its angular silhouette now looks sinister. A place to escape from, not to.

"Don't you lecture me about respect, you ingrate," Geoffrey snaps. She can see the veins in his head pulsing as he turns back to his dinner, cracking open a claw, and dunking it angrily in butter. So, this is the Geoffrey Clarke Faith has read so much about. The tyrant who never takes no for an answer. Or a giant baby in a bib, swallowing down lobster meat with a disgusting slurp.

She looks back to David, but he seems unperturbed by the outburst. Maybe he's used to them. "The islanders will be surprised, won't they?"

"They'll get over it," Geoffrey says, finally dabbing his mouth with a napkin. "Hell, they'll love it. The Clarke Fourth of July is the event of the summer. At least for these people."

David hesitates but ducks his head into a nod, conceding the fight to his father.

"Okay, glad that's settled. Time to get out there and show all the little gossip queens and bumpkins on this goddamn island that we have nothing to be ashamed of." Geoffrey throws his bunched-up napkin into the center of a puddle of butter and lobster parts on his plate. He rises from his chair, breathing heavily. He gives David a rough pat on the shoulder as he passes their side of the table. "I'll see you in the morning, son. Bright and early this time."

Faith waits for David to turn to her with some sort of mood-lightening grin or explanation, but he remains looking at his father's empty chair, a vacant expression on his face.

"Are you okay?" Faith gently puts a hand on David's arm. He flinches.

"Fine," he says, but she can tell that he barely registers her there. His mind is somewhere else.

Somewhere she isn't allowed to follow.

ORLA

Orla wakes up late, disoriented from a deep medication-induced sleep. Blinking, she takes in the end of the couch, the open window with the curtain billowing into the living room on the breeze. Her stomach sinks. She is still on Hadley. Still completely lost in life.

She forces herself upright and paws around for her phone, finding it between the cushions. It's nearly one in the afternoon already. She's overslept. Not that it matters. She has nowhere to be. She pulls herself up off the couch, her legs wobbling as she stands. She stretches and stumbles over to her open suitcase. Its contents are strewn from her bag in a messy radius. Blearily, she pulls on a pair of frayed jean shorts and an ancient men's Metallica T-shirt pilfered from a long-ago ex-boyfriend. Back from the first few years riding high after her first show, back when she actually dated.

She plods into the kitchen and rummages through the cupboards, where she scrounges up some ancient coffee grounds and a cafetiere and makes herself a cup of coffee, taking it out onto the back porch. She settles into a chair and tries to make herself relax. But the quiet feels eerie and dreamlike. It disorients her.

In New York there is always noise—the woman shouting on the street outside, the trash pickup, the drone of cars shooting down the

BQE a block away from her bedroom window. But here there is only a faint papery rustle of leaves, the intermittent screech of a seagull. Orla has often complained about all the noise in the city, but the sounds were kind of comforting she realizes now, signs of other human life. She stands up and takes her coffee inside, dropping it off by the sink. Then she grabs her purse and slings it over her shoulder, making a beeline for the front door, letting the screen bang behind her.

Hadley's one grocery store has changed since Orla was last on the island. She notices a fresh coat of paint brightens its drab warehouse ceiling. Danny's has also gotten bougier since she left. Walking the aisles with her basket she notes that alongside the classic island staples, the prepared stuffed clams, and Martin's hot dog buns, Danny's is now trading in heirloom beans, expensive tinned fish, dark bottles of organic Greek olive oil.

Orla finds that she is starving as she wanders around the store dropping random things into her basket, a box of expensive seeded crackers, a block of sharp cheddar, some Marcona almonds, a bag of grapes that seem to have nothing fancy about them aside from being nearly eight dollars. She is debating whether she will actually put in the effort to prepare a paper bag of gourmet pancake mix when a woman's voice interrupts her.

"Orla O'Connor? Is that you?"

Orla's shoulders hunch in dread. Spotted already. She slowly spins around, startled to find the wizened face of her fourth-grade teacher. "Mrs. Kemper," she says, forcing some cheer into her voice. It could be worse. Alice and Orla had loved Mrs. Kemper, a quirky woman who was always coming up with art projects; her classroom was a welcome scene of paint cups and spilled glue.

Her hand lands on Orla's arm, warm and smooth. "Fran, now. You're welcome to call me Fran. And no longer Mrs."

"Oh. I'm sorry," Orla stammers. "Fran."

"Oh, don't be. Marriage was the pits. For me at least. What about you? I hear you're in New York now. A famous artist." She smiles conspiratorially, and Orla feels her mouth go dry.

"Oh, hardly," she says, laughing awkwardly.

"Are your parents here?" She looks past Orla, down the cereal aisle.

"No, they're still in Florida," she says, and a strange heaviness descends on the conversation. You don't leave Hadley Island for seven years like they did and have nothing to answer for. Ms. Kemper continues staring at Orla intently, her mouth twisted up in a curious smile. It gives Orla the creeping sensation that the woman can read her thoughts. Orla looks down into her basket, trying to block her out.

"Well, I'm so glad to see you, Orla. You and Alice were always such a delight to have in class. So creative and full of imagination."

Orla's hand grows slippery around the handle of her basket. "Thank you, Ms. Kemper." She begins to back away toward the dairy section, eager to leave before Ms. Kemper asks for more details.

"You two always had so many plans. I'm glad you at least were able to go. To New York, I mean," she adds. Ms. Kemper's bright blue eyes bore into Orla. "I'm sure Alice would have wanted it for you."

Orla's foot comes up against something and she stumbles, catching herself on the edge of a cooler.

"Thank you, yes. I was the lucky one," Orla says, feeling the words change the shape of her mouth. Ms. Kemper doesn't realize that Alice was the one with all the plans. Orla was just her sidekick. Only a shadow of a person compared to Alice. She angles herself away from the cooler, prepared to dash away. "Well, have a nice summer, Ms. Kemper—I mean Fran."

Ms. Kemper wags a finger at her. "Oh, I'm sure I'll see you again. Can't hide on an island this small."

Orla rushes down the rest of the aisles now, grabbing an assortment of random items, and heads toward the checkout. She only starts to breathe normally when she emerges into the bright sunlight and begins back up the road toward home with her shopping bags.

*   *   *

They must have been coming to the end of their freshman year of high school when Alice first told Orla what the future had in store for them. Orla remembers them lying side by side in their usual position, backs down on her bed, legs up in the air against the wall. "For circulation," Alice had explained once, and Orla had never questioned it.

It was getting late in the evening, but it wasn't quite dark outside. A light breeze and the sounds of early summer floated in through the open window, the whispering rustle of fresh leaves and the hum of insects emerging from the ground.

They'd just eaten dinner downstairs with Orla's parents. Orla's dad had made some Indian-inspired curry he was proud of. "So cute," Alice had quipped about his hobby. Her own parents rarely cooked anything, relying on a string of frozen dinners and takeout from town.

"After we graduate, we'll go to New York," she'd said, passing Orla a half-full bag of Twizzlers. "It's the only place to be a serious artist."

Orla remembers agreeing quickly with her. "Oh, yeah. I always see myself there." But in truth she'd never really thought about leaving the island until Alice said it. Orla didn't actually consider herself a serious artist back then. She was, after all, only fifteen years old. Not yet truly ready to leave home. It was a childhood delusion maybe, the way you want to grasp on to things that are impossible to hold tight forever. But who wouldn't get swept up in Alice's vision? She had every detail plotted out for them.

"We'll apply to NYU and Columbia and the New School as a backup. We can get an apartment near campus." Alice had turned to Orla, her face flushed across the blanket. "I don't want to do the dorms if we don't have to."

"Me either," Orla had said, scrunching her nose with what she hoped was enough disdain, wanting to impress her best friend.

"Okay, good. We might need to share a room at first," she'd continued, barely pausing for breath as she listed off each element. There were things Orla would never have considered, how they'd get around New York and what they would wear, the events they'd have to attend to get noticed by gallerists. Alice's plans were airtight, each point shrewdly explained like she was making a legal case.

While she laid it out, Orla had taken a Twizzler and chewed on it quietly. The more Alice spoke of it all, the more real moving away became, and the more it secretly scared her. At that age it was hard for her to think about leaving the safety of the island to go somewhere big and unfamiliar like New York. Sensing her hesitancy, Alice turned her head toward Orla, looking at her over the comforter.

"You know who else lives in New York," she'd said, a devilish grin on her lips. Orla's heart had stretched anxiously under her ribs.

She felt her face flush. "Stop it."

"A very rich young man named David Clarke," she'd said, evoking Orla's massive crush, the one that had lasted all the way from the first time they'd met him at the beach at the end of sixth grade. That kept Orla waiting to see him summer after summer. "He'll be in his second year by then. Maybe at Columbia, isn't that where he said he was applying if his dad let him?"

Of course, Orla already knew that David lived in New York; Orla memorized information about David the way other kids did with celebrities or sports teams. She knew that David preferred dogs to cats, that he had watched every Adam Sandler movie ever made multiple times. She knew his favorite food was rigatoni Bolognese from Arturo's restaurant. And of course, she knew that he lived in a limestone Upper East Side town house just a few blocks from the Met.

The idea of being close to David Clarke made Orla's skin prickle. Alice twirled the licorice suggestively around her ring finger.

"You could go see David Clarke whenever you want to if you lived there," she said in a singsongy voice. Though they both knew it wasn't exactly true. What Alice really meant was that if Orla lived in New York, she could see David whenever *he* wanted her to. But the proximity was enough of an incentive to warm her up to Alice's grand plan for them.

Alice, on the other hand, wasn't concerned with local boy crushes; she wanted an adventure. She'd been extra full of restless energy in what would end up being the last year of her life. Sometimes Orla had trouble knowing which of Alice's plans were realistic and what was a fantasy.

But either way, when it came down to it, what other better things did Orla have to do but to go along with them? And Orla had to admit that Alice's vision of the two of them was tantalizing, like something out of a movie or a TV show. Real main character energy. Part of Orla always thought that they would ultimately return to Hadley. That somehow, the island was their destiny. How odd that she is here again, but stranger still is how Alice never left at all.

The air inside the house is cold as Orla drops the grocery bags on the kitchen counter. She leans over, putting her head into her hands. When she raises her head, she sees the Xanax bottle sitting tantalizingly on the counter. She picks it up and stares at it before knocking one of them out into her palm.

Orla knows that spending the summer here means she is going to have to face the pitying looks. And the familiar questions from those who are brave enough to ask, a sympathetic tone in their voice that doesn't do much to cover their titillation. *How are you holding up? Poor thing. What do you think made him do it? What do you think he did with the body? Didn't they say she'd been spending time with him, alone?*

That one made Orla seethe most of all. As though Alice had some-how seduced Henry Wright. As if Alice herself were to blame.

Orla had imagined the night Alice disappeared a million times over, playing out scenarios where her friend had survived. Where in another parallel life they were still able to go together to New York and ev-erything had gone exactly as Alice had planned it for them. But how would a fifteen-year-old have survived on her own? How would she have managed to swim across a huge open sound with no one knowing? Whatever happened to her out in the water with Henry, there was no chance that Alice had come away from it. Orla's fantasies of Alice having somehow made it through were only that, mixed with more than a little survivor's guilt.

She opens the bottle and takes out another pill, swallowing it down with a swig of cold coffee. Soon there will be nothing more to tie any of her family to this place. They have all suffered enough. The very least Orla can do now is to free them from it.

HENRY

Henry hits the switch on an electric kettle, filthy with hardwater stains. Back when Margie was in her prime, she would never have allowed it to get so bad, he thinks with a flash of guilt, as he pulls a mug printed with a faded image of Hadley's Osprey Point Lighthouse out of the dish drainer. He glances at the closed bedroom door and tries to make his footsteps lighter so as not to disturb her as he goes to the cupboard for the coffee canister.

Before things took a turn for the worse Margie was always keeping busy, bustling around the house sweeping nooks and crannies and wiping down the edges of things, her sturdy body fussing at the stove or shaking a rug off on the wraparound deck. Henry can still hear her faintly humming along to the radio, a little out of tune. He thought at the time that he could preserve them the way they were forever and keep them safe. That if they were on this rock nothing bad could ever touch them. He was oh so wrong.

Henry carries his mug across the living room past the full wall of windows that face the windward side of Hadley Island. They give him an unobstructed view from the pier in Port Mary all the way to the lighthouse perched on the end of a rocky cliff. Everything in between is within his purview. The telescope stands on its swivel in front of a broad dining table rendered unusable by its cover of newspapers and logbooks, old bills and an assortment of open charts.

Henry takes a long drink of coffee and bends down to look through the lens, noting that the ferry has arrived, disgorging a whole new crowd of tourists onto shore. They wander along the road into town, dispersing at the village, where they check into one of the B&Bs in the old Victorians off the main drag or move farther inland to various rental homes.

With a sharp jab in his chest, he moves the telescope once more to the Gallos' house. Henry had studied the property this morning, looking for broken branches or soil upturned by footprints, but found nothing in the thick-knit foliage covering the house. He doesn't know what he expects to see, but through the vines the house remains dark and quiet, the windows gray with dirt.

It must have been a trick of the mind that he saw there, a reflection in the glass cast from a fishing boat offshore. The O'Connors' house is quiet today too. Maybe the whole thing was just a dream. He is tempted to go back to the entry in his logbook and scribble it out entirely. It would certainly ease some of the anxiety that has gripped him since he woke up.

Henry pans left, following the rocky shoreline until it gives way to the perfectly manicured sand in front of the Clarkes' mansion. The staff have been preparing the house all week. He's watched them anxiously zigzagging across the lawn, putting out deck chairs and skimming the leaves off the swimming pool's surface. But now there is a row of black SUVs in the drive that weren't there before. The family must have come in last night while he was asleep. The Clarkes are not people to take a ferry anywhere. A private plane is much more their style.

He pauses to make a note in his logbook.

3:14pm. The Clarkes have returned. Will be keeping a close eye on them.

When he goes back to the eyepiece of the telescope, David Clarke is stepping out onto the veranda, his phone pressed to his ear. He is lean and tanned, his hair parted and combed into the same timeless, conservative style as his father's. Henry finds this amusing. The young man has been quite literally groomed for the role. Since the day he was born David has had only one direction in life, which was straight in line behind his father. In business and in life. Margie would appreciate the observation. He'll have to tell her when she wakes up.

The door behind David slides open and a woman comes out to stand next to him. The hem of her blue dress flutters in the wind as she leans toward him. David turns to her, putting his hand to her hip. Their heads bend together. Henry's eyes strain as he watches her stand on her tiptoes to kiss his cheek. She turns to the water and the sun catches her face. Henry's heart lurches. *Impossible.*

A scraping sound nearby startles Henry away from the telescope. He looks out the window down at the small blue boat pulling up to his little weatherworn dock. Jean is throwing a rope over the side. She heaves the boat in, looping the rope around the mooring to secure it. She had been having trouble getting someone to cover for her at the Crab, but clearly, she took care of that. Henry doesn't know what he'd do without her biweekly visits. She's been their lifeline, the one connection they've had with the outside. Through the window he puts a hand up in greeting. She returns the gesture, squinting up at him.

As Marjorie's younger sister, Jean has been providing for them for more than a decade, ever since the incident. She never let the town rumor mill sway her. Still, Henry is eternally grateful and more than a little bit mortified by her assistance. She unloads several paper bags of groceries from Danny's Market onto the dock, then pulls herself out of the boat. He should go down and help. Henry starts toward the door and then at the last moment he rushes back across the room. He covers the logbook with a map and swivels the telescope up, pointing it toward the sky. *I'm a stargazer,* is what he'd say if anyone ever asked. Though no one ever has.

"Hi, Henry. How's it been?" Jean bustles in, followed by a breath of ocean air. He takes the bags from her and walks them over to the counter.

"Fine, fine." He pauses, eager to tell her about the O'Connor girl and the light he saw in the Gallos' upstairs window. He'd like someone to reassure him. Of course, that might mean he has finally lost his mind out here and is seeing things, an equally worrying development. He stops himself. Jean has no idea about his hobby. Margie has always made sure of it.

He notices Jean looking at the bedroom door. It's shut now. It's been staying shut later and later, making his days more and more solitary. He swallows and turns back to the counter.

"How are things going with you, Jean?" he asks instead. His voice sounds loud and unnatural from lack of use. "How's the Crab?"

"Getting crowded already. I have a feeling it's going to be busy this summer." Jean bustles around the kitchen opening cupboards and putting things away. The arthritis in her leg has gotten worse lately, he notes. It drags very slightly on the wood floor.

"That's a good thing, isn't it?" he says absently, inspecting a can of peeled tomatoes. Even though Henry hasn't been to the Salty Crab in nearly fifteen years, through Jean he knows the ins and outs of the place as though he were a regular. Every special menu item and employee scuffle. Henry enjoys the chatter. Hearing about these people with their day-to-day problems and mundane situations almost makes him feel like one of them, like he is normal. And he knows that it is good for Jean to be able to talk freely to him in a way she can't with anyone on the island. After all, who does he have to tell?

"I know I should be grateful for business being good."

He can hear the guilt in her voice. "But what?" Henry asks quickly, putting the can into a cupboard with a whole stack of others. He doesn't really cook tomatoes but doesn't have the heart to tell her.

"I don't know what has gotten into people lately. They're always wanting gluten-free lobster rolls and asking if we have reposado, whatever that is. Not asking, *demanding*. And the look on their faces when I say no. This place is changing. And not for the better."

How much the island has transformed over the years is a common theme in their conversations. Hadley has always been exclusive and monied in the summer, but there was always something more laid-back about it than other East Coast getaways like the Hamptons or Martha's Vineyard. Perhaps because of its size and how isolated it is there was something more quaint and charming about the island than some of its brasher, more commercial neighbors. But over the past few years something has shifted. Henry can feel it even from here on his little outpost. It's been, as Jean put it bitterly once, *discovered.* The crowds are bigger, younger. Boats moor in front of the marina and blare music, the girls sunning themselves on the bows in barely-there bikinis. Port Mary is nothing like the sleepy fishing village where he'd grown up. Back then the wealthy people were mostly quiet and kept to themselves. But then again, Henry thinks, maybe it's the world that is changing. Not just Hadley Island. How would he know?

Jean unloads the bags, lining up various pantry items on the counter. She grunts with the effort. Henry tries to intercede. "You don't have to do that. I am perfectly capable of putting my own groceries away."

But Jean stubbornly picks up a coffee canister. "I don't do it for you. I do it for Margie."

Henry stands down, retreating to the other side of the kitchen island. He never could go against Margie's wishes.

"The Clarkes are back," Jean says, hobbling toward the fridge with a carton of milk.

"Oh, are they?" Henry tries to sound like this is news to him but miscalculates and it comes out too quickly. Jean glances up sharply. He looks away from her, distracting himself with the grocery haul.

He pulls a box out of one of the bags and looks down at the bright packaging. "What are these?" he says, grateful to change the subject. *Chocolate-covered nuggets with crisp rice coating.*

"Ice cream bars, just like the label says. They were on special." She shrugs. It's unlike her to buy him something so frivolous. Perplexed, he puts them into the freezer next to a frost-coated hunk of haddock.

Jean sighs heavily as she leans to place a bag of potatoes into the cupboard. She seems extra exhausted lately. He stops to watch. Is she moving slower than normal? Does she look slightly older? He relies on her for so much, the idea of it scares him. "Why don't you sit down a minute, Jean?" Henry tries again. "Have a cup of tea. I can do the rest."

She waves him off with a stiff flap of her hand. "No, no. There's no time to relax. I have to get back. Have a training session with the new hire. An island girl. She's good so far. Young but surprisingly bright. And a hard worker."

"Does her family live on the west side?" he asks, trying to sound neutral, though they both know the western part of the island is the side he can see.

Jean shakes her head. "No, she's from back in the village. Her mom is Eunice Collier."

"The drunk?"

"The very one."

Henry shakes his head. He's finding lately that some of the people in town are beginning to blur in his memory after so long away. Some may even be starting to disappear altogether. The thought is frightening and keeps him diligent about his logbooks.

"But Gemma is a good kid. You wouldn't know she's had it so rough from spending time with her. I'm grateful for her. Not easy to find a young person with a decent head on their shoulders these days." Jean folds the paper bags and puts them under the counter as Henry scans his memory for the young girl or her mother, but he comes up empty. The longer he spends away from the island, the more he doesn't know about it. No matter how hard he tries to keep up, things slip through the cracks. He can only know what he can see, after all.

"What does Gemma look like?" he asks. At this Jean turns sharply and stares at him. It passes quickly, but he can see in her arched brows something he'd rather not, something that makes him take a small step back and retreat into himself, going quiet until she leaves. He watches Jean limp down to the dock and get into her little boat, motoring back to the island, the question hanging unanswered in the air behind her.

ORLA

Orla spends the afternoon cleaning and sorting the upstairs bed-rooms. Better to be busy and productive than to let the lethargy she's felt these past months come for her here. It was already starting when she returned from the store. She'd finished putting the groceries away and just stood there in the kitchen for too long, her eyes going in and out of focus. She could feel it coming for her, like a hand slowly closing around her ankle, ready to drag her down. If she sat down right then, she realized, she might never get up again. So instead, she took another Xanax from the bottle on the counter and began to clean.

The really important things in the house, those with any deep sentimental or monetary value, have long since been shipped to Florida but there are still plenty of little things to sort through. She works methodically, sitting through boxes of mostly useless odds and ends, stacks of old bills and papers, folded-up blankets and towels; going through the extra boxes in her parents' bedroom; sweeping and scrubbing the floors while listening to a podcast. It feels surprisingly good to keep moving, to feel useful. She sorts diligently through boxes under beds and in cupboards, deciding what should be kept (very little) and discarded or donated (most of it) and forming piles of each. She hasn't stopped moving in hours and her brain has so far stayed away from the topics that brought her here, the well-trodden paths that lead to no place good.

She gathers armfuls of musty-smelling linens and blankets and takes them outside. Standing in the dappled sunlight Orla shakes them out, hanging them on the clothesline the way her mom used to. It soothes her. Orla likes the way tidying up makes her feel competent, even if only temporarily.

The sheets ripple gently in the breeze. Orla takes in a deep breath of the air that smells like sweetgrass and wonders what it would be like to live here again. She could keep the house for herself and stay. She begins to imagine herself painting seascapes and selling them at a shop downtown. Could she be happy here? Living next to the Gallo house? She narrows her eyes at the laundry to avoid looking next door as a flash of memory comes back to her. *Orla is chasing Alice across the lawn toward the water. They are young, elementary age, both in their swimsuits; their tan legs pump across the grass. Alice is excited. She's heard that a humpback whale has been spotted offshore and is determined to see it. "Wait, wait," Orla calls to her, but Alice just runs faster, yelling impatiently over her shoulder, "There's no time, Orla. Keep up!"* Orla hangs another sheet on the line as a new image crowds that one out. *The rush of waves, frothing white in the moonlight. And between crests, barely visible, Alice's hands reaching up for help as she sinks into the murky black.*

Back upstairs Orla washes the floors in the hallway and the bedrooms with Murphy Oil Soap. On her hands and knees, she furiously cleans, returning the sponge over and over to the soapy bucket, scrubbing at the wood as though she might also be able to remove the horrible pictures from her mind.

Satisfied by what she's done, she returns to her bedroom. Orla braces herself and twists the handle on the closet door.

It opens into a long crawl space lined on one side with rough wooden shelves. The space inside smells of must and mildew. On rainy days when they were young, it had been Orla and Alice's secret fort. Orla's hand grasps to the right, her muscle memory helping her quickly find the flimsy string that pulls the light on. A yellowy bulb illuminates a set of long shelves containing a variety of tattered boxes, plastic bins, and stacks of board games. The edge of an old cigar box catches her attention. It is decorated with an assortment of bright stickers. Curious, she reaches up and pulls it down.

Her chest tightens as she flips open the lid and looks down at an assortment of treasures she'd long since forgotten. A string of glass beads barely clinging to a threadbare cord. She remembers the way it lay on her sun-freckled wrist. How she couldn't stop touching it, running a bead back and forth along its cord. There is a selection of shells and small rocks she picked up on the beach, their edges chipped. None are particularly special, except for when she found each of them. One for each time she saw David Clarke.

A childhood crush was all it really was. Though it felt like love at the time. Their connection was intense for how young they were, Orla had thought then. But winters were long and gray on the island. They had a way of distorting things. The Clarkes' return each summer gave Orla something to look forward to, something to cling to all those cold empty months.

As soon as late June rolled around, Orla would begin her torturous wait. When the Clarkes' driveway filled with fancy cars, she knew David's first visit of the summer would be imminent. It could take a few days or sometimes just hours for David to free himself from his father's iron grip and come to find her. She never could quite picture what he was doing in the Clarke mansion before he showed up at her house, sometimes on a new bike, or once with a boat. Always in a way that let you know that David wasn't any old neighborhood kid, he was a Clarke.

That last year, before everything went to shit, she'd had to wait longer than normal for David to show. Days had passed since the cars had arrived in the drive. Orla became so morose that she was difficult even for Alice to be around. "He'll come, don't worry," she'd said, but Orla grew more inconsolable with each passing hour. She didn't even want to leave home in case he should arrive. Exasperated, Alice eventually abandoned her, leaving on her own for the beach while Orla moped inside, her eyes always at the windows.

She had to wait an entire agonizing week before she finally heard the honking in the driveway. It was an unfamiliar sound, and because of this she knew right away it was him. She fled the kitchen, where she'd been restlessly watching her dad make rose hip jam and bounded out onto the front lawn. The Bentley was silver and stunning and so foreign to Orla that David may as well have arrived by spaceship. Alice must have heard him first somehow, and by the time Orla got there, Alice was already outside, leaning against the car like she and David had been talking awhile.

"Look who's here," Alice said, her voice teasing. Orla gave her a hard stare, telling her to shut up. An anxious lump formed in her throat as she looked to David. But he seemed not to notice.

"Orla! Aren't you going to get in?" he called when he saw her in the doorway, smiling that mischievous half smile of his.

"Going into town with David," Orla yelled through the screen door to her parents, not bothering to wait for a response.

"You take the front," Alice said with a wink, jumping into the back seat.

Orla skipped down the steps and slid into the passenger seat. The car was one of his dad's, David explained, showing Orla how the top moved up and down with the flick of a button. He was sixteen to her fifteen. A whole year ahead. It meant a lot as a teenager. Each year was so precious, a large percentage of your life when you only have fifteen of them under your belt. David looked different that year. He'd filled out in some ways but slimmed in others. His cheeks looked narrower than before, his jawline more defined.

"What's been happening since I was last here? Give me all the Hadley gossip." His voice had changed too, grown deeper. There was something about it that gave her a queasy feeling in her stomach, the same way Alice's talk of the future did. It scared her.

"There's a new owner down at Mint Ship. And the storm in February tore up the beach, they had to bring in sand from the mainland to fix it," Orla started, but Alice had interrupted her.

"Nothing. Nothing ever happens on Hadley," she'd said, sounding hard and angry enough to stop Orla from continuing.

"Where are we going?" Orla asked, trying to change the subject.

"Hidden Beach, of course," David said, reaching an arm across to playfully ruffle her hair. "Where else?" Orla willed herself to relax. She leaned back and let the air stream through her fingers. David looked over at her, dropping one hand from the steering wheel and draping it over the back of her seat. She watched as his eyes lingered a moment on her bare shoulder. She realized then that he felt it too. As they sped toward the beach, Orla knew suddenly and surely that this was going to be the summer that changed everything for her.

In the closet Orla snaps the lid of the box closed, her heart thumping. She shoves it back onto the shelf. *There's no use for any of it now*, she thinks bitterly. She'll toss it in the trash, and everything else back here, too, before she puts the house on the market. The closet air grows warm and stale. The list of obligations grows in her mind as she turns back toward the closet door, her hand already reaching for the light pull.

Orla stops dead in her tracks when she sees the drawing. It's large and sprawling, a mural covering the plaster wall on both sides of the doorframe. She'd completely forgotten about it. Orla and Alice made it one rainy afternoon when they were in sixth grade, inspired by a book they'd read in school about a secret treasure map. Orla marvels at it now, tracing her finger along the thick lines of paint that depict all their favorite places on the island. There is Danny's Market and Hidden Beach, their name for the small patch of rocky cove between their houses and the Clarke mansion. Farther up by the doorframe said mansion stands above a wild swirl of waves. A depiction of David out on the edge of the lawn. And above the door, Alice and Orla, running through the water hand in hand.

Orla had almost forgotten how good an artist Alice was, even at such a young age. You can tell which lines belong to each of them. Orla's waver, tentative, afraid for her mistakes to become permanent. But Alice's are dark black and unafraid. Orla had learned so much from her. She can only imagine how good Alice would have become.

When Orla steps back into the bedroom, a bank of thick gray clouds has rolled in, low and ominous above the water. She picks up a basket of old sheets to donate and looks out the hall window. The waves are choppy now, their crests topped with frothy white. A fat drop of rain spatters the window and then another, like long fingernails tapping on the glass. A low rumble of thunder shivers through the atmosphere.

"Shit!" Orla yells, remembering the clothesline. She drops the basket on the floor and races downstairs, flying out onto the lawn just as the downpour begins. She yanks the wet sheets and blankets off the line, bunching them in her arms and sending clothespins flying into the grass. She pulls down the last quilt, an old one her late grandmother made for her as a girl. As it falls off the line, the backyard comes into full view. The air rushes from Orla's lungs. A slim figure in a black jacket stands in the middle of the lawn. The hood is pulled down over their eyes. Wet tendrils of dark hair cling to the slender shoulders.

Orla's body jerks back, clutching the wet blankets to her chest. The person also stands still, the rain splashing off the shoulders of their jacket. They waver slightly between the trees on the back edge of the lawn.

Orla blinks raindrops out of her eyes. She raises a hand from the blankets in a tentative wave. "Hello?" she tries to call out, but her voice comes out as a thin rasp.

The figure moves suddenly, sending another shock through Orla's system. It's a woman, Orla thinks, as she watches the black coat dart across the lawn and down toward the water, disappearing onto the slope of the beach. Over the rain Orla can barely hear the engine of a boat starting up. Now she breaks free from her trance, flailing and tripping over the soaking blankets as she races back into the house. She leaves a trail of dirty wet footprints on the freshly mopped floors. It is not until all the doors are bolted shut that she yanks the curtain aside, looking down over the bending branches toward the water. But all she can see is an empty beach getting battered with waves and beyond it through the creeping mist, the almost invisible outline of the Rock.

FAITH

By morning the weather has turned stormy. Dense clouds gather above Faith as she walks along the shoulder of the road toward town. The seagrass whips into her legs, and as she passes the beach a foghorn bellows. It seems like a bad omen, but Faith couldn't bear spending another day waiting around for David in the giant house with its sterile air and quiet hallways. As luxurious as it is, something about being there has started to make her feel uneasy. A strange creeping sensation prickling along her spine, like she is being observed. She'd sat on the side of their bed for a while staring into space and then before she could change her mind, she'd texted him, *I'm going into town.*

Always having somewhere to be and someone to go with is something she's taken for granted these last few years in New York. It's only been recently, since falling in with Elena, that Faith has been constantly around people, but she's gotten used to it quickly. She tries to remember the ring instead, glittering in its tufted box. Waiting for her.

The electricity in the air makes her pick up her pace until she reaches a bend in the road and Port Mary comes into view, a small strip of low buildings along the churning shoreline. Their bright colors look garish in the gloom. Faith hadn't had any destination in mind when she left, just a desperate need to get out of that house.

The town is more low-key than pictures online indicate. She's halfway through it in a few minutes. She finds herself at the ferry dock, looking out at the ocean. Waves knock at the boats moored out in the harbor, sending their masts swirling like bath toys. From here she can see the back decks of the restaurants she's read about. They are empty now, but their tables are set for dinner. Faith wonders if David will manage to bring her to one of them tonight or if she should prepare herself for another awkward family meal at the house. There is something deeply unpleasant about Geoffrey that she wasn't expecting.

She turns back to the road and peers into one of the shops, its windows displayed with sweatshirts and trinkets made from seashells.

The rain starts suddenly. It pummels the pavement, turning the sidewalk dark and slick. Barely able to see through the storm, Faith dashes toward the row of restaurants on the side of the pier. She ducks inside the first one she sees, a red-painted block of a building with a hand-painted sign that reads The Salty Crab swinging wildly in the wind above the doorway.

Inside it is darker than she would have expected, more of a bar than a regular restaurant. A handful of tables surrounds an old horseshoe bar already scattered with people, most of them staring quietly down into their drinks. Tom Petty plays on the jukebox over a clack of pool balls in the dimly lit bump-out in the back. *Leave it to me to seek refuge in a dive bar*, Faith thinks.

The bartender, a sturdy woman with a shock of curly silver hair, moves like she has worked in service for most of her life, her hands sure and steady on the taps as she pours another beer and slides it over to a man with a big gray mustache at the end of the bar. Faith hesitates, glancing back at the street where the rain is coming down in a torrent.

"Take a seat," the man says. He kicks out an empty stool next to him.

"Oh, I—" She looks behind her through the door to the rain pummeling the pavement.

"It'll be here a minute. This storm's not passing anytime soon. Stalled out just offshore." He shakes his head as he lifts the full beer to his mouth. The foam sticks to his mustache, making him appear walrus-like. "Might as well let Jean make you a drink."

Faith approaches the bar, cautiously claiming the empty stool a few down from his. She glances up at a dusty anchor hanging precariously from an ancient-looking rope above the bar. The old nautical maps on the walls are stained with a thick layer of grease. Below them a group of locals watch her from behind their pint glasses. Despite the long stares and bad lighting, Faith feels instantly at home inside the Salty Crab. These are her people. Or they were.

"Leave the poor girl alone," the bartender says, rolling her eyes. She slides a plastic-coated menu across the bar. "Take a look. I'll be right back."

"Try the clam cakes. Best on the island," the man says. Pale blue eyes sparkle from a web of squint lines when he speaks. He is wearing a faded T-shirt, its seams rippled with holes. The white of his beard make his deep tan even more pronounced. He hasn't stopped watching her since she came in. Faith wonders if she's made a mistake.

"What can I get you?" the bartender asks, resting a solid hip against the bar. Faith notices the ropy muscles in her forearms. She is a woman who has worked hard for a long time. It reminds her of home.

"I'll have the chowder and some clam cakes. I hear they're delicious," she says, looking sideways to catch the approval of the man next to her. The bartender nods, pulling the menu away. Then before she turns completely away, Faith adds, "Oh, and could I also have a beer, whatever your lightest is, mixed with tomato juice?"

The bartender gives her a quizzical look before she reaches down for a glass. "Not a drink order I've heard in a while."

A red beer, Faith's family called it when she was growing up. Her mom would make them in the heat of summer to beat whatever hang-over she was nursing. A can of V8 tipped into whatever light beer was on special from the Stop and Save. Her mom would pour one for each of them, putting more beer in her own glass. Faith had never admitted to anyone that she drank them, knowing somehow that it was odd and not wanting to get her mom into trouble. Jean raises her eyebrows ever so slightly but makes her the drink. Faith watches the beer swirl into the tomato juice, her mouth already watering.

Vile and *disgusting* were the words Elena had used the one time Faith ordered her favorite drink in her presence. They were on vacation in Tulum and terribly hungover. "Please never get that again. I don't want people to see me with you drinking it." She'd glared at Faith over her sunglasses. "Plus, it smells horrific."

And so, duly shamed, Faith hadn't allowed herself one since. Back then she was just starting to learn what was acceptable behavior among the monied class of people she'd suddenly found herself surrounded by and did not want to mess it up. There were unspoken rules, she was coming to understand. Faith was learning them over time through Elena's intensive exposure therapy as she brought her to catered parties at penthouse apartments and on weekends to the Hamptons. It was all in the details, she learned. And unless you were very careful it was all too easy to slip up and draw attention to yourself in ways that would not get you invited back. It was lucky Faith had Elena to teach her. But then, Faith was always a quick study. She could learn anything as long as there was a purpose behind it.

After Elena's scolding, even when Faith was tempted, she'd never allowed herself to order a red beer in New York, not wanting to make herself into some sort of conversation piece, as though it would draw a straight line from her to her humbler origins.

Now as she tastes the forbidden tang of the drink, Faith closes her eyes for a moment and is transported home, back to the bar where she was practically raised, a hole-in-the-wall if there ever was one, just off the highway a mile or so from her mom's place. It had a deer hunt game in the corner and a lineup of vintage beer cans on a shelf behind the bar way up by the ceiling. The whole place was stained with old cigarette smoke and grease from the kitchen, and it had a faint smell of spilled beer no matter how early in the day.

Faith can clearly picture her mom playing pool with her aunt Shelly in the back corner, the way her mom's smoker's cough crackled through the bar when she laughed too loudly, which usually meant she was starting to get drunk. She can see a very young version of herself eating french fries at the bar, chatting up Diane, the owner, or occasionally falling asleep below the pool table, the drunken chatter and jukebox music lulling her to sleep. Why does part of her long for it?

"Did you have Jean put tomato juice in your beer?" a voice interjects, jolting her out of the memory.

"It's a family tradition." Faith turns her head and smiles at the man, relieved not to be self-conscious for once.

"Cheers to that," he says. "Family is everything." She holds out her glass and lets him tap his against hers, a strange lump forming in her throat. Faith doubts David has ever set foot in here. She realizes that she's never been anywhere with him that isn't perfectly cultivated to bring you the most pristine dining experience, with the best food, where the wine list didn't include regional varietals. In other words, a place that isn't swarming with rich people.

"I'm Walter, welcoming committee here at the Crab," the man says.

"Self-appointed welcoming committee," Jean interjects, returning from the kitchen with Faith's food. "No one would hire him. That's why he had to retire from commercial fishing; not even the fish could handle his company." She smirks at her own joke.

"Yeah, yeah, Jean, I get it." Walter's T-shirt strains atop his beer belly as he leans back in his barstool. He looks at Faith a beat too long for comfort, a strange expression coming over his face. "You're familiar."

Her heart thuds reflexively. "No, it's my first time here. First time on Hadley Island at all."

"Are you sure? There's something about you. I swear I've met you before." He is still gazing at her, when a young girl steps up to the side of the bar. She is wearing a green apron with a red googly-eyed crab embroidered on the front.

"How's it going today, Gemma?" Walter asks. Faith notes the red flush that has crept into his cheeks from the alcohol. "Gemma is the only member of this fine new generation who seems to know how to work."

Faith suppresses a smile at hearing this kind of criticism coming from a man who is drinking beer midday on a Tuesday.

"I like your dress," Gemma says. She looks at Faith as though she might be some sort of celebrity. "It's Celine, right?"

"It is! Good eye. You follow fashion?" The girl nods, smiling shyly. Faith looks at her more closely, noting the on-trend bangs, the shirt that she has carefully buttoned up under her apron, the cutoffs with the patchwork. The dangling silver earrings. It is all so deliberately styled it is obvious to Faith that she has an eye for it. "You look like you do."

Gemma beams. "I love it. All of it. Not just the big-name designers, either; I love the small ones, too, the ones who do interesting and risky things. No one has any style here. You're from New York, aren't you? You can always tell when a New Yorker comes in." Her eyes are wide and shining. She's young and sweet, but also has a sharpness to her, a hunger. She's just like Faith must have been at her age. "I'm so jealous you live there."

"Oh, don't be. Really, it's so pretty here? Appreciate it while you can," Faith says before leaning forward and whispering conspiratorially, "But then get out. Was the best thing I ever did."

"Gemma, don't mean to interrupt your chitchat," Jean says insincerely, dropping a collection of drinks on the rubber mat. "When you're done, take these to table thirteen." Gemma gives Faith a little eye roll as she loads them onto the tray. When Jean has gone around to the other side of the bar, Gemma leans toward Faith. "I'm going to move to Paris soon," she whispers, her breath hot on Faith's cheek. "I'm saving up money at the Crab this summer so that I can go. I already know people who are going to put me up there in the fall. Got it all planned out."

Before Faith has time to respond, Jean comes around the side of the bar, her arms loaded with full beer glasses. "Gemma, I mean it. No time for dawdling."

There is a startling clap from Walter. "I got it now! You know, but Jean, tell me if it's true. Faith here is the spitting image of Alice Gallo!" he says. Faith's entire body jolts at the name of the dead girl.

"Stop it right now, Walter," Jean says, her voice thick with warning as she dries a glass. "You're drunk."

But Jean is studying Faith's face now, too, and it seems she doesn't like what she sees.

"This is only my second beer," he protests. "You know you see it too."

"Second beer and after two whiskeys, but it is striking," Jean concludes. "Where'd you say you're from?"

"I didn't, but New York, well, via Oklahoma," Faith admits, unsure how to process this new piece of information.

At this, Jean's shoulders drop, relieved. "You see, Walter? Oklahoma. There's no connection."

Faith's legs wobble as she jumps down off the barstool. The room has filled up with couples and tourists, their wet umbrellas collapsed at the sides of their tables as they settle in for an afternoon of drinking and eating.

"You take care," Walter says. The way he waves at her, she knows he doesn't expect to see her again.

"Nice to meet you," Faith says, giving him a genuine smile. She digs inside her ludicrously expensive straw purse for her wallet and leaves three twenties on the bar. Her mom's morals may have been mostly off-kilter, but she taught her daughter to always tip well, even if you're broke.

"Think of it like an investment in your future, kiddo," she'd said more than once on the drive home from the bar, her eyes red around the rims, a lit cigarette dangling from her fingertips. "You never know when you might need a friend."

Outside the rain has stopped. The sky has cleared and is streaked with yellowy poststorm clouds as Faith returns to the Clarke property. When she gets to the gate, she finds that the door she left from, straightforward enough on the inside that she paid it no mind, is only a sleek rectangular shape with no visible handle on the outside. She skims the surface with her hand, prying at the edge with her fingertips. She takes out her phone to text David and realizes she hasn't heard from him all day. Strange, as back in New York he was always checking in.

"Name." A mechanical voice crackles ominously above her. Faith jumps back, startled, and looks up. A red light blinks high above the gate. It is attached to a sleek black lens of a camera. It pivots, focusing in on her.

"Hello?" she calls up to it uncertainly, feeling suddenly quite vulnerable standing there in her sundress. She glances down the road, afraid for a moment that she'd wandered back to the wrong waterfront mansion. But it says it right there next to the gate, chiseled into a hulking piece of decorative granite: Clarke Residence.

"Name," the voice repeats without any intonation.

"I'm Faith, I'm staying here. I'm a guest of David's?" Faith explains, becoming less sure as she talks if she is talking to an automaton or an actual human.

There is a pause long enough for her to think she might be left out there all afternoon, but then some mechanism inside the door pops and it glides open, framing a view of the Clarke mansion in all its white marble glory. As soon as Faith walks through the door it slides shut and she can hear the lock closing. She walks up the front drive with a shiver in her spine. She glances up at the trees looking for more blinking lights, feeling like she is being watched.

Back inside, the house is still and quiet. Faith wanders from room to room, hoping she'll run into David. The lack of communication is starting to make her feel strange, like she is an interloper here. She goes from the foyer to a sort of lounge complete with a floor-to-ceiling humidor, peering down on a vast assortment of Cuban cigar boxes. Even in here the design is austere, the gleaming enamel banquettes and stuffed leather chairs all surprisingly unused and devoid of any personal items. The next room has two walls that look out at the water. It contains only a white grand piano in the center. The rooms all have a sparseness to them, all deathly quiet except for the low hum of climate control.

Faith wanders into a spacious living room with low-lying furniture so pristinely white it would be nerve-racking to sit on it. She stands up against the wall-size windows. The ocean undulates just past the lawn. She presses her forehead to the cool glass, watching the water rushing silently into shore. She gets the odd sensation she is watching it on a screen instead of in real life. She turns and marvels at the built-in bookshelf that contains a sparse assortment of curated vintage books and sleek objects. Faith is surprised to find a single photograph set on a shelf next to a minimalist blue glass orb.

It is black and white, taken on the front lawn of the house. The house was smaller then, Faith notes, picking the frame up off the shelf. The windows were far narrower and paned, and the veranda only stretched half the house. A teenage David stands on the lawn next to his father. Faith brings the picture up to her face to have a better look. He looks uncomfortable. But it can't be David, she realizes. The image seems far too old, taken back when pointed collars and high-waisted men's pants were in style. It must be Geoffrey with his own father, she realizes, uneasily. How strange that he and David could look so alike in childhood and so different from each other now. Behind Geoffrey and his father, three very young women lounge by the pool in skimpy low-rise bikinis. Geoffrey's friends perhaps. Faith looks around the bookshelf for more evidence of his family, but there seem to be no photographs anywhere of David, or perhaps more pointedly of his mother, who she has always been curious about but who David is reluctant to speak of. From what Faith has gathered online, she was once a famous socialite and model who left the family quite suddenly when he was barely a teenager.

"Addiction problems." David had sighed heavily on one of the rare times his mother had come up, after a few bottles of wine had made him a bit maudlin and reflective. "I've hardly heard from her since I was

a kid. Dad did what he could to help her out, but she was so far gone."
The rest of the story Faith had gleaned from old tabloids she found
online. But she knows it's something that has informed his life. How
could it not? Faith thinks how lonely it must have been for him growing up shuttled from place to austere place. There is nothing cozy about
this house. It is all glossy surfaces and sharp edges, no place for a child.
For the first time she almost pities him. For all her flaws, her mother
was a presence in Faith's life, whereas David, from all she has gathered,
was just alone.

A clock is ticking somewhere. Faith looks at the bar in the corner,
running her hand along the top-shelf liquors, most of which she's never
heard of. She lingers for a moment, tempted to make herself a drink. Her
buzz from earlier is already starting to wear off. She turns instead back
to the hallway. Farther on, it leads down into another wood-paneled
section of the house. Faith marvels that there is so much house for so
few people. What could you possibly do with it all? There is something
clinical and almost dead about it. Faith remembers again how Elena had
once told her that the way to gauge the value of a rich person was to
notice how much empty space they created.

Faith stops at the vibration of male voices behind a large wooden
door. She recognizes the sound of David's first, muffled. She is initially
relieved and steps closer, raising her hand to knock. "The girl, the girl."
Geoffrey's voice cuts in, his baritone assertive and angry. "I'm sick of
hearing about her."

Faith moves in closer and holds her breath, leaning up to the crack
in the doorframe.

David's strained reply is clearer now. "You might be tired of hearing
about it, but you can't erase things just because you want to. That's not
how it works."

"Don't you tell me about the way things work." Geoffrey's voice is
a warning rumble of thunder. "You owe me. I have always done only
what's best for you."

"I'm sorry, Dad. I appreciate all you've gone through to make things good for me—" David's voice is quieter now. Faith strains to listen. "You know this isn't something I *want* to revisit."

"Good. It's over then. There is nothing else to discuss."

Faith glances once again down the empty hallway. She should not be listening to this. But she doesn't move.

"And what about the other thing?" David's voice wavers so uncertainly Faith almost doesn't recognize it.

"What *about* her?" Geoffrey growls, dismissively.

"I wanted to know what you think. That's why I brought her."

Faith's stomach drops. They are talking about her.

She hears Geoffrey grunt in response. "I said my piece already about that situation. It's not right. Keep looking."

Faith's neck prickles as she waits for David's reply. But no more is said. Finally, there is a wooden thump, the rattle of a drawer as it slams shut. The heavy scrape of a chair on the floor sends Faith jumping back and rushing up to their room.

Faith says nothing when David returns several minutes later. How could she when she isn't supposed to know anything?

"How was the rest of your day? You said you went into town?" he asks. Is she imagining the flash of guilt on his face? "Sorry I didn't text you right back. I was immersed in business chatter. So incredibly boring and tedious. I wish I could have been with you."

"Didn't do much, just walked around a little and came back," she says, omitting her time at the Crab and the overheard conversation. Why tell David anything when he has secrets of his own? But he doesn't seem to notice her withholding anything. He is distracted by something on his phone. The togetherness she has felt leading up to this trip has dissolved. Faith feels like she might start to cry.

She is waiting for him to say something else, but when she turns her head back toward him and opens her eyes she can see the glow of his phone like a halo over his head.

She closes her eyes and tries to picture Alice Gallo.

HENRY

The fog blows in suddenly, a woolen blindfold that turns the windows of the house a blank gray. Even the sound of the waves is muffled as Henry steps out onto the deck. It is times like this, when there is no one to see, nothing to make a record of, that Henry feels like he is living on the edge of the world.

He is finally giving in to Margie's prodding. It's a good time to go take care of things. The fog will give him enough cover if he moves quickly.

With a growing sense of dread, he picks up a bucket and descends the stairs to the dock. He tries to avoid the sag in the steps, stepping lightly on the edges. He mentally adds them to the list of things he'll need to fix soon.

But he doesn't want to face all that now. One thing at a time. When he reaches the bottom of the steps he turns away from the dock and doubles back, ducking underneath the stairs instead. He carefully steps off the wood and up onto the rock below the house. It is dark down here. The entire thing has been shifting. The stilts are weatherworn and covered in wet moss, the bright green of it garish in the opaque light. Henry will need to replace some of them soon, before the entire house topples into the sea. His feet scrape along the jagged face of the rock, sending small stones flying.

He takes the familiar path under the house, ducking through the pylons, his feet slipping into the crags until he reaches the far side of the island, the one facing away from Hadley. Here the rock cleaves apart, giving way to a shallow divot filled with small stones. He slides down the angular face of the shale until his feet hit the pebbles below. It's lower here than anywhere else. Close to sea level. This is the only place on the Rock where the ground is soft enough to dig.

He looks for the marker, his heart thrumming as he scans the rocks, nervous at first that it has washed away. He finally finds it closer to shore than he remembers. It is simple, almost tragically so, a single heavy gray stone that stands out only because of its relative size and uniquely smooth surface streaked with a spiderweb of white lines.

Henry swallows. Margie was right, he's put it off for too long. The area has been hit by a recent storm surge, which, combined with a full moon, brought the tide farther in than he'd ever seen it. The small stones around the marker have washed away, forming a deep divot on either side, exposing more than he'd expected. The dampness has made its way through his thin shirt. He shivers. Now he'll have to make up for lost time.

Henry works diligently, moving back and forth to the water's edge to collect bucketfuls of sand and rocks. His muscles strain with the effort, dumping them into the opening and smoothing them into the cracks, making sure nothing is exposed. He hears a motor through the fog. A set of waves comes in soon after, a wake from some nearby boat. It sends water up to his ankles. Breathing heavily, Henry watches, helpless as some of the new sand washes away. The house creaks above him. The island itself has been slowly deteriorating, the rock breaking and shifting, pieces of it sliding into the sea as though it is trying to give away his secrets.

A foghorn blares offshore. The sound startles Henry and he slips. His leg slides into a crack in the rock. His yelp of pain is absorbed by the clouds. The rock opening is new, a sharp cut where it was once smooth. His shoe is wedged inside the opening. There is a dribble of bright blood on his leg when he finally pulls it free. He looks down, watching with a sick feeling in his stomach as it trickles down the side of his shoe and onto the wet rocks.

The sky is already beginning to clear as Henry staggers back toward the dock. He feels the sun on his back as though it has caught him doing something untoward. He rushes toward the safety of the house and the comfort of his telescope. He tries not to linger on what he's just done. But as he climbs the stairs up from the dock, he hears Margie's voice in his head, anyway: *We have no choice, Henry. It's the only place that makes sense to bury someone.*

Part Two

SIGNALS

FAITH

L et's go to the beach," Faith says, propping herself up on her hand and gazing over at David with the sultriest look she can muster. It's been a week since her trip to the Salty Crab and she's nearly forgotten about the dead girl. David has been himself this last week, only going off occasionally with his father. Otherwise, they'd been relaxed, if a bit shut in, spending time by the pool together, and in the evenings drinking wine on the dock, their feet dangling over the waves. Faith has become more comfortable thinking of herself as David's fiancée. She smiles when she imagines her life of ease and leisure, free from worry. All she needs now is the ring on her finger.

"The beach?" he mumbles, looking into his phone. She gently lifts it from his hand. His eyes turn to her, questioning. She moves toward him on her hands and knees.

"The beach. We are on an island, aren't we?" she teases him. "I hear the beaches are good here. Plus, I have this brand-new bikini I was hoping I could try out."

He cracks ever so slightly when she says this, and she knows she has his attention finally.

"That *is* very tempting. I'll need a visual. What does it look like?"

How annoying that men are so predictable,, but it's useful, she supposes, that they are easy to manipulate.

"Well, it's red," Faith starts. His hands are on her now, as she moves on top of him.

"Oh, how interesting."

"And very, very small," she continues. It's working. His hands are around her hips now, pulling her toward him.

"I'd love a look at this very small bikini. In fact, you should feel free to try it on right now." She forces herself to roll away. If she gives in too easily, she is afraid he'll abandon her once more. She pulls herself upright and winces theatrically like he's about to miss out on an amazing opportunity.

"Oh no, I'm afraid that won't be possible. See, I only wear my newest bikinis to the beach, so you'd have to take me somewhere if you wanted to see it." David seems to consider this a moment, propping his head up with his hand to gauge her seriousness.

"Sure, yes, of course we'll go," he pronounces, pulling her back on top of him.

"Finally!" she squeals happily. David is smiling now, too, looking once again like the man she knows and loves. Faith feels herself starting to relax as she straddles him, bending down until her hair hangs in a curtain over his face. Her plan is going to work. He reaches his lips up to hers. "Anything for you and your little bikini."

When they step out onto the driveway, a vintage white Porsche convertible is already waiting for them. They get in and zip down the drive and out onto the main road that loops around the island.

The heaviness that's been building inside her the last few days dissipates as soon as they leave through that giant gate at the end of the drive. Faith takes in big gulps of the ocean air, finally feeling like she can breathe.

The seagrass crimps in the wind as they fly past. The dunes give way to a view of the beach, the pale sand scattered with bright specks of towels and beach umbrellas. This is what she was imagining when she agreed to come to Hadley Island. This and, of course, him. She glances at David. His mouth is pinched as he takes a corner. She puts a hand on his arm, and he turns to her and smiles reassuringly. *It's all okay*, Faith tells herself. She's spent so much of her life on high alert waiting for the other shoe to drop, but maybe she was overthinking things.

When they swerve to a stop on the side of the road, Faith steps out of the car into the sandy parking lot feeling like she is truly on holiday for the first time. David pulls two folded beach chairs and an umbrella from the tiny back seat.

He leads her to a break in the dunes, where a narrow boardwalk fringed with seagrass opens up to the sparkling ocean.

"What do you think?" he asks when they arrive at a wide crescent beach hemmed in on both sides by stony hills and thick greenery.

"It's gorgeous." Faith looks out at the clear water.

"Whitest sand on the island, and clearest water too. Let's set up down there," he says, pointing to a rocky outcropping at the far end of the beach. She takes off her sandals as she follows him. They pass groups of sun-kissed teens, mothers under umbrellas slathering sunscreen on young children. Seagulls move in on bags of potato chips.

"We came here all the time growing up," David says, with the first bit of joy she's seen on his face since they've arrived.

"With your mom and dad?" Faith asks, surprised. She has trouble imagining Geoffrey relaxing at the beach. Faith knows little about David's mother other than that she was a famous model when she met Geoffrey Clarke. The tabloids she'd seen showed an astoundingly beautiful woman consumed by addiction problems.

David looks at her as though surprised by the suggestion.

"Dad was never much of a beach person." He smirks at the idea of it. "I came here with friends mostly. How's this?"

David stops, setting their things on a patch of soft sand.

"It's perfect," Faith says, happy to finally have him all to herself. David begins to set up the umbrella and Faith looks down the beach to where a father and young girl build a sandcastle on the beach. The scene is so sweet that Faith feels a pang of sadness that she never got to experience anything like it growing up. How lucky that little girl is to grow up coming here, to know the kind of safety of family vacations, to want for nothing. Faith realizes with a shock that soon enough this could be her family, her child. She allows the questions about David and his father to recede to the back of her mind. She longs for this life with an ache in her chest. Suddenly she wants nothing more than for David to propose, to seal the deal. She glances back at him, and he meets her look with a genuine smile.

"Now what about introducing me to this bikini of yours?"

She winks at him and pulls off her cover-up, a short white linen dress that ties in the front. She'd pulled no punches when choosing the suit. It is small and extremely well cut, accentuating her long legs and toned stomach. David turns to watch, shielding his eyes from the sun.

"So, glad you took the day off?" she says, dropping the cover-up onto the towel.

"Extremely." He grins as Faith digs a tube of sunscreen out of her straw bag. She applies it liberally, rubbing it into her legs slowly, soaking in David's attention, the first she's had of it in what feels like forever. The sun is already warm on her skin. The gentle lapping of waves and fine mist of salt water in the air soothe her. Maybe now she can relax. Maybe she can just be happy to be here. After all that she's gone through, surely she deserves it.

"Hey, could you get my back?" she asks, holding out the tube. When David doesn't respond, Faith turns to find that his eyes are no longer on her. She follows his gaze to the shoreline, where a woman stands ankle-deep in the waves, the weight on one leg pushing out her round hip. Her hair, the kind of thick, luxurious strawberry-colored silk Faith couldn't even dream of, is knotted on top of her head. And she is staring at David in a way that makes Faith suck in her breath.

The way David is looking back at her with undisguised fascination gives Faith a sharp twist of envy in her chest. The girl glances back at David casually at first and then does a double take, her mouth dropping open in surprise. Faith watches with dread as something intimate and unknowable passes between them.

"Who's that woman?" Faith whispers.

"What woman?" His voice is light and measured, but the levity is gone from his face. His hand grips the wooden edge of the beach chair.

"The one with the red hair," she pushes, as though it isn't obvious who she is talking about. She nods toward the woman who is making her way across the beach to them, a broad smile on her face. David makes too much of a show of trying to think about who she is talking about. "Oh, *Orla?* She's just someone I knew back when we were kids." He says it like he might have forgotten about her until right now. But it is obvious that isn't true.

"A girlfriend?" Faith feels strangely jealous.

"No! God no," he assures her, though his face is dark and inscrutable. "Just a girl I knew when we were both very young. I haven't seen her in a long time."

The woman's presence has done something to David. His shoulders are tense, like he is doing everything he can not to leap off his towel and go to her.

"Oh, why not?" Faith presses. Her voice must have grown impatient because David's head finally snaps toward her, freed from whatever spell he's been under. Orla's hair catches in the wind, a billowing flame-colored curtain, as she approaches.

"Well, whoever she is, it looks like she's coming over here."

ORLA

The air has that beginning-of-summer feel to it, clean and new, as Orla puts her feet cautiously into the surf. The water is crisp and so clear. She goes out another step, her chest buzzing nervously as the gentle waves swirl around her legs. Even if it was warm enough to dive in, Orla's fear would keep her from going out. Orla had once loved to swim, but now when she looks down into the water, all she sees is Alice. The tangle of her hair in every piece of seaweed. Her pale hands stretching up through the dark. A swell of icy water comes up around her feet and she feels Alice's fingers on her ankles. *Why didn't you save me?*

Orla shudders and turns back toward the shore.

And that is when she sees him, in *their* spot no less, lounging on the beach as though he doesn't have a care in the world. David Clarke looks exactly like he did in high school. If anything, he unfairly has become more handsome with age, his physique still slender but filled out, his jawline more defined. He leans back, letting the sun hit the flat ripple of his abdomen.

Next to him a woman pulls off her white cover-up, exposing a barely-there red bikini that shows off pieces of her toned core and long legs. She turns, shading her eyes as she decides which direction to place her towel. She is beautiful. Frustratingly so. But she is also familiar. Orla's heart pounds as she takes in the slim build and tan skin. She watches, riveted, as the woman pulls a tube out of her straw bag and begins to apply sunscreen, rubbing it thoroughly into each part of her body as though showing off how perfectly formed it is.

Orla glances down at her old one-piece and pale legs. Her feet look wide and bluish under the water. Nothing like the beach to make a person feel inadequate both in body and in life.

The woman sits down, finally finished with her performative lotion application as the man finishes putting up the umbrella. When he is done, he pulls himself fully upright and runs his fingers though his hair. He says something to the woman, who tilts her head up to look at him through her oversize sunglasses and smiles broadly. He turns and sits in one of the chairs.

In some ways the woman is exactly who Orla would have expected David to be with. Outwardly perfect. Inwardly, she is fairly certain, more shallow than a wading pool. Orla imagines that she is the kind of woman who won't ask too many questions or press him on where his money comes from or try to control what he does in his free time. Orla had always hoped for better from David but maybe that was naive of her. As much as he went on to her about breaking free from his father's clutches and doing his own thing one day, everyone must have known that David was always going to turn into Geoffrey. With his boarding schools and private planes, how could he have ever become anything else?

Now the woman beside him notices David staring. Orla watches the woman's glossed lips purse as she tries to suss out what is happening between them. Or perhaps to determine whether Orla is a threat. Her body buzzes self-consciously. Does she know about her and David's past? But there is no way she would know anything unless he told her, and Orla suspects very strongly that David never would.

Her first impulse is to flee. But then she'd be spending the whole summer hiding from him. She can't let him see her act afraid. There is only one thing for her to do. She starts toward them with a smile plastered to her face as she makes her way across the sand.

"Orla." David waves when she gets close enough, his face transforming into something less like shock and more like friendliness. "Is that you?" His voice is far deeper than she remembers, with a hint of Geoffrey's rumbling resonance to it.

"Hi!" she manages. She stands awkwardly as he rises from the towel and comes to join her, leaving the woman on her beach chair watching. He lowers his voice when he reaches her. "Didn't think you'd come back here," he says in a voice quiet enough for his companion not to hear him.

"I could say the same of you," Orla responds, her stomach churning anxiously. He's standing so close that she can see each of the freckles scattered across his taut, tan chest.

"I come every summer. Why wouldn't I?" He raises his shoulders in total innocence, but his voice is snippy. Orla stares back at him, trying to find the young boy she knew so well. He glances back to where the woman watches from her towel. She lowers her sunglasses and stares straight at her with Alice's eyes. Orla sucks in a breath.

"I see you brought a friend."

"Oh, yes, that's Faith." At the sound of her name, the woman pops up from her towel eagerly. *Too eagerly*, Orla thinks as she bounces effortlessly across the sand toward them.

"Hi," she says, pulling a piece of shiny hair from her face. Faith sticks her hand out and Orla is forced to go through the motions of shaking it. It is so delicate she feels like she might crush the bones inside.

"Orla is an artist back in New York," David says, a sarcastic edge to his voice that disorients her. His girlfriend doesn't seem to notice.

"Oh, amazing, what kind of art? Would I have seen it anywhere?" Faith asks in that annoying way nonartistic people ask about art. It sounds benign enough, but Orla can tell she is threatened.

"No, I'm sure not," Orla says, brushing it off.

"She's selling herself short. Orla's quite successful, actually," David says, dropping his arm around Faith's shoulders and pulling her toward him. Why does it seem like he's pretending? Orla swallows.

"What about you, what do you do?" Orla asks, dodging the attention.

There's an uncomfortable pause as Faith digs her perfect toe into the sand. "I'm actually between things at the moment," she says, glancing up at David. *Already getting money from Daddy Warbucks,* Orla thinks ungenerously. She is starting to get dizzy in the open sun like this. Her knees wobble dangerously. What would it be like to collapse onto the sand in front of them? Would she ever recover?

"I have to go, actually," she says quickly, feeling like she might pass out. "Meeting someone. Just so busy, you know. Lots of, um, island things to do. People to catch up with."

"Yeah, I bet," David says. She turns away from them and flees, stumbling across the sand toward the parking lot. As she regains her footing, Orla is horrified to find herself still attracted to him.

HENRY

Jean's boat pulls into the dock below Henry's window. Henry straightens his shirt, wishing he'd thought to check on the state of his hair in the bathroom. He starts to raise his hand to wave and stops short. There is a young girl with Jean this time. Surprising. His heart twists anxiously as she follows Jean up the steps, holding up fistfuls of brown shopping bags from Danny's.

"Morning, Henry," says Jean, and he sees now that her hand is wrapped with a thick white bar towel. "Had to bring this one along to help."

"Hello," he says, his voice rough from lack of use. "Are you Gemma?"

Jean pauses at the door, and Henry sees the slight panic in her eyes. "I should have brought one of the kitchen staff but they're all so busy this time of year. Gemma, why don't you leave those and wait down by the boat."

But the girl has already stepped into the house with the bags. She gives Henry an easy smile. "Where should I put these?" Henry hasn't seen a new person in the house in so long. He tries not to stare as she moves around the kitchen island.

"Please, let me," Henry says, taking the bags by the handles. He has all but forgotten what young people look like, the slight awkwardness to them, as if they are still new in their skin. She reminds Henry of the young egrets he often watches fish down on the rocks. Their gawky bills as they dive their heads into the water, like they are pretending to be adults. He tries harder not to stare.

Jean watches nervously. "We'll be in and out," she says, glancing behind her at the door as though worried someone might be watching.

"She didn't want the help, but I insisted," Gemma says, plucking at a stack of small beaded bracelets on her wrist, her plump cheeks flushed with youthful enthusiasm.

"That sounds like Jean," Henry says, getting a glare from his sister-in-law in return. "What happened there?" He points at her hand. A small spot of bright red has soaked through the towel.

"It's nothing, slicing lemons. I just went clean through it," Jean says. Her eyes shift between him and Gemma and she steps awkwardly between them, forcing Gemma to step away. Henry knows why. His neck goes hot with shame.

"That looks quite bad," he says of the growing stain.

"See, that's what *I* said," Gemma interjects from the living room. She is looking around his house, taking it all in. Henry sees his home through her eyes and is filled with embarrassment at the cracks in the walls, the chipping linoleum. He cringes at the piles of papers on the table, the small mountain of laundry, still unfolded against the corner by the washer. She picks up an old clay sculpture of a bird Margie made back when she was in her short-lived pottery-making phase.

"Careful," Henry says quickly, unable to bear the thought of it breaking. She puts it back and continues on, craning her neck to look through the telescope. Henry panics for a moment, trying to remember. It must have been pointed at the Clarkes' house.

"You can see everything with this, can't you?" She moves it.

"I usually just watch the stars," he says quickly. Jean's eyes flick toward him at this obvious lie.

"Let's hurry up and unload things, Gemma," Jean says, and Gemma reluctantly steps away from the window and comes to help in the kitchen. Jean pounds around pointing at drawers and doors.

The three of them work in tandem, Gemma lining up cans of tuna and bags of pasta on the counter for them to put away. Henry stops and holds up another unfamiliar item, wrapped this time in brown paper packaging. He looks from it to Jean, questioning.

"Oh, that. It's some sort of fancy new chocolate cookie. Thought you might want to try 'em," she says brusquely. "I noticed the ice creams were a hit." Henry ducks his head shyly. He hadn't eaten anything so decadent in years. He'd offered one to Margie when he opened the box, but she'd refused. She'd shrunk lately, he noticed, a lump forming in his chest. The comforting width of her hips whittling down so that her pants formed little flaps on each side. "You go ahead, though," she'd encouraged him before turning heavily toward the bedroom. He finished them off in four days, eating one after dinner each night. They were possibly the best thing he'd ever tasted. His mouth waters at the thought of another sweet treat.

"Why don't you both stay and have one?" he asks Jean, beginning to clear the newspaper from the top of the table. He should have cleaned up a little, he thinks guiltily, pulling a pile of old newspapers into the seat of one of the dining chairs. "I could make some tea."

But Jean shakes her head quickly. "Nope. No. We have to get back to the Crab. Going to be a big day with that Bermuda sailing race. Let's go, Gemma. *Chop chop.* No time to waste."

Jean folds a paper bag, and something wet spatters onto the floor.

"Your hand, Jean," Henry says. The blood has soaked through the towel and left an arc of dark drops along the floor.

"Damn it," Jean says, looking like she might break down. "I don't have the time for this."

"You do. It'll only take a minute." Henry leads her to a kitchen stool. "Sit," he says. He removes the soaked bandage from her hand.

"That looks quite deep," he says of the gash. It gapes open, quickly pooling with blood when he releases pressure on it. He finds an ancient tube of ointment and squeezes it into the cut, wrapping her hand again with a fresh dish towel, tighter this time, and pinning it in place with an old fishing lure.

"Be careful, or it'll get infected." He looks at the towel where the blood has already started to soak through again.

"I'll be fine." She sighs.

"You look so in love," Gemma says, startling them both.

She is across the kitchen, looking at a photo high up on the wall. It is of Margie and Henry on their wedding day. In it Margie is wearing a flowered dress. "None of that virginal princess stuff for me," she'd said emphatically, which was more than fine by Henry. The ceremony was held at the lighthouse on the far edge looking out over the sea. Henry wore a brown suit and a blue dotted tie that flapped insanely in the wind as they stood to say their vows. They'd only invited a few people: their parents, who were still alive then, and Jean, of course. Always Jean.

"Do you take this woman?" the officiant had started, and a seagull had swooped down and nearly landed on his head. "I object!" Margie had joked in her best impression of a seagull screech. The photo was taken immediately after, when Henry's and Margie's heads were thrown back in laughter.

"Is this your wedding day?" Gemma's young, clear voice interrupts Henry's memory.

"Let's go, Gemma," Jean says, frustrated. "No time for all this chit-chat."

"Yes, it's been fifty-five years now," he says quietly, looking to the bedroom to see if Margie heard, but there's no sign of her stirring. He thinks she'll be sad to have missed a visitor.

"I mean it." Jean takes Gemma by the shoulders and steers her firmly toward the door. "We have work to do." Henry says goodbye, then watches Jean rush the girl down to the dock. Once they are in the boat Jean looks back up at the house. He sees the relief spread across her face when they pull out into the water.

Henry goes to make another coffee when he sees Gemma's little beaded bracelet left in the center of the counter. Its white beads are made from some sort of shell strung on a thin piece of blue elastic. It's a gift, he thinks, picking up the bracelet. She's left it for him. His heart beats faster as he strains to pull it on over his large hand. It fits him, though the beads do not dangle delicately the way they did on her arm. They are tight along his wrist. He leaves it there, liking the feel of it, and goes back to the telescope with a new cup of coffee. The lens is focused on the back of a row of old buildings down by the docks. They've been repainted since the Clarkes took over the property. Back before the family started buying up every private marina on the island, the murky sand in front of them was always the best place for clamming. Henry had once gone every Sunday, bringing home a bucketful to cook with tomatoes and herbs in the evening. Until the day *she'd* shown up there.

He'd been ankle-deep in the surf, using his feet to scan the surface for air pockets, when a young voice had cut through the air behind him. "I said, excuse me." Henry had turned back to see the girl calling to him from shore. He'd looked around, unsure to whom she was talking, but there seemed to be no one else around. Worried she was in some sort of trouble, he made his way back, a bucket of clams in one hand. She rushed to meet him. She was dressed plainly, in shorts and a red V-neck T-shirt. A backpack hung over one shoulder.

"Hi, I'm—"

"Alice Gallo," he finished. "I know who you are." She stopped and smiled, following him up to where he'd left his shoes by the side of the building. He'd never spoken to her before, only seen her. But she didn't seem surprised he knew who she was. On an island this small, everyone knows everyone else. Up close, with her large dark eyes and heart-shaped face, it was clear she was already the kind of pretty that gets young women into trouble.

"Yes, that's right. Well, I was just wondering, do you think I could draw you?" Alice had said.

"Me?" he'd barked, feeling his face grow hot.

"Yes, you," she'd replied, her face serious. "It's for an art project, for school."

"I shouldn't." He'd shifted uncomfortably, the bucket getting heavy in his hands. Margie would be expecting him soon.

"Oh, please. It'll only take a little while. We could do it right here." She gestured to the wharf building.

"We'll need to be quick about it." Henry glanced out toward the Rock, wondering if Margie would be able to see him here.

"Yes, thank you!" Alice said, clapping her hands together in excitement. It was this gesture that reminded Henry that she was still just a child. She kicked over an orange bucket and set it in front of the wall where the red paint peeled through to the wood below.

"Here, sit on this, if you don't mind."

"Are you sure you don't want a better background?" he asked as she dropped her bag to the ground and began to pull out a box of pencils and a large drawing pad.

"Nah, this is more real. I like the texture, don't you? Seems cooler."

"I guess so," he'd said, not knowing what was cool about something falling apart.

"What should I do?" he asked, afraid for a moment she would want him to smile. Would his teeth look crooked? Would he be able to hold it on his face?

"Nothing. Just be yourself," she said, as though it were really that easy.

Henry swallowed and followed her to the bucket, sitting down primly on top. Alice pulled her hair back from her face and twisted it, securing it with one of her pencils. Then she got to work. Every so often she'd squint at him and then back to the page. Henry couldn't see what she was drawing but her concentration on him made him squirm. Henry had grown up debilitatingly shy. In school his lanky frame made it hard for him to disappear and he was often the target of bullies who followed him home from school, hurling hunks of seaweed at him as he raced home.

Would Alice laugh at him also? But the girl was all business. As she drew, she chattered in a friendly way, telling him about the art college she was planning on applying to in New York, commenting on the weather, asking him about the Rock. The conversation relaxed him, and he was amazed at the ease with which she conducted herself. She seemed older than her age, he'd thought, which couldn't have been more than fifteen or so. He found himself sitting up a little straighter as they spoke. She'd been drawing for about fifteen minutes when a hard scraping of wheels came from the side of the building. A car door opened and shut. And then footsteps crunched on the gravel.

"Alice?" It was the young Clarke boy, David. "I didn't know you'd be busy, sorry," he said, a strange implying tone in his voice that immediately made Henry shrink back and want to disappear again.

"We can finish later, okay?" Alice had said to Henry. "I'll find you." He'd ducked his head in a shy nod, slipping his socks and shoes on under David's disdainful gaze, feeling as though he had done something untoward. He'd snatched up the bucket of clams. He could hear the Clarke boy's voice as he walked down the dock to his boat, as it carried toward Henry over the wind: "What are you doing with that weirdo?"

FAITH

"Well, well, if it isn't Alice Gallo back from the dead," Walter says from his stool when Faith walks into the Salty Crab.

"Yep," Faith says, wondering if coming back here so soon was a bad idea. "It's me. Couldn't stay away." The truth was she had no idea where to go.

"Not at the beach like the rest of 'em?" Walter asks, his eyes traveling around the near-empty bar.

"No, I've actually had enough beach time for a little while," she says wryly, sliding onto a stool a few down from his.

The beach had been packed by the time she and David had left. Faith had closed her eyes and made a silent wish that they could have been included. Instead, they sat together tensely. Orla's visit had upended things. David was distracted and snippy with her.

"I really wish you'd tell me what is going on," she'd said gently after enough time had passed and the lack of conversation was beginning to feel like a punishment. But David had only retreated further from her.

"I'm going to jump in," he'd said, not inviting her to join him. Faith had watched, her vision blurring behind her sunglasses as he walked out into the water, not even pausing in the cold. He'd raised his arms above his head, the muscles in his back tensing as he dove under the waves.

The David she thought she knew had once again dropped away. Maybe they'd been together once, she'd thought, watching the bob of his head as he swam parallel to the shore. He'd seemed back to normal when he returned, giving her a smile as he dried off. He looked at his phone and his eyebrows furrowed.

"What?" she'd asked, still anxious.

"Just got a text from Dad. Looks like I have some meetings today after all," David had said. She could detect some relief in his voice, as though Geoffrey had provided a convenient escape from her potential prying into his past. He had the look in his eyes again, the same one he'd had that first week they were here. There was no use trying to talk to him when he was like this. He would be impenetrable. When they got to the parking lot, she'd held back.

"You go on," she'd said, "I'll walk. I'd like to enjoy the beautiful day." It had come out snottier than she'd meant, but Faith couldn't bear the thought of returning to the house only to wait around all day. If David noticed, he didn't show it. He tossed their beach gear into the back of the Porsche and got in alone, not looking back as he sped off toward the estate. She'd finally turned the other way, toward town where she knew the Crab would be waiting for her along with all the town gossip she'd need to find out who Orla was and whether she was a threat.

"You're back," Jean says flatly, coming around the bar. Faith can't tell whether Jean thinks this is a good thing. These New Englanders are impossible to read.

"I am," she says, wondering if the goodwill she'd felt at the end of her last visit was imagined.

"One of your tomato cocktails?"

"Just a Coke this time," Faith says. "And some of those clam cakes, please."

Walter leans back and takes a long drink of his beer, staring at her. *There is something creepy about Walter*, she thinks for the first time. When he smiles, it feels a bit too familiar. "Didn't have a chance to ask you where you're staying last time. You must be in a rental."

"I'm here with my boyfriend," she says quickly, happy in the moment that it is true. Faith catches herself before she says the word *fiancé*. *Too soon*, she scolds herself. *Don't be getting ahead of yourself.*

"Local boy?" Jean asks. Her hand is thickly bandaged, and she winces as she wipes down the bar.

"Not exactly. He comes every summer, though. David Clarke."

Jean freezes behind the bar. Walter puts his glass down and refocuses his attention on her. "David Clarke? You're serious?"

Faith nods. Of course, everyone would have heard of Hadley Island's billionaire family. Jean's eyes are wide and fearful.

"You're staying up there on the hill in that big mansion of theirs, hoo boy." Walter whistles under his breath.

"What do you mean? Have you been there?" Faith asks.

"Only to do some seafood deliveries for one of their parties, years ago now. But that place made me glad to not be rich."

Faith wants to ask what he means. Jean has turned away but not before Faith can see the trouble on her face. She yanks glasses from the dishwasher, her eyebrows furrowed.

"That family never comes down from their castle, do they?" Walter asks.

"Oh, I'm sure they must come out to dinner here sometimes?" As she says it Faith realizes that it is probably not true.

Jean lets out a bitter laugh. "Maybe some of the other restaurants in town, but definitely never to the Crab if they do. This isn't exactly the Clarkes' thing."

When Jean goes to the other side of the bar, Faith turns back to Walter, whose eyes are in fact starting to droop. She recognizes this stage of drunk well. He has two choices now, either go home and sleep it off or power through and keep tipping them back until he reaches a state of delirium. She suspects Walter is an expert in the latter. "Do people really not like the Clarkes?" Faith asks him.

"Well, let's be honest. Geoffrey is an all-around prick. And that son of his, sorry, your boyfriend, well," he lets out a dry chuckle. "He gets away with whatever he wants, don't he."

Jean is moving around now, avoiding eye contact as she busily unloads the washer and begins to stack beer glasses, but Faith can tell she wants to say something more.

The girl—Faith hears Geoffrey's voice again from behind the office door—*I'm tired of thinking about her.* Maybe she'd been wrong about the conversation. Maybe they hadn't been talking about her at all.

"Alice Gallo, what happened to her," Faith says.

"She drowned," Jean says quickly. Walter hesitates before nodding in agreement.

"No way to survive out there. You'd have to be an Olympic swimmer." Walter glances at the back windows, which frame a view of glittering blue waves. Hard to imagine anything bad happening on a day like today. "And nowhere to swim to even if you were strong enough."

"Your boyfriend didn't tell you all this?" Jean finally asks.

"He did," Faith says quickly. "Kind of. David said he knew Alice a little?"

Jean's eyes cloud. "More than a little. They were close. Inseparable. Spent the whole summer together every year traipsing around the island. I always wondered what kind of trouble they were getting into. The three of them, those two and Orla O'Connor."

Faith's chest constricts at Orla's name.

"They were with her the night the girl died. Did he tell you that?" Walter prods.

"Was this on the Fourth of July?" Faith ventures.

"That's right. Night of the big Clarke party. Or always used to be, haven't had it since that year."

"They're having it again this year," she says, nervously tracing a pattern into the sweat on her Coke glass. Something is happening that she doesn't quite understand. She can feel it in the air, as though the Clarkes coming up had shifted the air around her. Walter and Jean are staring at her.

"Now why would they do a thing like that?" Jean snaps.

"Apparently something to do with the mooring for Geoffrey's new yacht." Jean's head swivels toward her. Her eyes narrow.

"That's what they told you?" Walter snorts, amused. This annoys her. She's not an idiot. But it bothers her even more that she would be kept in the dark by David.

"What other reason would they have?" she asks.

"Maybe they want folks around here to think certain things about them." He shrugs, drinking from his beer.

"What kinds of things?" Faith doesn't know what Walter is getting at, but she doesn't like it.

He raises a finger and wags it. "There have been people circling that family for years. Anyone that rich has things to hide. Big money equals big secrets." He coughs, wiping his mouth with the back of a leathery hand.

"Having to do with Alice Gallo?" Faith pries. His eyes go big above his glass.

"Did I say that?" He recoils as though she were the one gossiping. "I don't think I said that. Though that snobby little twit never made things easy for anyone." Faith isn't sure if he is talking about David or Geoffrey now. She waits, hoping he'll continue, but he is maudlin now, looking down into his beer like he wonders where it's gone.

"I heard the man living out on the island killed her, that he drowned her purposely after he did something to her." The idea of it is so terrifying that Faith shudders when she says the last part.

Walter's head snaps up at her. "Shhhh, don't let Jean hear you say that. Henry Wright is her brother-in-law, you know?"

"I had no idea." Faith gazes at Jean, whose mouth is twisted in worry as she struggles to slice a lemon into wedges with her bandaged hand. She sighs, placing her head into her good hand for a moment before she shuffles to the side of the bar.

Walter sniffs. "She doesn't like when people speculate, but of course they do. Who wouldn't? Miracle Henry isn't in prison on the mainland after all that."

"After what?"

"Henry has always been an odd bird. But I don't think anyone thought he was any trouble until he got friendly with young Alice. People saw him talking to her back behind the old wharf. He was a bit obsessed with her, it seems. And then, well. Poor thing."

Faith glances at Jean, who is now leaning up against the far side of the bar, the receiver of an old landline pressed up to her ear. "Gemma, it's Jean again. Not sure where you went. You were a lifesaver this morning, but I need you back tonight. We have a band in, you'll make some good money." She wraps the cord around her hand anxiously.

"What happened to Alice's family?" Faith pries, a sick feeling taking hold of her.

Walter looks up, surprised that she doesn't already know. "They left a big ol' house behind, a couple blocks down Harbor Street." He jerks a thumb at the wall of the bar. "Just up and went to the mainland. Let it go to ruin."

ORLA

O rla's fingers struggle with the top of the Xanax bottle. It's lighter than expected. She's horrified to discover a thin layer of pills rattling around on the bottom. The bottle was meant to last her entire trip. *For emergencies only,* she'd repeated to herself when she filled the prescription. She pulls out one pill and wavers, trying to decide if she should save it. Running into David Clarke definitely qualifies as an emergency. She's been waiting for this to happen for years now.

She had been on the lookout for David when she first moved to the city. As a downtown artist, Orla was flying in very different circles than the billionaire's son. And she had tried her hardest to keep it that way, graciously declining events held on the Upper East Side and avoiding parties with his kind of people.

"What kind of people, Orla?" her exasperated agent had asked her.

"Rich assholes," she'd explained, not telling him the whole story.

"You mean the kind of people who buy art?" He sighed. But he'd given in. Her "no Finance Bro event" addendum had remained in full effect until he dropped her after the disaster show. The years in between passed and the worry of running into David receded to the back of her consciousness. Eventually he became more of a myth than an actual person, popping up occasionally in news items about Geoffrey, photos of the two of them in a conference room or taking long strides toward a helicopter. David always in his father's shadow. Whenever Orla ran across one of them, she would get a tight feeling in her chest, but even that reaction had diminished over time. David was just someone she once knew, but no longer. Someone she'd rather forget about.

But now, as she braces herself against the kitchen counter, on the brink of a massive panic attack, Orla realizes that seeing David in person is something else altogether. She hadn't realized he was still even coming to Hadley, not after everything. And she certainly didn't want to run into him now, not like this. How dumb of her to think she could avoid anyone on an island this small.

She tosses two Xanax into her mouth and washes them down with a palmful of water from the sink. It wasn't just seeing David that threw her. It was that woman, Faith. With her long tan legs and her shiny brown hair. And that name. *Ridiculous.* She should have known he'd date someone like that. And didn't she bear an uncanny resemblance to Alice? More than Orla would ever care to admit. Her chest tightens as she pulls on a striped cotton sweater and storms out to the back porch.

How could she revert so quickly to her childhood self? The one who was insecure and jealous. She can feel the blood rush up to her cheeks. She tries to imagine how he must have seen her in her old swimsuit with her hair unbrushed. The humiliation of all of it. Orla is even more disturbed that even after everything that happened, she still wants David to see her a certain way. After all this time, how pathetic is she? As if any of it matters. Disgusted with herself, Orla flops into an old rattan lounge chair. She pulls her knees up to her chest and looks toward Alice's house.

The trees between her and the Gallo house twist angrily into Orla's peripheral vison. A large maple is covered in untended vines that have run amok, creeping claustrophobically up the trunk and out across the branches. The entirety of it ripples in the breeze.

Orla finds herself sketching the shapes of the woods in her mind, the dark silhouettes of the trees, the negative space where the light spills through the branches, and beyond, the angles of what is left of Alice's house in the background. Her fingers suddenly itch to be active, to help her mind escape thoughts of David and his new love interest and the vision in her yard of the young woman in the hood.

Instinctively, Orla reaches down to the low table in front of her. This was the place where she and Alice spent most of their time together drawing. She pulls open the drawer below and isn't too surprised to find one of her old sketchbooks still inside. A few pencils roll out from under it as she lifts it out. The whole of it is warped from humidity and its edges are fraying. She flips through the first few pages. Sketches of the beach and a few sailboat studies all done with college applications in mind. Then, as if to chronicle the exact time that Alice disappeared, the rest of the book is blank.

Orla starts to draw and her mind calms into a pleasant buzz of concentration. The scratch of the pencil eases her anxiety. It reminds Orla that she had actually loved drawing once. Back in school. With Alice. Before it became art with a capital A. A breeze rushes up the lawn and pulls at the page. It has the scent of woodsmoke on the back of it. The smell is melancholy, and it reminds Orla of their last summer together.

David was the one who had invited Orla and Alice to the bonfire. There would be weed, he promised. And one of his friends was going to be making gin and tonics. "Jeremy is obsessed with them apparently." David had shrugged, but she could tell he was trying to act cool about it all.

Orla realized then with a twist in her stomach that this was not going to a summer full of bare feet and ice cream cones and hot dogs down on the pier. That wouldn't be enough for them anymore. This summer already had a restlessness to it that prior ones hadn't. They were getting older. Things were changing, whether Orla was ready for them to or not.

David had raised his eyebrows at them, an invitation and a challenge all in one.

"I love gin and tonics," Alice said. Orla turned to look at her, screwing her eyes up as though to say *you've never had a gin and tonic*. Alice had shrugged and said, "We'll be there, won't we, Orla?" She gave Orla a meaningful stare.

"Of course," Orla had said, returning the look.

That night David had pulled up to Orla's house in a blue Lamborghini. He was running through his father's entire collection, he explained when she got in. Trying to decide which was his favorite so that he might know what to buy when he was on his own. He was trying to impress her, Orla realized, flattered by the attention.

When they went next door to pick up Alice, she wasn't home. Her mom, a stylish but frail woman, came to the door instead. A tiny cigarette smoldered between her fingers as she looked out through the screen door. Orla had never seen her smoking before. "I thought she was already out with you," she'd said. Her face rippled with concern. "She's always off god knows where lately."

She's only ever with me, Orla had thought. But even she hadn't seen Alice as often as normal recently. She hadn't thought much about it either way, assuming she'd been at home. After all, where would Alice go without Orla?

"I'm sure she's fine. We said we'd go to the beach later. Maybe she's there already," Orla said to comfort Alice's mother as much as herself.

"If you see her, tell her to come home by dinner. She's always going off lately, not telling me anything," her mother said, shaking her head. Orla peered past her one last time into the gloom of the house before skipping back to the car.

"She's not there," she'd told David as she'd jumped back into the car. "Maybe she'll meet us there?"

"That's strange," David said, looking more concerned than she wanted him to.

But Orla was right. As the sun was going down, Alice had arrived at the bonfire in a pair of short white denim cutoffs and a cropped white top that showed off her even tan and slim arms. She was wearing a stack of gold bracelets Orla had never seen before. They jangled as she dropped down onto the blanket across from Orla.

"You like?" she'd asked. Orla had nodded noncommittally. But the truth was that Alice's outfit made her feel insecure. The top displayed her flat tan stomach and tiny waist. Orla's own body, which had started to develop, made her feel large and indelicate next to Alice. Her sundress suddenly seemed young and unsophisticated. Her pale legs looked too wide whenever she gazed down at them.

Alice's outfit felt almost like an act of betrayal. There was something different about her, something distant and unfamiliar. But the real kick to the gut came moments later when David reemerged from the water, his skin prickled with cold, his hair slicked back from the waves.

"You're here!" he'd said, the relief in his voice palpable as he picked up his towel. He gazed down at them in a way that made Orla suck in her stomach and toss her hair back, but she noticed his eyes linger on Alice.

"Would never miss a hang with you two," she'd said, leaning back and meeting his gaze.

"Hey, you ever get that Rocky Road?" he said in a way that felt like an inside joke.

"What Rocky Road?" Orla asked, trying to keep her voice steady.

"Nothing," Alice said quickly, still looking at David. Something passed between them that made Orla's heart dive into her stomach. David turned to Orla, his voice even and light.

"I saw Alice down by the ferry the other night. She was going to buy an ice cream, or so she says, but Mint Ship was closed."

"When was this?" Orla asked, her head toggling between the two of them. Alice shrugged stiffly, trying to end the conversation.

"Last Friday, I think? I was out with Dad talking to some official down in the boatyard." Orla had spent that evening with her stomach in knots waiting for David by the window and slowly losing hope as the dusk dissolved into night. The idea of the two of them meeting without her and Alice not saying anything made her want to climb out of her skin.

David looked down the beach to where the others had gathered. Orla could make out the cups being passed around. A bonfire was growing in the midst of them, sending orange flames into the fading blue sky. "Oh, Jeremy's here. I'm going to go get us drinks. What do you two want?"

"Gin and tonic," Alice said quickly.

"You don't drink gin," Orla protested.

"I do now," she said, and David chuckled like she'd said something clever. Again, Orla noticed something between them, a secret look that made her feel young and dumb.

"You saw David last Friday?" Orla hissed as soon as he started away from them. She didn't know if she was more hurt by her friend or that David didn't come to her first. "Why didn't you say something?"

"I didn't want to upset you. You were waiting for him all that time." Alice shrugged. Orla could have killed her.

"Or maybe you didn't actually want me to see him," Orla fumed bitterly, stinging from the weird buzz of intimacy she'd seen between them. Her heart dropped at the idea of them alone together.

"That is such bullshit. I asked you to come with me," Alice said, annoyed.

"You still should have told me!" Orla insisted, her voice rising. "I could have come down there and met you, I could have—"

"And then what, Orla?" Alice snapped. "You get there and he's gone already, and I have to watch you freak out like you are now? Besides, I had other things to do. It wasn't a big deal."

"Not to you it wasn't."

"Orla, honestly, this obsession with David has gotten out of control. You two aren't even dating."

Orla reeled back from the hurtful words feeling like she'd been slapped. Alice knew how much David meant to her, how close they'd been to kissing last summer, how he'd held her hand on the beach once as they'd raced back from a thunderstorm. Orla sat in stunned quiet waiting for her to retract it. But instead, Alice stood up suddenly.

"This is stupid." She picked up her purse as Orla watched in shock. "You're ridiculous, you know."

"*I* am ridiculous?" Orla said, feeling her face get hot. "It's ridiculous that you'd hide something like that from me."

From above Alice looked angrily down at Orla on the blanket, her face barely lit by the flicker of the fire. "I have my own shit to deal with. Grow up, Orla. It's not all about you." She stormed off down the beach.

There was still time. Orla waited for her to turn around. She would accept an apology from Alice if she came back, she decided quickly. It wasn't worth them fighting about. But Alice's body got smaller and smaller as she walked down the beach.

"Where's Alice going?" David asked, returning with the drinks.

Orla shrugged, taking a cup from him. She was relieved that it looked clear and fizzy like a Sprite. "She had something to do that she thinks is more important than spending time with her friends, I guess," Orla said, a bitter edge to her voice.

David turned to look at her. "Has she been going off by herself a lot?" he asked, caring more than Orla wanted him to.

"No more than usual." Orla realized as she said it, though, that because of the week she'd wasted waiting for David to show up, she hadn't seen Alice much recently.

"This summer is weird, isn't it?" she asked him, trying to bring his focus back to her. She took a big sip of the gin and tonic to show David that she was just as game, just as fun as Alice. She tried not to choke when she tasted how vile it was. Like Lysol.

"It's been . . . interesting that's for sure," he answered cryptically, downing his own drink and grimacing. *Interesting how*, she thought. But there was something different about David that year, something moody and unapproachable that stopped her from asking. She leaned back into the sand and tried to look casual.

"I'm excited for your party this Fourth. My parents aren't going this year. They said I can come on my own." But David didn't say anything.

He gazed past her with a brooding look on his face. A horrible plum-meting feeling took hold of Orla's chest as she looked behind her and realized that his eyes were still following Alice down the beach.

Orla can no longer see the paper well enough to keep working. She lowers the pencil and sits back, raising her arms up in a stretch. Draw-ing has taken away some of her anxiety, she's pleased to notice. It always does. *The magic of focus*, one of her art teachers always called the feeling of getting lost in the rhythm. Orla holds up the paper, squinting at it now with a critic's eye. The linework is good enough; she's always been a technically proficient drawer. But it is missing something, the thing that at a gallery would make a person stop and look. To move closer.

She is about to tear it up when there is a sharp crackle of branches just beside the porch. She puts her pencil down and peers through the screen out into the dark tangle of the woods waiting for a rabbit to scamper from the brush or a deer to emerge. She holds her breath lis-tening to the leaves, their papery rustle camouflaging whatever is out there. The stillness makes Orla's scalp prickle. She gets the horrible sen-sation that someone else is out there too. That they are doing the same as her, holding their breath, each of them waiting for the other to make a move. For a moment Orla thought she saw her again, the figure of a woman slipping through the trees.

"Hello?" Her voice wavers as she calls out to the dark. "I know you're out there. I can see you."

At this lie there is a rush of movement between the trees. Orla jerks back from the screen, hands gripping her chest at the blur of snapping branches and moving limbs as someone crashes away from her into the woods.

HENRY

While he waits impatiently for the sun to go down Henry makes himself dinner, chopping up peppers and onions and frying them in olive oil with slices of sausage and sliding them onto a piece of toasted bread. Nothing fancy, but it does the trick. Henry once loved to cook. Back when he and Margie still went places, he put so much energy into their meals, blackening whitefish and taking the boat out to collect clams by the beach to make linguini alle vongole. But it's hard to be inspired day in and day out. He sets a plate on the edge of the counter for Margie.

Henry brings his plate to the telescope and looks out at the diners congregating on the back decks of restaurants to watch the sunset. He recognizes Steven Hanson, one of the island's most respected firefighters, sitting with his wife and their children, a steel gray tower of chilled oysters between them. Henry wonders if Steven's family knows about the affair he's been having with one of his colleagues at the station. Henry has watched Steven meet her late at night when he's meant to be on his shifts, sneaking up the rickety back staircase to her apartment above the liquor store.

A few tables over two twentysomething couples sit at a table overlooking the water. They are all young and beautiful, relaxing on vacation. He watches as a server fills their glasses from a bottle of rosé sitting in the center of their table. The woman closest to him reaches for her glass, her bare shoulders catching the fading sunlight. Henry appreciates the shape of them, the way the muscles move across her back as she lifts the wine to her lips, smiling coyly at her dinner companions. He feels a stab of envy.

If there is one thing Henry misses about being part of the rest of the world here, it is having company with his meals. Now that it is summer, he likes to pretend he is dining with them. He watches quietly as bottles of wine are uncorked and poured, the plates of calamari and baskets of bread are served. People smile and laugh and sip from glasses with stems and reach for bread.

A piece of sausage drops from his plate, bouncing against his chest and leaving a circle of grease on his shirt before splatting onto the floor. Henry sighs, wondering how he would even handle being at a restaurant anymore. Would he be presentable, or would he stare rudely and dribble food on his shirt? The thought of it tugs at him in an unpleasant way and he quickly refocuses his attention on the ferry pulling in.

It's nearly nine when the last red sliver of sun disappears over the edge of the water. Now he brings the telescope up the shore and watches, his breath shallow with anticipation as the lights in the houses along the water start to go on, setting each of them like tiny stages. Windows looking onto the street are nearly always curtained, but lucky for him no one worries about being seen from the water. Who is out here besides a few fishermen? Henry scurries over each of the houses with his telescope, watching the people inside move like shadow puppets.

He eagerly moves the telescope first to the far left, looking for Orla, but there is no sign of life in the O'Connors' house. The windows are black and opaque. His chest heaves with anxiety. She couldn't have left the island, though. Not yet. He'd been watching carefully enough, monitoring each ferry in and out of Port Mary. He'd have seen that red hair. Like a beacon. *Or a warning.*

Henry swallows nervously, panning farther right and up over a
ridge to the Clarkes' mansion, where every light seems to be turned on.
No one worries about conserving electricity at that house. He watches
as a team of private chefs prepare something in the kitchen. He goes
toward the living room. It is spacious and austerely furnished with
low-lying white sofas and a huge swooping light fixture. It is empty
except for the young woman he saw earlier on the porch, who is there
alone perched on the edge of one of the sofas. She is dressed as though
she is ready for dinner out somewhere fancier than exists on the island
of Hadley. Her hair is done in loose waves just past her shoulders,
and she is wearing a dark pink dress printed with some sort of yellow
flowers. It's remarkable, he thinks, how much she looks like an older
version of Alice; even her mannerisms are the same. He watches her
crossed legs bob impatiently, her eyes traveling back to the doorway,
waiting.

The woman stands abruptly, crossing the room to a mahogany bar.
She glances behind her to the doorway before uncorking a bottle and
pouring herself a glass of something clear. She adds a few ice cubes and
a splash of something pink. He can see the glint of a silver spoon as she
mixes it. Now she walks with it toward the window, her forehead creases
as she looks out across the bay toward him. Henry feels bad for her all
alone in that house. *Where is David?*

Henry finds him for her. Farther to the left, past several darkened
windows in a wood-paneled office lit by a single desk lamp. Both the
Clarke men are there. They look tense. Geoffrey leans back in a large
chair behind an oversize desk while David paces the length of the office
in front of him. His mouth is moving quickly, his fists clenching and
unclenching with each stride. He turns toward his father and stops. His
hands flop at his sides as though he is a young child having a tantrum.
Henry almost expects him to stomp his feet.

At this display the elder Clarke's face folds in obvious displeasure.
He leans back and turns away from his son toward the window, and
for one terrifying moment it seems his angry glare reaches through the

telescope. Henry's throat goes dry. He steps back, breathing deeply to regain his composure.

When he returns to the room, David has dropped onto a low sofa across from the desk. He cradles his head in his hands. Geoffrey stands above David. He looks calmer now, but his face is still red as he says something to his son. Then he turns away, his lips tight, and storms out of the office. There is a long pause before David finally lifts his head. He wipes his face with the heels of his hands and then stands up, following Geoffrey out of the office. They both disappear into the hallway, out of Henry's view, leaving the office light on to be turned off by one of the invisible staff of silent stagehands that skitter around and manage their employers' privileged lives.

"You're watching the Clarkes again, aren't you." He hears Margie's voice behind him, a bitter edge to it. Henry doesn't turn around. He doesn't need to. He already knows the disgusted expression on her face, the one she reserves especially for the Clarkes.

"David looks fairly miserable," Henry says, knowing she'll like this.

"It's a great mystery of the world how the rich seem determined to make themselves miserable." Margie has never liked the Clarke family, not even before the incident. Of course, behind Geoffrey's back most of the islanders hated the Clarkes. It was no secret that Geoffrey was an all-around prick.

Despite his massive fortune, Geoffrey was known to never leave a tip or to pay any of his staff on time. But no one hated him as much as they feared him. His stinginess was matched only by his pettiness. Because it was also known that with one phone call Geoffrey Clarke could end your career or have your son expelled from school. Ruin your life. And where would you be then? Trapped on an island where everyone knew one another. No one on Hadley could afford to take that risk.

"What is happening over there now?" Margie asks as Henry peers through the telescope. In between sentences he hears the sound of her chewing. "I feel like I can see something happening on the lawn."

"I thought you didn't want me to look," he protests, giving her a hard time. She snorts. He knows that it is pointless to try to hide the tents that have started going up out on the lawn of the mansion. They are getting ready for some sort of event.

"Preparations," he says simply, trying not to get Margie worked up.

"What kind of preparations? Geoffrey installing some sort of throne for himself?" she asks suspiciously, pacing behind him.

Henry wasn't planning on mentioning the woman but finds he can't help himself. "And David seems to have a new love interest."

This juicy tidbit stops his wife in her tracks. He can hear her breathing heavily as she decides how she feels about it. "Pretty and young, no doubt?"

He doesn't answer.

"Well, she won't last long," she says simply. "That family goes through women like old newspapers."

"That's not true," he interjects. "Geoffrey was married a good ten years to that one, ah, what's her name?"

"Bethany Shaw? Oh, and look what became of her. Drug addiction! Depression! And then, a sudden disappearance? You're only proving my point."

"Oh, come on now," Henry says. She's beginning to make him tired. Besides, he knows this timeworn line of conversation all too well. "We don't know anything about his ex-wife."

He looks back from the window as Margie throws her hands into the air and turns on her heels back to the kitchen, where she angrily starts cleaning up dinner, banging her plate into the sink and running water in a way that lets him know she is exasperated.

Henry turns back to the telescope in time to watch David Clarke enter the living room alone. His face has transformed from distraught to confident in the walk from his father's office, and his stooped shoulders have straightened. The woman leaps up off the sofa when she sees him. She greets him with a kiss, which he returns eagerly, a foxlike smile on his lips, his fingers pressing indentations into the bare skin on her back.

Even before the incident, Henry always felt like Margie's distaste for the entire Clarke family was extreme. After all, why should he have anything against the family personally just because they were wealthy? But now the very thought of the Clarke family sends Henry's body into revolt. He can feel a version of it starting now, the strange rubbery sensation that takes over his legs and travels up through his body. It forces him to take a step back and sink into his chair before his knees give out.

"We should have known to be afraid of those people is all I'm saying," Margie calls from the kitchen, pointing the dish sponge angrily. "There is something sick about them."

Hours later Henry opens his eyes, looking up into the skylight of their little bedroom. The moonlight glows against the beadboard walls. Nature is surprisingly bright on its own, when the stars are out and the moon is nearly full and reflecting off the water like it is tonight. Margie is turned away from him in bed, the lumpy form of her body below the thin quilt unmoving. The old digital alarm clock on the nightstand reads 2 a.m. Henry climbs out of bed and goes to the living room. It isn't unusual for him to be awake right now. He rarely sleeps more than a few hours at a time these days, often startling awake, with some unnamable dread clawing at his spine.

He read an interesting article once about how wolves who become separated from their packs sleep in fits and starts same as he does. It's a form of self-protection, a way to stay vigilant when you are isolated and more vulnerable to threats. At least that's how it feels to Henry. They'd never meant for it to be this way, not permanently at least.

We'll let the talk die down on the island, Margie had said all those years ago. *Then we'll start going back in.* But they never have. Occasionally in the first few years one of them would bring it up, musing about how they could take the boat into Port Mary for dinner or go to one of the town's parades. But then doubt would cloud the other's eyes. They had Jean to bring them groceries, after all, and there was no real reason to go back, no one they really wanted to see. Or perhaps more accurately, no one who wanted to see them anymore. It had been painfully clear when no one had stood by them after it came out that Henry was a suspect in the girl's death. No one wanted to touch the Wrights after that.

It became harder and harder for them to pretend that they were just taking some time away, that the plan was to go back one day. And Henry began to worry that all this time spent hiding in plain sight across the water only made him seem more guilty.

He goes to the main room and turns on the lamp and then pads to the kitchen and pops down the lever on the kettle and prepares a cup of tea. The backs of his eyes ache from lack of sleep as he bends and looks through the telescope.

The beach is empty, eerily lit by the dim glow of a single halogen lamp from the parking lot behind it. Henry takes the telescope on its familiar route starting at the ferry dock. It is quiet. The ferry bobs lonely with its yellowy circles of light reflecting on the water. He moves slowly up Harbor Street, catching the front lights of the Salty Crab going off for the night. He would wait for her to lock up, but he knows that Jean won't be leaving anytime soon. She'll still have the till to sort, the floors to scrub. On weekends it's rare she makes it back home before three in the morning. He often watches her as she locks the front doors and disappears back into the village toward her house on the east side of the island.

Henry stops on a figure stumbling up the road. A man, by the shape of his shoulders. His image goes in and out of focus as he moves toward the edge of town.

At first Henry worries that he's hurt but then realizes the man is drunk. He stops for a moment and sways. An arm reaches up, tilting back a bottle of something. He's probably gone out and forgotten where he is staying. Summer often does this sort of thing to people, Henry has observed. He's watched it before, as though all the nice weather and beach time, the relaxed pace of life here, turns them into idiots, making them do things they wouldn't ordinarily do. Reckless things. Each summer there are more of them. The man wavers in the dark, but before Henry can get a better look at him, he disappears behind a thicket of wild rose hips.

Now Henry sees the outline of a woman, her torso bent as she trudges up the hill away from town. He follows her with his telescope, focusing, trying to get a better view. She is young, he guesses, based on the way she walks bent forward like she is carrying a backpack. He sees the flash of a white skirt as she passes under the streetlight before she moves behind the same dense grove. Henry holds his breath, imagining the two of them passing in the night, the drunk man and the young girl. His body starts to thrum nervously as he moves the telescope back and forth, timing the footfall of the girl with the open view of the road past the rose-hip bushes. He shuffles impatiently as the clock ticks behind him on the kitchen wall, staring intently at the empty road until his eyes grow bleary.

But they never emerge.

ORLA

The curtains billow into the living room like the tails of ghosts. Orla closes her eyes, blocking them out. Her heart thrums. Her mind spins in useless circles. All the movement outside, the leaves in the wind, the waves lapping at the dock, has her on edge. It could be that the Xanax is making her paranoid. She's lost track of the time between doses and taken too much of it. She should know better.

She's going to need to leave Hadley she decides suddenly. She'll tell her father she couldn't do it. She'll get a job in New York selling tourist crap or waiting tables, she doesn't care. She just has to finish with the house and then she can leave. She has only to get rid of the furniture now, fill a few nail holes, and tackle the upstairs closet of course. She'll work all day tomorrow. Then she will get the hell off this island. The plan soothes her enough to lull her into a partial sleep, and a memory of Alice comes to her.

"What about our plan?" Orla had asked quietly when she saw Alice the next time. They were at the lighthouse for a picnic hosted by Orla's family. It was a yearly tradition, and much like everything it was different that year. Even the weather seemed more volatile. The wind plastered their sundresses against their backs and whipped their hair across their faces.

"I have a new plan," Alice said, casting her eyes down at the lineup of food on the folding table.

They hadn't spoken since the bonfire night on the beach. Orla had waited for an apology, but Alice hadn't offered one. Her bedroom window had been dark the last few days. Orla picked up a hot dog from a tray and dressed it with ketchup. She found herself nervous in her friend's presence for the first time. Alice pulled out a can of Coke from a cooler.

"What is it?" Orla put her hot dog down and leaned across the picnic table. But Alice had raised her eyebrows, taking a sip of Coke as Orla's mother ran past them to secure piles of paper plates with rocks.

Alice pulled her hair out of her face. "It's always so intense up here. Why do we do this every year?"

"Tradition," Orla said. Alice rolled her eyes. "What's the plan?"

"It's something I've been working on," Alice said cryptically. "I promised I wouldn't tell anyone."

"Promised who?"

Orla's father came over and interrupted them, all joyful naive dad bluster. "Be sure and get some of that curried chicken salad before it all gets scooped up," he said. "It's my new recipe."

"Looks amazing," Alice said as she gave him a dazzling smile.

"But I still want to do *our* plan," Orla said when her dad left. She had come around to the idea of New York. The idea of David and her being together had taken hold of her fully. "We'll go to school in the fall and get an apartment. We'll do all the things you said."

"You don't understand." Alice finally looked at her, frustrated. "I can't."

"What are you talking about? Yes, you can. You have to." Orla began to panic. Without Alice there was nothing. No apartment. No art school. No David.

"No, Orla. You don't get it. Do you know how much money art school costs?" Alice twisted on the bench to look back toward her mom.

She stood off to the side of the gathering drinking a plastic cupful of wine and talking with the dad of one of their school friends. Her thin dress flapped in the breeze. She looked even frailer than normal, Orla noted, her face drawn.

Alice shook her head, dejected. "My dad left, so I'll need to help my mom. Somehow."

"Oh my god, when?"

"Memorial Day weekend. He got on the ferry and just didn't come back. My mom has been so depressed. She barely gets out of bed except to go down to the liquor store."

"I'm so sorry." Orla leapt up and hugged her friend, relief spreading through her. All the feelings she'd been having about Alice betraying her were wrong. This was the reason she'd been acting strangely. It wasn't Orla. And most important, it wasn't David.

"She'll be okay, I think. Don't worry about me, though. Like I said, new plan."

Alice looked down at her plate. To one side, Orla's parents conversed with a group of locals next to the grill. Orla couldn't imagine what Alice must be going through.

"What do you mean?" Orla asked, confused. Alice had turned back into that enigmatic girl from the bonfire, the one she hardly knew.

"There are other ways of making it besides school, you know?" Alice said, giving Orla a little wink.

"Like what? There's no job you can get around here that will pay us enough for college, not without a degree," Orla protested.

"Who said it was a job?" Alice said cryptically.

"I don't know what you're talking about," Orla said, getting frustrated.

"Oh, Orla, sometimes you are just so . . . young."

Orla had pulled back, stung by Alice yet again.

"When you know the right people and they can put you in touch with whoever you want, you can skip all the other stuff." Alice said it as though explaining to someone much younger than her.

"But I thought you wanted to go to school."

"I want to draw. And I want to be successful at it. But honestly? School has always just been a means to an end." She flipped her hair away from her face, a gesture Orla hadn't seen before.

"And how are we going to meet people like that on Hadley?" Orla said, unconvinced.

"You haven't been paying attention, Orla," Alice had said in that newly adult voice, thin with impatience. Orla looked up to see David crossing the field toward them. "It's summer. There are influential people everywhere. If you know how to look for them."

A loud bang vibrates through the house. Orla's eyes fly open. Her body startles into a sitting position on the sofa. She thrashes, struggling to unwind her legs from the blanket as the pounding starts back up, incessant, coming from the front of the house. She turns her head to the front door. It rattles again as whoever is out there slams their fist to it frantically.

Orla's body goes rigid. She's left a lamp on in the corner of the room. It was meant to comfort her but now she feels exposed; the light spilling through the too-sheer curtains would have already given her away. Orla pictures the rigid form of the woman. The thin legs and oversize coat. The damp curls spilling from inside the hood. She'll be standing on the front steps. Waiting for her.

Orla drops onto the floor sick with fear. There are no neighbors near enough to hear her cries. There will be no one to help her. The knocking starts again, harder now. She crawls on her hands and knees in a mad scramble through the living room looking for something to defend herself with. Orla snatches a fireplace poker from its holder.

She closes her eyes for a moment and takes a deep breath. The banging on the front door continues, turning to a rhythmic thud as she moves in a low crouch to the front door.

Her own breath rattles along with it as she stands next to it, feeling the vibrations of a fist pounding on the other side.

Whoever it is, they are not going to stop. They know she is here. She will have to confront them. She rises to her full height and raises the poker above her shoulders, holding it like a baseball bat so that she can get a good enough swing if needed. But her body shakes with fear.

"What do you want?" she cries out in a shaky sob.

"Orla?" The muffled reply is amused, familiar. A man's voice. "It's me."

"David?" Orla's voice wobbles. Her body goes weak with relief.

"Jesus Christ, Orla, let me in."

She pulls the door open a crack. He stands in the shadows of the doorway with a cocky smirk on his face.

"Orla! Did I wake you?" His voice sounds teasing, like showing up at nearly two in the morning unannounced is normal behavior. She pulls the door fully open. He takes her in, scanning her ragged pajama bottoms and baggy T-shirt. He raises his eyebrows, amused when he gets to the poker. "Oh, were you just about to club me? Glad I knocked."

Asshole, Orla thinks. So full of jokes even when he knows that he terrified her. She lowers the poker slowly. Her heart is still racing.

David gives her a grin, rocking back confidently on his heels. His shirt is damp and unbuttoned partway, exposing a V of skin on his upper chest. His chin is covered in uncharacteristically messy stubble. He has a brand-new bottle of something in his hand.

He moves toward her, and she braces herself for a hug but instead he brushes past her into the house.

"Oh, did you want to come inside?" Orla asks sarcastically, glancing back at the dark empty street behind him before she shuts the door and locks it. He is nearly to the kitchen by the time she catches up with him. She can smell booze on him, mixed with the lingering aroma of some kind of expensive aftershave.

"Yes, thank you." David thrusts the bottle out at her.

"What is this?"

"Tequila. Let's have some," he says brusquely. He walks into the dining room. Orla trails behind.

"No, I meant what are you doing here?"

"Can't a man pay a visit to his dear old friend?" he asks, a sarcastic edge to his voice. He leaves the dining room, moving past her farther into the house, going from room to room, searching for something.

Finally, he spins unsteadily back toward her. "Where is your bar?"

"We don't have a bar. We are normal people. We keep our glasses in the kitchen," she says, trying to give him a hard time though her voice is shaking.

"Of course." David chuckles. He sways as he puts his fingers up into air quotes. "Normal people." Looking at him closer Orla wonders if he might be on the verge of some sort of breakdown. His eyes are webbed with angry red lines. He teeters on his heels like he might fall over. She recognizes the signs of someone who is sleep-deprived and stressed.

Orla leads him into the kitchen and pulls a lowball glass out of a cabinet. She hesitates, knowing she shouldn't, and takes out a second glass as well.

"Oh, Orla, I've missed you," he says, leaning back against the counter as she drops ice into the glasses.

Orla's heart thumps, wanting him to shut up and to continue talking in equal amounts. She opens the bottle and tips a generous pour into her glass and a slightly smaller one for him.

"You were always my best friend on Hadley. So strange without you here all these years."

Orla tries not to let the compliment affect her, but it does. David Clarke was always good at flattery. It was the kind of thing that could make a person start to get ideas about themselves; if they weren't careful, they might even start to think that they were special. Orla moves away from him, going back into the living room with the drinks so he can't see the sudden flush that's come into her cheeks.

David drops onto the couch and makes himself at home, leaning back and propping his feet across the coffee table. His shoes are dripping wet. Thick clumps of sand break free from the treads and land on the wood.

"Cheers." He reaches his glass out, clinking it with hers.

How many years had she imagined it like this, minus the dirty shoes? David Clarke and her sharing a drink with no one else in sight. Orla's fingers tremble as she tilts the glass back, letting the tequila flow against the back of her throat. It is smooth and delicious. After the spike of adrenaline, it tastes like pure relief.

"So. What are you doing here?" she demands, dropping into the chair across from him.

"That's not very nice," he says, pretend hurt. He was always a bit of a baby when he was drinking. She'd forgotten that about him until now.

"You're wasted," she says with a snort.

"I thought you'd be glad to see me. Can't I come visit an old friend?" He swirls his glass arrogantly.

Orla glances at the grandfather clock in the corner. "At one thirty in the morning?"

"Well, you ran off at the beach. Didn't let us finish the conversation. What was I supposed to do?"

"Oh, right. I'm sure your girlfriend wanted me to bring my towel over and sit down with the two of you."

He ignores her tone, looking around the room as though seeing it for the first time. She flinches when he sees her drawing out on the coffee table. "I always think about you being in this house. So funny you've actually been in New York all this time, but I always picture you here. We left things so strangely between us all those years ago. And then both of us ended up in New York. How come we never got dinner?" His hairline is receding slightly, she notices. It doesn't diminish her attraction to him.

"*Get dinner?*" she asks, incredulous. Orla is starting to get the impression he is toying with her. "Why would we have?"

"I don't know, I suppose we have a lot in common being from this place. And of course, there is Alice. Do you think about her?" He veers off topic.

"Of course I do," she snaps. "She was my best friend."

"What do you remember about that night?" he asks. Orla looks away, wishing for the very first time in her life that he would leave.

"Not much," she lies. She remembers all of it. *The hand on Alice's knee. Her hand around the glass. The spectacular dress, falling off her shoulder. The way her eyes moved below her lids trying to stay awake. The fear in David's eyes when Orla turned to him.*

"Why are you asking me now?" she says, snapping back to the unlikely reality of him holding the glass in her parents' living room.

"I've just been thinking about it lately." He's going somewhere with this that Orla isn't sure she wants to follow. He is close to her now. He smells like a combination of expensive things, crisp cotton, luxurious body products. David's shirt hangs half opened in front of her. Orla has the desire to raise her hand to his chest; she could push a finger through the space, touch his skin underneath. His neck is perfect. Inhuman. She pulls back, horrified by herself. After all this time, after what happened to Alice. *No.*

Orla stands abruptly and crosses her arms over her chest. "Why are you here, David?"

He smiles crookedly into his drink. "Like I said, just catching up with my old friend."

"I don't believe you," Orla says. "What do *you* remember?"

Men like him always ignore the questions they don't want to answer. *It's a shame really*, Orla thinks, watching David cross the room and pour another drink. He has a presence so few do, not to mention the resources. He could have done so much more with himself, could have been something other than his father's protégé. Her heart thumps as his eyes fall on her unfinished drawing. She should have gotten rid of it.

"Very nice, Orla."

He smiles a bit ruefully at it, like he is looking at the colorings of a small child.

"I saw your show."

"What?" She feels the room begin to spin. "When?"

"The one you had in New York, the first one." He sips his drink, watching her closely. "That was the big one, wasn't it? The one that made your career?"

Orla's chest seizes up at the mention of that first show of pencil drawings. She cringes at the memory of the opening. The fancy dress she'd worn, the hands she'd shaken. The photos snapped for the society pages.

"I didn't see you there," Orla says, not believing him.

"No, I was going to say hi. I thought I might even try to reconcile, but then you were just so popular. Surrounded by all those artsy Brooklyn people. The *belle of the ball*. I watched you enjoying yourself and I thought, she's made it. I was thrilled for you. But then I saw the art. There were so many familiar faces on that wall. All from Hadley. I thought it felt a bit . . . familiar. But then I saw the one of Jean. You know which one I mean. The black-and-white one, with the little lines around the hair. It's a stunning image. Impossible to forget, really." He gives her a hard look. "They were Alice's."

"I made them my own," Orla starts to protest. She puts her empty glass down, feeling woozy.

"Oh, Orla. Let's not," David tsks. He leans arrogantly against the mantel, his head lolling around. She wants to smack it. "We both know Henry would never have sat for a portrait for you."

"You never said anything." Her cheeks are hot with the shame of it all. She had tried to cover it up for so long, thought that if she proved herself as a competent artist without Alice, she could somehow erase what she'd done.

He looks down into his glass and frowns. "There was a moment when I was angry. I left with every intention of calling the gallery the next morning and telling them you were a fraud but then I thought, why bother? Why not just give it to her? She's been through a lot, and she has so little of, well . . . anything."

Orla turns her head away, trying not to let it show how much the words hurt her. She'd tried to leave it all behind her. As her career limped forward it was all anyone ever wanted to talk about—the creepy pen drawings of all the people from Hadley that Alice had spent that last summer making. People who meant nothing to the collectors who have them hanging in their private collections but who are easily recognizable to anyone from here. How could she have been so careless? She had thought after all this time that she was safe. But she was wrong.

"Will you say anything?" she asks in a whisper. She wants to stop him, to block his exit. To hold him hostage and make him listen to her until he understands why she did what she did. Until he can see the way she cared for him, the way she would spend each summer endlessly waiting for him to pay attention to her.

"No. Not unless you do."

"What is that supposed to mean?" She stares at him.

"You know exactly what I mean."

FAITH

F aith wakes up with the sheets twisted around her legs. Her heart races as she pulls herself free. She's been having the same nightmare she's had ever since she was a kid. Sometimes in the dream she is naked, standing up in front of everyone she knows, exposed. Other times she is on trial, up on a stand suspended above a faceless jury of strangers as they murmur her guilt, begging them for understanding. The details vary but the feeling is always the same. She is caught out, unprepared, and the people she thought she could trust have turned against her.

This time Faith is tied up, her arms bound behind her as someone familiar but unnamed holds a knife to her throat and yells at her to confess. Even as she is having it, Faith knows it's just a dream, the circumstances are so familiar. But it doesn't lessen the urgency. The voices come from all around her, low murmurs that promise her that if she confesses, she will be freed. But she doesn't believe them. She can't. No matter the circumstances of the dream, the theme stays the same. She is caught. And she never comes out unscathed. She is exposed to everyone as a fraud.

Panicked, she looks toward David, worried she may have called out in her sleep like she sometimes does with the dream, but when she turns to find him, blinking into the unfamiliar darkness, David isn't in bed next to her. The air in the bedroom is unnaturally still. The bathroom light is off; David isn't there either. She puts an arm out and feels that the sheet on his side of the bed is cold. Now fully awake, she rolls over and grabs her phone off the bedside table. 2:55 a.m.

It's 3 am! Where are you? Faith starts to text him, her heart pumping. There was a time barely over a week ago when she wouldn't have hesitated to send it, but now she stops herself. Maybe he's just gone downstairs for a glass of water. She's probably being paranoid. She tries to close her eyes again but her brain whirs in the dark, spitting up images of Geoffrey Clarke, his mouth full of lobster, and the woman, Orla, walking through the sand, her long red hair whipping in the wind and David's eyes trailing her as she walked away.

Faith's eyes fly all the way open.

She won't sleep until she knows where he is. She gets out of bed. One of David's sweatshirts is draped over the back of a chair, and she takes it and pulls it on over her lacy shorts and tank before she slips out into the dark hallway.

Faith starts down the stairs but stops in her tracks at the sound of a door opening below. She ducks down and looks past the banister out over the landing. A pale beam of light momentarily shoots across the floor and someone steps inside, shutting the door behind them. He leans heavily against the wall and pulls out a phone. Faith exhales, relieved, taking in David's familiar shoulders, the cut of his favorite T-shirt. She moves to the edge of the step and opens her mouth to call out to him but there is something in his face, now lit above his cell phone, the grim set of his jaw and downturn of his lips that makes Faith crouch farther into the shadows of the stairs.

She watches the rapid rise and fall of his chest. It's exaggerated like when he comes back from a run. He folds his body toward the wall, pressing a number into a security system that makes a green light flash. There is a low beep, and Faith watches, holding her breath, as he turns back again. He runs his hands over his face and his shoulders sag as though he's exhausted. He drops his arms and lifts his head, gazing up into the stairwell.

Faith ducks back onto the landing. There is something about his demeanor that feels private, and she doesn't want him to see her there. Below, his footsteps echo on the tile of the foyer.

She turns and quickly tiptoes back up the stairs and into their bedroom. Dashing across the room, she yanks the sweatshirt over her head and climbs back into bed, rolling onto her side just as she hears the click of the door opening again. David slips into the bedroom moments later, shutting the door quietly behind him.

Her ears roar in the dark. She wants to turn the light on, to ask him what he was doing outside at three in the morning fully dressed, but something in the image of his face grimacing over the glow of his phone stops her. Instead, she lies there as still as she can while she hears the soft rustle of his shirt being removed. She focuses on keeping her breathing steady. He will tell her in the morning. He'll have to.

She listens to the swish of fabric as he undresses in the dark. When he finally lies down, pushing his legs under the crisp white sheet next to her, Faith can smell something on him, sharp and acrid and then, on the back of it, a waft of the sea.

In the morning, David's body meets Faith's under the sheets. Barely awake, she lets him pull her closer, enjoying the warmth of his skin on hers. She feels his lips on her shoulder blade just as the memory of the night comes back to her. "David," she begins, her heart racing as she thinks of the empty bed, the foreign way he held himself against the door, as though he were trying to hide from something.

"Yeah?" David mumbles, kissing the back of her neck. But the words dissolve in her mouth as he pulls her toward him. The sex is rougher than usual. She might have enjoyed it, the way he pulls at her, grabbing her hips as though he can't get enough of her, but this time she feels detached. His face moves above her, nearly unfamiliar. She looks up at him again. *Who are you?*

She replays the words she overheard outside Geoffrey's office. There was a scraping sound after he spoke, wasn't there? A drawer closing. And then, perhaps, the metallic twist of a key in a lock?

While Faith waits for David to shower, she gets a text from Elena.

How is everything on your island paradise? You are so lucky, Fay! It is boiling in the city. And the smell. My god. I need to get out of here.

Faith can picture Elena swishing self-importantly along Sixth Avenue, tanned legs flashing, tapping on her phone as she walks to work. The thought of her best friend and of the city with its buzzing energy fills Faith with unexpected longing.

She texts her back. *It's been interesting.*

Oh? I'm not sure I like the sound of that. Interesting how?

Faith begins to type. *Have you heard of Orla O'Connor? Apparently, she's some sort of artist in NYC.* Faith's finger hovers over the send button. She knows that telling Elena anything has its risks. Behind her in the bathroom the water goes off.

In the end her curiosity wins, and she presses send. Elena's text bubble appears immediately then disappears.

"Who are you texting?"

Faith quickly turns the screen off, tucking the phone against her palm. "Oh god, you startled me." Faith's chest is still tight as she turns to look at David in his towel. "It's just Elena. Apparently, there's a heat wave in the city and it's miserable there." Can he hear the strain in her voice? He stares at her a beat and then comes to her, puts a hand on the nape of her neck, and leans in close. Faith's skin tingles, her heart pumping frantically. For a split second she thinks he is going to say something. But he kisses her instead on the temple and goes to the closet. "Well, tell Elena hi for me."

"Will do," she squeaks out, not sure why she is feeling so anxious.

Her heart is still pounding when she looks back down at her phone. Elena has texted back.

Never heard of her. She can't be that important.

David's muffled voice calls from the dressing room. "Should we go have breakfast on the veranda?"

Faith is surprised by this. "Are you sure? Aren't you going to go off and do some mysterious financial work somewhere with your father?"

"Well, I may have to do that later, but I was hoping to spend the time with you first." Faith hesitates.

Their plates are filled with poached eggs and bowls of sliced exotic fruits flown in from some other, far more tropical island. An assortment of French pastries sits on a marble tray on the center of the table; the shine on their perfect lamination suggests that they too were imported recently, perhaps flown in this morning. Faith takes a bite of a croissant.

"Good?" David asks, watching her.

"Yes." She almost hates to admit that somehow it's even better than the ones she tried in the cafés of Paris when she went with Elena several years ago. David seems nearly relaxed now, more so than he's been since they arrived. He's uncharacteristically chipper for someone who was up in the middle of the night. He takes another piece of bread from the tray on the table and slathers it with butter. His appetite is certainly intact, she notes.

A massive white yacht is pulling into view just offshore. Faith counts five decks, angled aerodynamically on top of one another. On board she can make out the smudges of white-uniformed staff rushing around on the decks.

"What is that?" She drops her napkin on the table and leaps up from her chair, going straight to the railing to look at the massive white yacht that's pulled into the harbor.

Behind her, David reluctantly rises from his breakfast and goes to stand next to her. "This must be Dad's new toy," David says. Faith lowers her sunglasses.

"His toy?"

"Yes, it's been his hobby the last few years."

"It's huge."

"Dad never is half-assed about his interests," he says, amused. "If it's worth doing, it's worth overdoing. I think that's what he always says."

David folds his arms on the railing and leans out. Faith has been waiting for him to tell her what he was doing out so late, but she is starting to realize that is not going to happen unless she presses him.

"Are you okay?" she asks him.

"Of course, why wouldn't I be?" He says it too quickly. The yacht is reflected in his sunglasses. So this is how it's going to be.

"Well, there was the thing on the beach—" she starts, her stomach sinking.

"Fay, I told you she was just a friend, are we going to keep talking about this?" David says, cutting her off, the same irritation creeping into his voice as was there before.

"There was something else I wanted to ask you about."

He turns, his eyes obscured by his glasses. "Go on?"

"Son!"

David stands up straight as Geoffrey comes out to the veranda, ignoring the two of them as he goes to the railing and looks out at the yacht. His father's skin looks pale and vaguely unhealthy in the bright sunlight.

There is a small flicker of a smile on his face, Faith notices. One she hasn't seen before. Perhaps Geoffrey Clarke is capable of joy after all.

"There she is." He sighs. "*Ophelia*—the second one, of course. Been waiting for her to be finished for about three years now."

Why do men always call a boat *she*? Faith wonders. Probably because a boat is something they like to own, steering them whichever way they like. An illusion, though, isn't it? When the ocean is really in charge.

"Why the second?" Faith asks, keeping her voice light.

"The first one was sold off years ago," David replies quickly.

"This one is better," Geoffrey snaps. His fingers grip at the railing.

Faith lowers her sunglasses, looking out at the boat, where staff continue to dash around on the yacht, busily preparing for Geoffrey's arrival.

"Over a hundred meters long," Geoffrey says proudly. "See, David, the party you are dreading is already paying off dividends. This mooring just came through last night. What's-his-name down at the harbor rang me up and said it magically opened up for us. Took me a lifetime to get a mooring in front of my own damn property."

"Where will you take it?" Faith asks him.

He doesn't look at her as he answers, his eyes fixed out at the water. "Newport probably. Possibly Martha's Vineyard if those assholes let us moor."

"Dad had a bad experience with the port there. Said his last yacht was too big, not up to code," David says, glancing at Faith. He raises his eyebrows to let her know not to push the topic.

"It was bullshit, and they know it. They were just trying to punish me." Geoffrey's voice rises into an intimidating growl. Faith takes a peek at David. His mouth flicks downward, distracted. Geoffrey leans past her and speaks to his son. "David, let me show you the offices."

"You coming?" he calls back at them as he starts to walk away.

"Be right there," David says, giving Faith a helpless smile as he makes a quick stop at the table and slurps the rest of his coffee down. "I guess we are going to look at Dad's new yacht."

But Geoffrey holds up a thick hand. "Only David. I have some things to talk to my son about."

David begins to follow his father. "We'll go for dinner instead, okay?" he says. "I won't be long. Promise."

"Coming, David?" Geoffrey growls.

"Yes, of course."

"Then hurry the fuck up."

Without breaking stride, they arrive at the dock and step onto a small white speedboat. She watches as it cuts through the water toward the *Ophelia II.*

After they leave, Faith steps softly down the hall to Geoffrey Clarke's office. She stands in the silence for a beat making sure there's no sign of any staff, but the hall is dark and empty. She twists the handle and slips inside, shutting the door carefully behind her.

The office smells like leather and something slightly sour she can't place. The desk is almost comically large. Its top is arranged with an assortment of the kinds of things she'd always imagined men like Geoffrey would own, a marble globe, each country marked with a different color stone. Her heart thumps as she sinks into his leather chair and examines the keyhole in his desk drawer. She's relieved to find it's an antique, punched through a polished brass plate, probably at least a hundred years old. Analog designs are always easier to navigate than something new and electronic.

To pick a lock all you need is relatively dexterous fingers and time. As a child Faith had both. She'd started picking locks out of sheer necessity as she increasingly found herself locked out of her house when her mom stayed out at night.

Faith had gone to the public library and asked for books about locksmithing, raising the eyebrows of the uptight librarian. She pored over them, learning how different locks functioned and what she needed to do to release them. To practice, one evening she'd left her mom drinking at the bar and had snuck home and picked the lock on her front door. It had opened with minimal trouble, the spring giving way just like the books she'd read had suggested, and the door had opened easily. She found the mechanics of locks were satisfyingly predictable, unlike the rest of her life.

After that there were other doors. Faith was deliberate, choosing only those houses that were dark and empty. At first, she took very little—a single diamond ring, a tennis necklace, a watch—so that the owner, upon discovering the item missing, would always wonder if it had just been misplaced, sucked up in the vacuum, or dropped behind a bureau.

But those were just the first in a series of indiscretions, slowly becoming more daring than the last. Each brought her closer to something she would regret, something she wouldn't be able to come back from.

The house was dark when she'd arrived. She'd been careful in selecting this one, the mansion of a rich socialite who had lost her husband. Faith had followed the woman for days, shadowing her to nail appointments and salon visits. She seemed to have few friends; a discovery that made Faith so sad she almost gave up. But then she saw the bracelet. It dangled loosely from the woman's wrist when she handed over the keys to a valet at an expensive restaurant. She was meeting a man this time. *Good for her*, Faith had thought as she sat on a bench outside and watched them through the window as they ate. He had slicked-back hair and was touching her.

There had been signs she should have noticed from the start. The door to the house was already unlocked, the alarm system switched off. Faith had crept up into the house, her feet soft on the staircase that elegantly curved up to the second floor.

She couldn't find the bracelet. There must have been a safe somewhere, she had begun to realize with frustration. She was about to leave when a low moan came from behind a door. She should have left then, gone home and forgotten all about it, but instead she crept toward it. She flicked on the light to find the woman curled up on the floor of the bathroom covered in blood. She'd been hit on the head with something very hard. Her eyes went in and out of focus as Faith cradled the woman's head in her lap.

"He took everything," she gasped. "He said he loved me."

"Shhhh."

Faith had called the ambulance then. As the sirens neared, the woman gently took her last breath, and Faith's survival instinct had kicked in. When the police came, they found only her fingerprints. Faith was already on her way to New York.

Faith moves around Geoffrey Clarke's desk now. It is a surprisingly simple case really, she notes, moving around it to the inside and looking at the drawers. In her mind she can see the intricate set of brass sliders and gears that will need to shift for the inner toggles to align. And for that all you need is a simple hairpin. Faith pulls one from the underside of her ponytail, opening the prongs slightly to increase the tension. She slides it into the lock, feeling the metal scrape against the interior workings. She feels them fall one by one into place until the spring inside gives way and the drawer moves slightly forward with a satisfying pop.

She pauses now, her fingers resting lightly on the handles, and glances at the door before sliding the heavy wooden drawer open. Inside is a grid of wooden compartments. Faith realizes she doesn't know what she is looking for at all. There is little in the drawer. A heavy brass letter opener with a compass on the hilt, the key to some sort of Mercedes, a bar of chocolate—which, Faith notes, is opened—with several large bites taken from the top. That's it. She starts to shut the drawer, and notices the compartments shift ever so slightly forward. They are in a solid wooden piece resting inside the drawer.

Her chest constricts as she lifts it up, releasing a loud scrape. She pauses, her ears roaring, waiting for any sounds in the hall. Peeking below she sees a shiny blue envelope. She slides it out and opens it.

Inside, there is a thin stack of photographs. They are glossy prints, the kind people used to get from a disposable camera that they'd get developed at the drugstore. Faith holds the photos delicately by the edges to avoid smudging them as she flips through. In one, Geoffrey Clarke is standing on a dock in front of a very tall boat. He is younger, less gray in his hair, his spine stacked a little straighter.

The name of the boat is painted next to him, *Ophelia*. This must be the original. Faith flips to the next. This is of David and his father standing next to each other. She hasn't seen any other photographs of David as a teen. She brings it closer. Their faces are overexposed, pale and flat in the glare of the flash. Geoffrey, a crystal tumbler full of something in his hand, gives a crooked grin. His hand rests heavily on his son's shoulder. David is smaller and slighter as a teen. His head looks almost wobbly on his shoulders. His teeth are clenched in an unnatural smile. His eyes focus on something or someone out of the frame. They are standing next to a railing. Behind them the sky is a hazy black.

The last pictures are group shots. There are several men Faith doesn't recognize. They're wearing polo shirts and tan shorts. Silver watches hang heavy around their wrists. They are smoking cigars. David stands next to them awkwardly. His hand clasps his arm nervously. The reflection in the window has caught something across the room. Faith holds it up toward the window, squinting. The flash has caught it at an angle. A sofa across the room. Something is there, pieces of it reflecting the flash like the scales of a fish. Faith walks to the window and carefully pulls back the curtain just enough to send a beam of bright sunlight onto the image. Something protrudes from underneath the fabric; it doubles and blurs in the reflection, but she can make out a slender leg and a small foot.

She returns the photos to the envelope and slides the drawer back into place just as a brisk set of footsteps come from the hall. She freezes, waiting as they go past, receding into the distance. Now she moves to the next drawer.

A copy of Geoffrey Clarke's book, *The Success Manual*, sits on the top. It had to have been published at least three decades ago now and looks it, with its dated blocky neon font. A photo of Geoffrey on the back shows him smiling arrogantly. He had no hint of a beard back then and much thicker hair. He looks remarkably like David. Faith shudders and goes to put it back into the drawer when a stack of pages below it catches her eye.

She tilts her head to read the top page. It is a nondisclosure agreement.

Faith has never seen one in real life. She scans the page until she gets to the bottom, where a name is signed in shaky blue ink.

Bernice Gallo

The page below it is another NDA. It reads the same. There is a whole stack of them there, all reading the same. Only the signatures are different. She looks back at the first one. The date next to the signature is the same, July 5, 2008.

Orla O'Connor

She is still trying to make sense of it all when more footsteps sound in the hallway. They grow louder and pause outside the door. She ducks down under the desk as the door opens. A throat being cleared. She can see a pair of shiny Italian shoes. They stop a few paces from the desk.

An incoming text dings loudly on her phone, and she quickly smothers it with her hand as though to shush it. Below the desk she freezes. She begins to panic, wondering how she could possibly explain herself. She watches the feet shuffle back and forth, then turn abruptly back to the door, tapping loudly as they disappear from sight. She hears the door as it closes again. Faith lets out a slow uneasy breath, unsure how she wasn't caught. Faith slides the papers back into the drawer. Then she creeps sheepishly back out into the hall, run-walking away from the office door. She hears something mechanical as she walks down the hall, followed by a familiar beep. Faith is heavy with dread as she keeps going. She doesn't need to look this time to know a camera is following her. It's only once she is safely back in her room that she remembers the text and looks at her phone.

The message from Elena reads: *Call me. But only when you are alone.*

HENRY

L ate in the afternoon there is an unexpected pounding on the screen door. Henry has spent all day dealing with a new crack that had sprung up overnight. It is common to have cracks in the walls; the pylons below the house tended to shift ever so slightly. But the night had been particularly windy, angry gusts rattling at the walls, and he awoke to the sound of splitting wood. Rushing into the main room, he found a new crack traveling from the floor up to the ceiling. Water was already leaking through, streaming down the walls.

"If you don't fix that today it will grow," Margie had said. Henry had sighed as he continued not wanting to face it. "It will spread and spread. This whole place could go down before you know it."

Of course, Margie was right. A crack that big would need instant attention. Dismayed that he'd have to forfeit most of the day's observation time to repairing it, he'd dragged supplies out of the closet and mixed up some plaster. Up close the wall was crisscrossed with a web of plaster lines from previous repairs, and he saw this crack was even worse than he thought. He'd swallowed anxiously as he took in the fissure, wider than any he'd seen before. The first coat of plaster sank into the crack, making multiple coats necessary. It was still a garish thing to look at, a wet river of gray that traveled in a jagged lightning bolt down the wall.

"Just a minute," Henry calls loudly to whoever is banging on the door. Glancing at the logbook still open on the table, he rushes back and sloppily slides a large tidal chart across the top of it, smudging it with plaster. No one else needs to know about Matilda Warren's trip down to the water in her bathrobe last night. He'd watched in shock as the octogenarian had slipped it off and dove into the waves completely nude, gracefully swimming out into the cove in the dying light. When he turns back, Jean hasn't listened to him and has already opened the door. She barges inside. Her cheeks are red from the wind, her graying hair frizzled by the ocean air. This time she has no grocery bags.

"I need you to tell me what you know about Gemma." The words fall out of her.

"Who?" Henry asks, trying to keep up. His heart thuds.

"Gemma," Jean says again, impatient. "The young girl I hired at the Crab. The one who came to the house."

"What about her?"

"She's gone," Jean's voice crackles.

Henry's chest seizes. "What do you mean *gone*?"

"Just gone. Vanished. What else can I say?" She throws her hands up, her fingers stiff with frustration. "The police came by the Crab just after close."

Henry puts his hand to his cheek, worrying his fingers up along the grit of his stubble. "When was this? What night?" Fear has started to gnaw at his insides.

"Last time I saw her was right after I was here with you."

Jean paces in front of the windows. "I knew it. I thought she was a good worker. That she wouldn't have gone and quit with no notice like this. But I called her mother, and she hadn't seen her either. That stupid woman. I should have said something sooner, should have gone to the police. It could have been useful."

Henry recalls the slim figure of a young woman cutting up Harbor Street and the man going in the other direction. How they'd disappeared behind the thicket of rose hips on the side of the road. He'd moved his telescope, waiting for them to emerge, but they never did. He had brushed it off, assuming maybe they had met each other and gone off together onto the beach. He itches to page through his logbook, to be sure of the details. He would have written it down.

"What's wrong, Henry?" Jean stops pacing and looks at Henry suspiciously.

She stands at the edge of his table catching her breath.

"Nothing, I—" Henry backs away. He wishes Jean would go. He needs to think, to look back in the book.

"You saw something, didn't you?" Her face pales.

"Me? No! What would I have—" he starts feebly, glancing anxiously toward the table, hoping she can't see the edge of the logbook peeking out from under the tidal chart. He darts toward the kitchen, where he keeps his back to her and fusses with the kettle. But Jean is relentless. She follows him.

"You did, didn't you? What did you see? *What did you see, Henry?*" Her voice is coarse and desperate. It sends him stumbling back toward the kitchen island.

"I don't know what you mean." It comes out more gruffly than he intends. His mind is whirring, trying to recall the details of that night. The shadow on the road. "Lower your voice, please." His eyes flick toward the bedroom. Henry puts the water on and fills the kettle, trying to drown her out.

"Was it her? Was it Gemma?" She is right next to him now.

"Jean, please stop." He turns the faucet up higher. He is getting angry. What right does she have to barge in? Jean shouldn't be here. This isn't her day to come.

"Don't think I don't know, Henry," Jean says quietly. "I'd have to be an idiot not to know after all these years."

Henry grips the counter. The blood rushes into his face, fizzing at the top of his head, where his hair has started to thin.

"Know what, Jean?" He tries to laugh. He could never lie to her. Not outright. Not even by omission.

She snaps her palm up, quieting him. "I know that you spend your days holed up here spying on people. Now, I've never said anything. But you must know Margie and I never have had a secret."

"Whatever you're thinking, you're wrong." He couldn't let her think about him that way. His only friend.

"I—" Henry slumps over. He supposes he thought that his and Margie's life was theirs alone, but he should have known better. The way she and her sister spent so much of their time together, ankle-deep in the mud offshore looking for clams or sitting out on the dock, bottles of beer in hand, their voices dulled by the wind so that all he could make out were the occasional sharp cackles passing between them.

He hears Jean behind him. She is leaving. Good. But her footsteps carry on deeper into the living room. *Oh god. No.* He turns back to see her marching across the room toward the table, where the thin tidal chart teeters precariously on top of his latest logbook.

"No! Stay away from those, Jean," Henry croaks, running toward the table. Jean reaches it first, lunging for the tidal chart. Henry intercepts her and tries to cover it with his thin torso. Their arms tangle as they scramble. He is surprised to find that Jean is stronger than him, and nimbler as well. Her hand easily shoots under his rib cage and takes hold of the edge of the chart. There is a loud rip as she yanks the sheet away. There is a thundering of paper as it slides to the ground in two giant pieces, revealing the logbook below, still open to this morning's observations.

Henry pants, watching in horror as she snatches it up and retreats with it to the far side of the table. She flips through the pages, something awful taking hold of her features. Her eyes narrow. How could he have let this happen? Henry watches helplessly as she examines a page.

"June fourteenth, Orla O'Connor returns," she reads out loud. Her eyes snap up to look at him before she turns the page. "Guess you didn't need me to tell you."

"Jean," Henry starts, his voice shaking. How can he make her understand that it is just something he does, that there is no harm in it, none really? She is shaking her head.

"It was none of my business. I always thought it was a strange thing to do, this obsession you have with watching, but probably not harming anyone. Now I'm not so sure."

Henry retreats, his shoulders hunched in shame. "Please, Jean. It's only a hobby."

"Oh, really, Henry? Spying on people is a hobby?" She turns the page in the logbook and points to her own name: "4:12 a.m., Jean leaves the Crab." Jean lowers the book and gives him a look that skewers his heart in two. "Spying on me, too, then, are you?"

"It's not so creepy as it seems. I swear. I just wanted to make sure you're okay."

"And if I'm not? What are you going to do, Henry? Jump in your boat and come for me?"

He stares at her startled. What is she implying? She draws closer to him. "Oh yes, I know about *her*, too, Henry. The young girl. The other one." She lowers her voice to a hiss. "Alice."

Henry reels back. He didn't think Margie would have told her that. He thought that it would have been a secret. He'll have to tell her that there are things too dangerous to talk about with Jean. He stands up straighter now. "You weren't meant to be here. This is our house. *Our* things. What right do you have to show up here unannounced and, and—?"

They are both breathing heavily now, eyeing each other across the table warily as though afraid to make the next move.

"I don't care what you do, Henry. This—" She flaps a frantic hand at the corner of the table. "This is your business. But I swear to you, if you know something about that sweet girl and you don't tell me? I will never forgive you, Henry Wright."

Henry quickly does the calculation in his head. He can't afford to lose Jean. She is their one thin tether to reality, the only person who cares. There is something else that is happening, filling him up with a weak, fuzzy feeling. He is relieved that he's not the only one who has carried it all this time. That she's been carrying it all this time also.

"I saw something," he exhales.

"When?" she asks quickly.

He puts his hand out for the logbook, and Jean hands it over to him. He turns the pages until he finds the entry. "Wednesday. It was mostly a shadow in the streetlight. A woman walking down Harbor Street toward the Clarkes that night. And a man as well, coming from the other way."

"And?" she asks.

"That's it," he says, feeling flustered. "They disappeared."

"What do you mean?" Jean narrows her eyes at him.

"Just that there was a man coming the other way, and they sort of converged."

"Could you see who?"

He shakes his head. His mouth opens and closes helplessly. Jean looks at him for a moment as though she is trying to decide whether or not to believe it. Then she presses her fingers into her eyes.

"Jean, are you all right?" He trails behind her as she walks to the door.

"No. I'm afraid," she says.

"I'm sure it's nothing. I'm sure the girl will be okay." His heart twists with the desire to make it better. For Jean or for himself, he isn't sure. He puts his hand out toward her shoulder, wanting to comfort her, but he stops himself. It hovers just above, where she can't see it. He can feel the bracelet Gemma gave him. It digs into his skin, hidden just below the cuff of his shirt.

"I'm not afraid only for Gemma, Henry. I'm afraid for you." She stops but does not turn to face him. Instead, she lets her body fall, exhausted, slumped into the doorframe.

"For me?" He almost laughs. But Jean's face is stricken when she finally turns around to face him. Her eyes water dangerously. Henry can't bear to see her crying.

"Jean, please don't worry, I—" He tries to comfort her.

She stiffens and turns back, walking through the door and onto the deck; when she reaches the stairs, she stops. "They will come for you, Henry. They will lock you up. And this time no one will be able to protect you."

"But Margie . . ." he begins helplessly. She gives him a look. It is stern mixed with pity.

"Now, I know it's been hard for you," she starts as the panic begins to fill his chest.

No no no. He backs away from her. His limbs feel weak. *Please don't say it.*

"Margie wouldn't want me to let you keep going like this. It's not . . . healthy." Jean sighs, ignoring his pleas and stepping toward him. "Stop it, Henry. She's dead! Dead! You can't keep walking around this little place pretending she is still alive."

He lets out a low moan and covers his eyes.

How hard he'd tried to convince his wife to leave the island for medical care, begged her to go to the mainland. "I'll go with you," he'd pleaded.

Margie would hear none of it. "Those doctors, you can't trust them. They'll say I need treatment, and the next thing you know I'll be hooked up to a bunch of tubes and machines and god knows what else." She'd bustled around behind the counter, rubbing it down with a rag as though scrubbing away any idea he might have of her going anywhere.

Henry opens his mouth now to speak, but whatever words he might come up with are lodged firmly in his throat.

He flees back inside as soon as the motor starts.

"Besides," Margie had said, swatting him playfully on the knee as she brushed past him toward the kitchen. "What would you do without me here?"

Eight years on and Henry still doesn't know.

ORLA

They were of course supposed to go to New York together, Alice and Orla. But it was only Orla who went in the end. Her parents came on the ferry to the mainland, where they put her on a bus that would take her to the city all by herself. It was a blustery day and she had vomited twice in the ferry's miniature bathroom as they chugged across the sound.

"I'm sorry this isn't happening the way you wanted, Orla," her mom had said, but she failed to hide the relief on her face that Orla was finally leaving. Orla's father had said nothing but hugged her to his thick chest. She couldn't blame them. Orla couldn't have been easy to be around; she had spent the last two years of high school in a state of total depression. With Alice and David both gone, the color drained out of her life. She stumbled between classes, disengaged. She knew it was a miracle that they let her graduate at all. When the letter arrived from the New School, she almost didn't open it. Her parents, however, insisted.

"Why not try it out, Orla?" her dad had said while her mom nodded encouragingly next to him. "Will be good for you to have a change of scenery."

From the bus window Orla had watched as they turned back to board the ferry home. She had to grip the seat below her legs to keep herself from leaping up and running after them. She didn't know if she could do it. New York alone was almost unthinkable. Without Alice. Without David. Orla no longer even knew who she was.

At art school she was quiet and cautious. She felt disassociated from the others who were excited to be mingling and socializing completely free from the confines of their families for the first time. But Orla didn't know how to do any of it without Alice, wasn't sure how to be the kind of person who went to parties or made new friends. She had always relied on Alice for that.

So instead of developing friendships or dating, Orla studied. She took the core art classes she needed and tried to work on her craft the best she could. She painted hundreds of still lifes and nude models, learned the basics of every major medium, gouache to clay. At the end of each day, she would hole up in her dorm room with a sandwich from the deli and draw. Aside from the paths she took through Washington Square Park every day, she barely even looked at the city.

Despite all her hard work, nothing she was making had any spark of inspiration.

Somehow, though, Orla managed to pass her classes. She was focused in a way she hadn't been before. After all her effort, she was technically proficient. Art school is like that, she came to realize by the beginning of her senior year. If you can pay your way, and you do the work, they are bound to give you a degree whether you are any good or not. Instead of finding it depressing, this became a comfort to Orla.

She knew by then that art the way that Alice had imagined it, the capital "A" art of paintings and sculptures housed in museums and galleries, wasn't going to be part of her life. She would have to pivot after graduation, to find a job in graphic design or maybe even advertising. It felt good in a way, knowing she was near the end. She only had her senior project to complete and then she would be released from it all. She had started to feel lighter, to spend more time out in the world. Soon she would be able to stop living out the childhood dreams of a dead girl. And maybe then, she hoped, she would be free from the stomach-turning memories that haunted her whenever she was alone at night, flashing against the backs of her eyelids just as she drifted off to sleep.

Two sets of legs. One young and thin with slightly knobby knees that suggest they aren't quite yet done growing. The other is older, covered in a map of veins and leg hair. The feet clad in some sort of ugly expensive-looking sneaker. The hand on her knee. The horrible scream. The wet hair curling below the water.

Orla had moved into an on-campus studio apartment by then, an upgrade, as it was somewhere she could spend her time completely alone. But she was packing to leave. She was going through all her art, getting ready to toss it, when she found the tube, still taped shut. She had forgotten all about Alice's drawings. She'd brought them to New York for sentimental reasons. But maybe there was something else she could do.

Orla unrolled the drawings onto the floor. They were a series of portraits, all of people they knew on Hadley. There was a picture of Jean, with her jagged lines. And then of course, Henry Wright with his bare feet and his hooded eyes. The angular lines halting around the corners of his mouth, the large worker's fingers. They were ordinary, but in the careful details Alice had made them beautiful. And Orla had the idea suddenly that Alice would be her project.

She mounted the fragile drawings on thick stock and cut the frayed edges off. The way she smoothed them out, coating them with a thick layer of varnish, gave them a professional quality they hadn't had before. A sort of polish that made them glow from within their frames.

It was something she could still give her, Orla rationalized, as she prepared each piece for display. It would be her final farewell to the idea of being an artist, and a send-off to Alice, whose work would be shown in New York just like she'd dreamed of all those times, feet propped on the wall next to Orla's bed. Orla even felt a sense of misguided pride when she took them into the gallery at school and lined them up to be hung. She was bringing Alice's art to New York. The way Alice had always wanted. She was doing her a favor. Or maybe it was all a lie Orla told herself. That it wasn't going to harm anyone, and that Alice's genius could be a gift to her best friend who was left behind. That she could get away with it.

Orla's thesis adviser, Ruth, a thirtysomething woman with tattoos and hair razor-cut to her chin, someone who had dismissed Orla as boring, stopped to stare. It was only when Ruth leaned in to look more closely, appreciating the thin lines of charcoal that some chord of apprehension plucked inside of Orla.

"Wow, Orla. These are so raw, so powerful. The lines are so controlled. I always knew you were technically very good, but these almost remind me of Käthe Kollwitz's charcoals. More modern, though, and even more lively."

The anxiety Orla felt in that moment began to dissipate as they got closer to the show. She was nearly on the other side of college, ready to pivot to whatever real-world drudgery awaited her. She was almost looking forward to finally becoming a normal person. And then everything went wrong.

A famous gallerist showed up to the senior exhibit. Ruth found Orla in the corner of the gallery, quietly sipping from a plastic cup of oaky white wine. "Dom Castro is here." Her voice was singsongy and her eyes shiny like she'd just been standing in the wind.

"Who?" Orla said, feeling cornered.

"He runs Vestments," she said, waiting for Orla to respond appropriately. When she didn't, Ruth got impatient. "Orla. Come on. It's the most influential gallery in the city right now, aside from, like, *the Gagosian*." That one Orla had heard of. Her chest constricted.

"He wants to meet you. He says he wants to show your work." She grabbed Orla by the wrist. She knew as Ruth dragged her across the room that she had made a major error in judgment. Orla wanted to tell her then that the drawings weren't even hers. But as a man with slicked-back hair reached out to shake her hand, Orla found it was already too late to say anything.

So, Alice's drawings were not just a success, they were a triumph. A rare fluke of time and space rarely afforded to any artist at any point in their career let alone one in her early twenties. The gallery show had sold out before it even opened. But the opening was still spectacular. Orla doubts that Alice herself would have been able to dream up what came next. How she went from reclusive nobody to the art world's darling in a matter of months. The invitations to show her work, the write-up in *Vogue* complete with a photo of Orla wearing a Balenciaga gown with a pair of Nikes, her head tilted arrogantly to one side.

Orla had known it was wrong. But she couldn't say that the drawings weren't hers, not then. She would have been publicly shamed and, worse, after all that she went through, she would have her degree revoked. She needed to live in this new reality, to make it her own. So instead, she studied Alice's drawings and followed as best she could the same techniques, creating several more shows from the work she produced.

They were not the blowout successes that the first had been, but they were passable enough to keep collectors salivating. It almost didn't matter if they were as good as the first set, which Orla knew they weren't. By then everyone wanted an "Orla OC," as she had begun to go by.

Plus, Orla was finally starting to enjoy her new life, the one where her phone was lighting up with texts and she suddenly had places to be. The new people in her life filled up the empty place where Alice had been. They helped her forget.

As the delusion really settled in, she had begun to gain confidence. Orla liked the new version of herself with the fashion industry friends and cool bangs.

She even began to convince herself that Alice's genius and her own were actually intertwined. Orla could show some of her own paintings, she decided. She started a series of monochromatic boxes, their tops opened to reveal their empty insides. She painted them late into the night in a fervor. It was that last desperate attempt that did her in. First the bad reviews poured in and then after the show, everything slowed to a pathetic trickle.

Her astronomical success, like most, had been a quick hot flame. And then it was over.

Orla looks down at the kitchen table at the drawing she's started of Alice's house. The branches twist like they are moving. The dark windows appear through them as sunken eyes. Maybe there is something there. A flutter of hope builds in her chest. If there were just more contrast to it perhaps. Orla is suddenly desperate to prove that she has talent. David is wrong about her. She just needs to finish this drawing and she can take it back to New York and ask her agent to find her a new gallery. She can turn her career around. And maybe then her life will follow.

Remembering a box in the closet marked Art Supplies, Orla leaves the drawing sitting next to her nearly empty tequila glass and goes upstairs. She makes a beeline for the closet door, swinging it open, and steps inside reaching for the flimsy string to turn on the single bulb.

The shelves in the back remain dark as she puts her hand up and feels for the box. She finally finds the edge and pulls down an old green plastic pencil box. She undoes the latch and holds it under the light bulb as she paws through it, an invisible film of ancient eraser dust and pencil shavings making her fingers slippery.

At the bottom of the box Orla finds what she is looking for, a narrow packet of vine charcoal still in its plastic wrapper. It's been there since high school art class. That will work. She tucks the box under her arm and turns back to the door quickly, eager to leave the closet. As she reaches back up for the light switch, she is confronted with the hand-drawn mural on the back of the closet wall. Her heart jerks violently up into her chest. Before she can fully comprehend what she is looking at, she starts screaming.

The box of art supplies falls to the floor with an angry clatter,

sending pens and pencils rolling loudly across the hardwood into the
dark corners of the closet. It isn't Alice and Orla's drawing. Not anymore.
It's been changed. Orla's knees buckle. The faces of the two of them so
carefully rendered by Alice have been scribbled over with coarse black
Sharpie, looped into furious scribbles over the eyes so that only their
mouths remain. And David, the entirety of him is blacked out. Then
there is the Rock. The house's windows have been filled in crudely with
black paint. It drips all the way down the side of the wall, pooling in a
sticky puddle on the floor of the closet.

FAITH

Faith almost misses it. She has to double back to the wooded lot to find the shape of an eave peeking out from between the branches. From there, she can almost trace the shape of the house camouflaged behind all that wild greenery. She glances back down the road to make sure no one is watching her and then steps into the woods.

The trees thin a bit as she draws closer to the property. Now she can see the side of a railing and past that a window clouded with dirt. Faith pulls aside a branch, noting the broken underbrush below her feet. Someone else has been here recently. She moves along the side of the house, carefully stepping up onto the porch. She jumps back as her foot nearly goes through a rotted piece of board.

She takes the hem of her dress in her hand and uses it to wipe a patch of the window. She leans forward, pressing her nose to the smudged glass. The house is still furnished, she's surprised to see. The sofa and chairs stand around a low table that's set with a tray as though ready for tea. But the walls are in bad shape, the floor so warped that one of the chairs sits at an angle on top of it. It's just a sad empty house.

The sunlight filters through the camouflage of branches. They cast an array of dizzying shadows through the underbrush. Her eyes dilate. There is a flash of something in the woods near the house, and everything around her is moving, tilting. She retreats quickly to the edge of the wooded patch stumbling out onto the lawn of the neighboring house.

Rattled, she makes her way back along the side of the house next door. This house is well kept, its grounds manicured. Her breath slows as she walks quickly along the side of it toward the road. A large bay window juts off the side and she pauses, looking through the gap in the thin linen curtains at a wide stone hearth and warm wood floors draped with worn throw rugs. Framed photos hang on the walls. Faith glimpses a candid family portrait where a mother and father embrace a child with flame-red hair. Her heart starts to pound faster as she takes in the assortment of pencils scattered across the dining table. This must be Orla's house.

She looks closer now, curious, pressing her face up to the glass. She had felt threatened by Orla on the beach, but now Faith feels a pang of deep envy at the life Orla must have had growing up in a house like this. She imagines the dinners spent gathered around the table, a Christmas tree put up in the corner, the security of these sturdy walls during a howling storm. It's hard to imagine a little girl like that becoming the woman she saw on the beach with so much unhappiness etched on her face. Faith finds herself getting irrationally angry at Orla. She probably doesn't even realize how fortunate she is.

Faith squeezes her eyes shut for a moment, trying to reset herself. She remembers why she is here. The dead friend next door. There's nothing lucky about that. When she opens them back up, she sees it: a light blue shirt draped across the back of one of the chairs facing away from the window. Faith sucks in a breath as she realizes that it's David's.

As soon as she's back at the Clarkes' estate, Faith rushes up the stairs to their bedroom.

She goes straight into the dressing room. David's clothes dangle, neatly pressed on hangers now. The suitcase is tucked against the back wall. She yanks it out and unzips it. It is completely empty. She paws through it anyway, lifting every flap, her fingers scraping the sides, looking for the little red bag with the box inside. He must have moved it. Frantic, she goes to his clothes, hanging in their neat rows above. She runs her hands over each of his shirts searching every pocket for the bulge of the little red box. But she can't find it anywhere.

The ring is gone. Maybe it was never meant for her to begin with.

When she leaves the closet, David is standing in the middle of the bedroom.

"Oh!" Faith clutches her chest. "I didn't hear you come in. What are you doing?"

"I was just looking for you," he says, a strained smile on his face. "But maybe you're busy?"

She holds up the sweater, grateful to have grabbed it at the last second. "It's getting cold out." A funny look passes over his face. Fear twists in her stomach. He doesn't believe her. "Why were you looking for me?" she asks, her throat suddenly parched.

He is staring at her. "I thought we could go to the lighthouse."

"Now?" She glances through the windows, a thick band of clouds is moving in, below them the ocean is churning, the waves tipped with white.

"It'll clear up," he says. She marvels at the certainty with which he says it. Like he has power over the weather. Had he always been like this, so full of arrogance and bravado, and she had just ignored it?

"David, are you sure?"

"You've wanted to go all this time, I thought you'd be into it?" he says, and it feels like he is challenging her. "I had the kitchen staff pack us up some wine and cheese."

Reluctantly she follows him out to the driveway where a car is already waiting for them. A Mercedes this time. She thinks of the key in Geoffrey's desk drawer and wonders if this is the car it belongs to. If so, would David have gone into the drawer to retrieve it? Would he have seen the NDAs, remembered the photos? Of course she can't ask him any of it. Not any more than she can confront him about the shirt on Orla O'Connor's chair. David is silent, focused on the road. He hardly looks like he is in the mood for a picnic, she thinks, bracing herself as a gust of wind hits the side of the car. The Mercedes swerves, making her carsick as it follows the pitch of the road up toward the lighthouse. It is a stark whitewashed box of a building supporting a black-and-white painted tower anchored to the rocky ledge of a tall cliff. The waves foam angrily against it.

As they grow closer the light in the top of the tower flashes above the tree line. *A warning*, Faith thinks out of nowhere. She glances at David. His brows are tight over his eyes giving nothing away as they park the car in a sandy lot near the edge of a windswept field.

There are only a few cars in the parking lot. As David goes to get something out of the trunk, she watches a couple packing up their chairs.

"Going to be a disappointing sunset tonight with these clouds coming in," she hears the woman say to her partner as they wrangle a golden retriever into the back seat of their car. The clouds roll quickly past, their purple underbellies swollen with rain.

"Should we go back?" Faith asks.

"It'll be fine." David picks up the basket and tucks a rolled-up picnic blanket under one arm. He gives her a tense smile as they leave the parking lot. They trudge silently through the tall stands of seagrass toward an open field at the foot of the lighthouse. It stretches from the building out toward the edge of the cliff. The sky grows darker; the woman in the parking lot was right, the sunset tonight would be gray and dull, the sun snuffing out uneventfully on the horizon. David wordlessly reaches for her hand as they walk. She lets him take it. His grip is tight, his fingers digging into the edges of her hand.

The trail wraps around the front of the lighthouse to the edge of the cliff. It's colder than it was back at the house. The wind blows up off the water in heavy gusts whipping at her dress.

The guardrail tapers off and Faith looks down over the edge. Far below, the waves collide with the rocks, sending a fine spray up into the atmosphere. She can feel it on her skin, in her hair. This island, it has a way of attaching itself to you. David stops walking nearly mid-step and turns toward her.

"Faith . . ." For a moment she thinks he's going to tell her something important, but he seems to change his mind. "Here okay?"

She nods. He unfurls the picnic blanket, and they sit. David uncorks a bottle of wine and pours two glasses. Faith kicks off her sandals and stretches her bare feet out over the edge of the rocks feeling the spray of the waves. Out in the distance the waves toss a small fishing boat around. Faith can make out the tiny figure of a fisherman on its deck. He throws out a lobster cage.

"I wanted to apologize. I didn't expect to be swept up with work from dawn till dusk. I wanted to take you out, explore the island."

"That would have been nice," she says.

She used to think she knew David so well that she could tell what he was thinking but she wonders now if she was wrong. If they were always two very separate people and she had only imagined their closeness. But now she looks up at him and he raises his glass to hers.

"Who'd have ever thought you could be bored by a mansion?" she adds in an offhanded way, taking a sip.

He must not have expected her to agree with him so quickly. "I didn't know that hanging out by the pool was such a hardship on you. Honestly, Faith." She draws back, stung.

"You've completely disappeared, David. I don't even know where you are half the time."

David stiffens. Then he shakes his head in disbelief. "I've been doing my *job*."

Before she can stop herself, she shoots back, "In the middle of the night?"

"What's that supposed to mean?" he demands, but she can tell by the way he tenses up that he knows exactly what she means.

"You came to bed at three a.m. Where were you?" she pushes.

"Now you're spying on me in my own house. That's great." His eyes dart around. Cornered.

"I woke up and you weren't there," Faith cries, feeling called out. "What was I meant to do?"

"I don't know. Go back to bed like a normal person?"

Faith's chest hurts. They've never fought like this before. There is a meanness in his voice that has never been there before. There is also a challenge in her own voice that he has never heard. She feels like they are beginning to spin off the rails. Faith should stop before it's too late. She knows she should apologize, to reel it back if she wants to keep things okay between them. But the ring is gone. And so is the girl, Gemma. Faith has less and less to lose.

"Were you with Orla?" she asks him quietly.

"What? Why would I be with Orla?" he scoffs. "Of course not. Look, your obsession with her has really gotten out of control." He looks down at her, a sneer on his perfect face. For the first time he looks ugly to her.

"You're lying to me," she says before she can stop herself. "I saw your shirt. You left it at her house."

David watches, stunned, from the side of the blanket. The wine has tipped over and is spilled on the blanket between them. The little picnic is ruined, but Faith no longer cares.

She stands up and slips into her shoes as he sputters angrily, "I invite you into my home and you sneak around spying on me and digging up things from my past?" He abruptly stops speaking.

"I never pegged you for the jealous type," he says at last, shaking his head. Faith's stomach sinks.

"There's another girl missing, about the same age as your friend Alice was," Faith says, even quieter. "But maybe you already knew that?"

At this David leaps up from the blanket. He advances on her and she stumbles back across the grass. "Where did you hear that?"

"It's a small town, David. People talk."

"My father has never done anything wrong," David insists, his voice rising angrily.

Startled, Faith looks at him. "Why do you say that? I never once mentioned your father."

David is staring at her now and breathing heavily. Why did it take her so long to see who he is? All this time she'd thought of David as the victim, assuming he was being manipulated by his father out of a sense of duty, but maybe it was deeper than that. Maybe they were protecting each other. She was wrong about David. Wrong about it all. Her mother would have told her that men like David were nothing but trouble.

David storms petulantly toward the car, leaving the picnic behind for someone else to clean up. Faith can see right into him now. He isn't angry anymore. He is afraid.

HENRY

Henry tries to carry on as normal with his routine, but his fingers fumble as he cooks up a piece of haddock and some potatoes, and he does something wrong, forgets to put enough oil in the pan and turns the burner up too high and the fish sticks to the cast iron and turns black. He tries to eat it, but he can feel bones sticking in his throat when he takes a bite. Henry's appetite isn't good anyway. He takes his dinner out to the deck and throws it onto the rocks for the seagulls to devour.

Then he goes to the telescope and looks.

He goes first to the docks by Port Mary. There is a lineup of people, all unfamiliar. The ferry bobs at the dock, preparing for the return trip. The restaurants are busy. People linger over gratuitous plates of lobster, piles of fried calamari, and bright yellow rings of banana peppers. They finish off bottles of wine, smiling and laughing like nothing has happened. Like a girl isn't missing. Like Henry isn't a suspect. Like Margie isn't dead.

He lets the telescope go out of focus and fall from his hand. He isn't in the mood to watch anymore. He's lost interest in the comings and goings on Hadley. His logbook is unmarked since his last entry when Jean made her unexpected visit.

Henry knows how lucky he was that Edward Robertson was the town's detective fifteen years ago. Without him there to talk people down, they would have locked him up. Or worse.

Henry swallows, thinking about the last time.

When Alice Gallo was declared missing, a mob had formed outside the station overnight. In the early morning they'd filed into Hadley's little community center and sat on folding chairs. The camera people there had schlepped their equipment all the way from the mainland. There were sharply dressed news reporters holding microphones too. A press conference, they'd called it.

By the time they had brought Henry in, David Clarke was already talking. He looked pale and shaken. He hunched down, his teeth chattering.

"We were out on the b-boat," David stuttered. "We'd been drinking." He had said this part with what sounded like deep remorse.

"And then what?" the reporter prodded.

"I don't know exactly," he mumbled. "I fell asleep. And when I woke up Orla was screaming and Alice was gone. I ran over and Orla was looking down into the water. There was a boat there in the dark, rowing away from us."

"Did you get a look at who was in it, David?" the reporter had asked, putting a paternal hand on his shoulder.

"Him," David said pointing, "Henry Wright. He had Alice in the bottom of the boat. I could see her dress."

There was a collective gasp from the crowd.

"Now hold up," Ed had said, holding up a palm to quiet the room. "This is just to gather information; there will be a fair trial here."

"What direction did they go?" the reporter asked.

"Away, back to his house," David said, and then he had raised his head and looked straight into the camera. "Please, I need you to find her. She's one of my best friends."

Henry was standing dumbfounded, his clothes still damp, when the reporters descended on him and shoved their microphones into his face.

"Is it true? What were you doing out there in the water?"

"I saw the young girl in distress. I was only trying to help," he'd tried to explain but Geoffrey Clarke had appeared then in the doorway. His arrival quieted the room as people stopped talking to watch him swagger up the aisle. His presence filled up the small community room, a rarity, like seeing a celebrity in the flesh.

His voice sent a ripple through the room.

"This wasn't the first time you went looking for Alice, though, was it, Henry? There are people who saw the two of you behind the old wharf building. She even told David that you were obsessed with her."

Henry had hunched in shame. Had she really said that? "No, it wasn't like that. She'd been the one to find me," Henry had whimpered as the crowd gasped, titillated by this new piece of information.

"Blaming the victim is a bad look, Henry." Geoffrey had shaken his head sadly, though Henry thought he was not actually sad.

"You said you saw her. Do you often look for girls, Henry?"

"I look at everything. I like to watch—"

"You have it there, straight from his mouth. *He likes to watch!*" Geoffrey appealed to the crowd, twisting his face into a theatric look of disgust.

Henry's mouth clamped shut. He looked around the room. Nearly all in attendance were familiar. They were kids he'd come up with, all grown up. Childhood neighbors and classmates, his dentist and doctor, the owner of the local deli. Most of them people he'd known his whole life. But their faces were unfamiliar to him now, their eyes closed off to his pleas for understanding. A few had held their hands to their chests in shock while several others curled their lips back in disgust; they had already turned on him.

"Now, now," Ed had interjected from the side of the room where he'd been taking questions. "I said there was no proof of anything at all. We are still investigating."

"Just a child," Geoffrey tutted, stepping in front of the policeman. "And they're going to let him go with a slap on the wrist."

"There's no clear evidence that Henry had anything to do with it," Ed insisted. "Please let's all allow the process to do its job."

All eyes went to Geoffrey, who spun toward the crowd raising his hands in question. "The process?" he scoffed. "I don't know about you, but I expect my police force not to pussyfoot around when a young girl's life is at stake." A buzz of angry conversation rippled across the room. Henry swore that he could see Geoffrey grow taller in front of him as he was egged on.

"My own son saw that man take his friend onto his boat." The murmurs grew louder, angrier.

"But that's just n-not t-true," Henry stuttered.

"Did you go out to find the girl, Henry?" the reporter was asking him.

"Yes, I went out to find her, but she wasn't there. I . . ." Henry looked helplessly to David, whose head dropped down toward his lap. Henry remembered how kindly Alice had treated him all those times, chatting with him and asking him questions. He'd felt like she was a friend by the end of their last drawing session. He'd been nervous to see the finished drawing, afraid of facing himself, but when she had turned the sketch pad toward him, he felt only a swell of pride. How well she'd captured him. His imperfections were there, the deep grooves in his cheeks, the receding hairline, but they seemed to lend him a certain quiet dignity, something he'd never seen fully in himself. But she did. She was a special girl, and they were out to hurt her. He thought of the men on the boat and how they had loomed over Alice. Anger rose up in his chest. Finding his voice, he leaned over and spoke directly into the microphone. "Something bad was happening out there on that boat."

"Oh, something bad?" Geoffrey waved his palms at the crowd in mock fear. "Was it *really* something bad or did you see my son and his friends having fun the way teenagers do? I think you decided to spy on them and got jealous when you saw your creepy little crush there with someone her own age. What kind of perversions do you have that make you want to watch teenagers?"

"No," Henry said. "It was you." The truth of it was, Henry didn't know what he saw, not exactly.

"And he's delusional as well. I wasn't even on the yacht, Henry. I was at the party. Ask anyone here. They all saw me." There were low voices as the attendees conferred among themselves. They had seen him, hadn't they? Geoffrey had been in rare form that night, shaking hands, slapping backs. You couldn't miss him.

"No, you were there," Henry protested. "I saw you and others too. Not kids, grown men." But his words were lost in the voices of the crowd. Henry could hear Margie's voice trying to defend him. He strained his eyes trying to find her.

"Do you like to watch people?" the newscaster prodded him.

"That man"—Geoffrey waved his hand in Henry's face—"was looking at children through a telescope. He says himself he does it all the time."

An outraged murmur rippled across the auditorium. As they jeered at him, Henry became less sure of himself. What if it really wasn't Geoffrey he'd seen, but his son? "Please, Geoffrey, let's let the law decide all this," Ed begged, but he was losing steam against the crowd, who were growing louder and more disgruntled by the second.

Henry finally found Margie in the far back of the room. She was standing along the wall, her face pale under the fluorescent lighting. Her eyes wide with fear. Margie had been the one who suggested they leave. *These provincial people,* she'd always complained, *I can't bear it here anymore.*

"Why you are protecting him?" Geoffrey boomed at Ed Robertson. "You have no other credible suspects, and you have a witness. Unless you are trying to hide something also?"

"That's a disgusting lie. I'm protecting the law. Not him." Ed was growing visibly nervous as the murmurs from the islanders grew louder and angrier.

At this Geoffrey Clarke spun back on his heels and raised his eyebrows, addressing the room again. "My son, David, came forward and told the police right away, but they ignored him. That man is strange, we all know it. We give him a pass, but look at him. Who goes and lives on a tiny little island like that unless they have something to hide? Why else would a man move his wife out there, so far away from the rest of us, unless he was disturbed?"

Ed cut in. "We found nothing at the Wright residence to suggest—"

But Geoffrey had found his footing now. The crowd was his. He turned on the officer.

"How long did it take you to get a warrant? See, he can't even answer? Well, I will, it was hours. I say that gave him plenty of time to do what he wanted with her. And to hide the evidence."

The crowd gasped at the implication.

"God no, I never—" Henry had tried to defend himself, sickened by the very nature of the accusation. The jeers of the crowd grew louder and the overhead light suddenly became very hot on his face. He had one clear thought then: If only he had written it all down, he could prove it.

"If my son isn't a good enough witness for you people, he isn't alone. The girl saw him too." Geoffrey pointed at Orla O'Connor. Her head dropped to her chest.

"It's okay, dear, you can tell us," the reporter said, his voice dripping with performative empathy.

"I saw him," she said through the hair that had fallen in front of her face. When she looked up, her eyes were red from crying. "We went to look, and she was gone."

"And then what? What did you see, dear?"

"Henry Wright was in the water. And I saw Alice in his boat."

At this the roar from the public had been so intense the police had become visibly nervous. They whisked Henry away from the blur of angry villagers and out a back door to a police car.

We'll never be able to leave now, Margie had said after that night. The terror of their predicament was all over her face. *Unless it's for good.* But both of them knew that wasn't an option, not really. Hadley was all either of them had ever known. It was home. And they weren't the types to start over. They were creatures of comfort. Homebodies. They had each other, though; that was what mattered.

"Ed was the only one who stopped them from hauling you off like vigilantes," Margie, shaken, had repeated later. The fear in her voice had turned to anger when they were back in their chairs, safely on their little island and settled in for the night. Henry hadn't wanted to think then about the people he'd known all his life having it in for him.

"We don't know what they would have done," he'd said, turning his attention toward the water, ready to put the whole thing behind him. But Margie wasn't ready to let it go. She shuffled angrily in her chair.

"I do," she'd said, pulling the blanket tightly around her and shuddering. "Geoffrey would have had them tear you limb from limb. You, or anyone else that threatened to expose his terrible little secrets."

ORLA

The liquor store is set in a tiny strip mall next to a launderette right in the center of Port Mary. Orla walks toward it. She'd walked into town in a fearful trance, the painting in the closet forcing her out of the house and onto the road.

Her fingers fumble as she pulls open the door. A quick search on her phone showed that all the hotels on the island are booked through to July 5. Not that she could afford it even if they weren't. She'd debated calling the police. But what could she show them other than a mess of childish drawings? She can't even be sure. It *is* dark in the closet, she tells herself. And Orla hasn't slept more than a few hours a night since she arrived. The humidity, it could do things to ink, couldn't it? Make it slide. Make it run down walls. Black out eyes. Her back quivers with the memory of it.

But the idea of being questioned by the Hadley Police Department makes her feel nearly as sick as the paint dripping down the closet wall.

There is only one way out of this nightmare and that is to sell the house and leave Hadley as quickly as humanly possible. Coming here was supposed to heal her, but it has brought nothing but pain.

Orla finds a bottle of the same tequila David had brought to her house. She's developed a taste for it, particularly since the Xanax has run out. It isn't as expensive as she'd thought. Orla takes the largest bottle from the shelf—she'll need it if she is going to survive another night in that house—and walks slowly toward the front of the store. The rows of bottles comfort her, as does the gawky kid who rings her up at the register. The world is still as it should be. Her breathing has begun to return to normal as she steps back out into the night. She looks out at the curve of the restaurants' glittering reflections on the water. The clinking of silverware and dinner conversations are barely audible in the distance over the lap of waves against the pylons.

Orla crosses the cracked pavement to the pier, her sandals crunching across the debris of broken clamshells dropped by hungry seagulls. Orla doesn't know how she'll go back to the house. The drips of paint play on the backs of her eyelids whenever she blinks. Before Alice died Orla never believed in ghosts. But now she sees them everywhere. As she leans back and allows her eyes to close, she sees a flash of the drawing, mutilated by thick black lines.

She jerks them open just as the lights blink out at the Crab. There is only one light on the dock, and it's sending an orb of foggy light down on the bench. The air is thick with humidity. Beyond the periphery of the light, Orla can hear but not see the water as it rushes past. The moored boats clang and creak out there in the dark. She wonders what it would be like to sleep outside. There's no way it would go unnoticed someplace like this. What a way to make her grand public reentry to Hadley—arrested for sleeping on a bench along the harbor. She'll have to go back to the house. But she is going to need help. She pulls the tequila bottle out of its bag and fumbles with the top, her body thrumming with nerves.

"Need a hand with that?" She jerks with fright at the voice behind her. A bearded man comes into the light. He sways slightly as he walks, and Orla realizes he must have come from the Crab. She wonders how much he's had to drink and how long he's been standing there like that, watching her. Her body tenses as she looks past him at the desolate road.

"I was just l-l-leaving," she stutters, calculating how fast she could run. He reaches into his pocket, and something silver flashes in his hand; he unfolds it into a short knife as he advances on her.

"No, please I—" Orla pulls back, preparing to run away until she realizes it is a fish scaler. He reaches for the bottle.

"May I?" She lets him lift the bottle from her hands and watches him use the blade on it to take off the plastic and lift the cork.

"You should see your face right now." He is smirking. "Saw someone over here, thought you might need help, but now I see it's you. Heard rumors you were back. You don't recognize me, do you?" He steps away from her, sitting down on the next bench over. Orla peers over at the weathered face and realizes there is something familiar about him.

"I'm sorry. It's been so long."

He flops into the bench next to hers. "It's Walter Severson. I knew your parents way back when. I know, haven't aged a day, right?" He grins, revealing a row of stained, crooked teeth. She remembers him now. A surprisingly handsome man in his younger years. He's aged. Badly. He was always around town working odd jobs.

Orla offers him the bottle, feeling like she should be polite, but he declines, patting his chest. "Beer guy myself. Can't do the hard stuff anymore." Orla can tell he is lying. He pulls out a packet of cigarettes and tips one to his lips. He offers her the packet, but she shakes her head.

"I heard from Jean you were back, but I almost didn't believe her." He looks out at the harbor, the red of the cigarette glowing as he takes a deep drag.

"Jean knows?"

Walter drapes a weathered hand across the back of his bench. His skin is deeply tan but bears a crisscross of white scars from years on a fishing boat. He is the kind of person Orla could never quite explain to rich people in New York. He is Hadley Island through and through, the type who would never leave. There is something about him that is also in her. Like a piece of home. Or a secret you try to bury.

"Surprised you'd show up back here actually." His eyes don't open all the way, and she can see only the small slivers of blue under his lids, so bright they nearly glow in the dark.

"I am too," Orla says quietly.

"Why'd you come then?"

She takes a long swig out of the bottle. She has no reason not to answer truthfully. "I'm going to sell the house." It feels good to have at least one of her secrets out in the open.

"Oh, okay." He shrugs as though it makes sense.

"What? You don't think I'm a traitor?" Orla says, surprised he isn't more reactive.

"Maybe. Or maybe you just want to start over," he says. "Nothing wrong with that. People do it every day."

"Not here," she says. Walter smiles a little at that.

"Not me," he agrees. "Nothing running away would fix for me. And besides that, I'm comfortable here. Got my place. Got the Crab. And this view." Walter gestures out at the black nothingness in front of them. "Speaking of, Jean's not too happy you're back."

"She doesn't like me," Orla says, reverting.

"I think it was just what you did to her brother-in-law," Walter says matter-of-factly.

"I didn't do anything to him," Orla protests.

"Well, you told the police that he killed your little friend."

"I didn't. I only said I saw him there. Which I did."

"Okay, okay," he says, raising his eyebrows like *don't kill the messenger*.

"You don't believe me?" Orla's heart pumps a bit faster.

"I didn't say that. Did I say that?" Walter puts his palms up to show his innocence. "I don't take sides. I'm like Austria."

"I think you mean Switzerland," Orla says. She's becoming annoyed now. Walter is an idiot. She should never have engaged with him.

"Don't know. Never been there."

She stands up and is preparing to leave, when he says, "I hear David Clarke has a new girlfriend."

"Does he? I wouldn't know." Now she can see he is toying with her, trying to get a rise. That's what small-town people do when they're bored. Create their own gossip.

"Oh, I met her. Faith." Walter rolls the name around in his mouth.

"That ridiculous name," she mutters, remembering the woman on the beach. The way she looked at Orla. *Would I have seen any of your art?* Walter stretches back against the bench, entertained.

"Yeah, she came into the Crab alone a few times," he says. "Nice girl. Smart too. Pretty, like Alice was."

Orla takes a swig of tequila. The thought of Faith makes her feel sick to her stomach.

Walter smiles, he's enjoying this. "You don't like it. Still have a crush on David Clarke after all this time, don't you?"

"What would you know about that?" she snaps. "No, I don't. I hate him actually. I just don't see why he deserves to be happy."

"Well, you don't have to worry, she won't last. Trust me," he says. "Look at what happened to the other one, to David's mom."

"What do you mean? I thought she left them." Orla barely remembers the beautiful woman who teetered in the background, worry gnawing on her face until one summer she was gone. She'd gone into treatment, David said, and never brought it up again.

"You could say that. Or you could say that she was put into circumstances that made it impossible to stay."

"You're saying Geoffrey got her addicted to painkillers so he could get rid of her?"

"Me? I'm saying nothing." He twists an invisible lock near his lips.

Orla lets out an angry laugh. "None of those Clarke men could ever commit to someone."

"Maybe they just like their freedom," Walter posits, insincerely.

"Maybe they are just selfish assholes," Orla snaps at him.

"Whooo, okay. You have a real chip on your shoulder, lady." Walter pulls himself down to the other end of his bench and studies her.

"Could say the same about you," Orla replies. She stands up as though to storm off but realizes she isn't sure where she is going.

"You never really bounced back from all that drama with Alice, did you? Maybe time to move on?"

"Maybe it's survivor's guilt," she says quietly, crossing her arms in front of her.

"Maybe," Walter says, though he doesn't sound entirely convinced.

Orla has had quite enough of Walter and his bullshit.

"There's another girl missing, you know? Gemma, works down at the Crab or did until a week ago."

A shudder rattles Orla's spine as he continues, "They'll probably be going after Henry again."

"Why? What do you know?" Her chest heaves.

Walter shrugs. "The police have some evidence on him. At least that's what my sources say." He gives her one last long stare, and then he stubs the cigarette out on the side of the bench and begins to walk away.

Orla starts in the other direction, following the dark curve of the road up past the beach toward home.

FAITH

On July 1, the cars begin to arrive at the Clarke estate without warning. Black town cars, four of them in total, pulling in through the main gate and moving up the drive like a funeral procession. Faith watches from the bedroom window as they stop at the main entryway, disgorging an assortment of middle-aged men clad in pressed khaki pants and shorts that look like dress pants cut off at the knee—leisure wear for rich old conservatives.

Faith goes down to the kitchen for an iced tea and sees they've already gathered on the veranda. There is a tight pack of them. The scent of cigar smoke hangs in the air. An occasional loud, humorless chuckle rises up from among them. Faith observes them from behind the glass, feeling like she's watching some sort of nature special. David is out there with them. She'd pretended to be asleep this morning as he'd slipped out of bed. The last week has been tense, distrust simmering between them, though they pretend it isn't. They have eaten together, making idle chitchat about the weather, and the party, coming up now in just a few days. Faith wonders what will happen. Will they be able to salvage it or should she start looking for new jobs and apartments with roommates? Geoffrey saunters out to the veranda and is immediately folded into the center of the men, the alpha male.

David spots her watching and comes into the kitchen next to her. He kisses her cheek. She flinches at the roughness of his stubble on her face. "Who are they?"

"Dad's friends," he answers simply.

"You don't like them?" Faith says. He gives her a look.

"I didn't say that," he says quickly. When he sees her expression, he explains, "Look, they're a certain type of man, right? From a different generation. It's not that I like them or don't like them, they just are."

She looks up at David. *Are what?*

"Let's get out of here," David says, taking her hand and pulling her away from the veranda.

"Where to?" she asks him, trying to find the lightness in her voice. She isn't going to say anything until she knows more.

"Wherever you want," he says, leading her toward the main door. "I'll have Jim bring round a car."

"There's something going on in town, an oyster festival or something," Faith says, remembering the flyer she saw stapled to a board next to the town hall.

"That'll be perfect." He seems almost desperate to leave now, picking up his pace, and Faith wonders what he wants to escape.

"I have to change first," Faith says, hesitating at the bottom of the stairs. She is wearing only a black one-piece swimsuit and a pair of gauze pants.

"You look great just as you are," David says, his eyes pleading with her. She gives in.

Geoffrey Clarke steps into the foyer, cutting them off at the pass.

"Where are you dragging my son off to?" he booms.

"Faith and I were about to go downtown for the Oyster Festival," David says quickly. "Some local thing. We shouldn't be gone long."

Geoffrey eyes the two of them. Faith can tell he is calculating something.

"I'd like to come," Geoffrey says. "Would be good to show my face around town before the party, don't you think?"

David pales. "Are you sure, Dad? I thought you were taking the boys down to the course later." Geoffrey returns a defiant look.

"I think the boys can wait. Or they can come with. They love an oyster. You know that."

"Aw, Dad, I was hoping that me and Faith—"

"What? Did you want a little private time? Don't want your old pops tagging along on your little date?" Geoffrey says this last part antagonistically. Even though it is true that Faith desperately wants time alone with David, she won't let Geoffrey see her sweating it. She gets the feeling he is toying with her. She puts a serene smile on her face.

"It's fine, David," Faith says, putting a hand to his arm. She turns to Geoffrey. "You are more than welcome to come. The more the merrier; besides, David and I get plenty of time alone together in New York."

Geoffrey returns an aggressive smile that shows her she's gotten to him. "Thank you, Faith. That's very generous."

"Jimmy!" he calls out, pushing past them to the door. "We'll need three cars. SUVs. I'm bringing the boys."

The air at the festival is briny with shucked oysters. Rows of white catering tents are set up at the site of an old fort next to a low concrete barracks in front of the sea. And Faith feels like part of an invading army as she walks next to David, behind all the men.

They come up to a stall where a father and son work in tandem. The young boy dumps a bucket of ice into the tray while the father lays out gray oyster shells on top. Behind them an oven lets out plumes of woodsmoke.

"Freshly harvested," the man calls out to them, balking when he sees Geoffrey Clarke moving toward the front of the pack.

"Crooked Clarke Bake," Geoffrey reads from the menu as the oyster seller sweats in front of him. "What's that?"

"I'm sure it's just a joke, right?" David says. "Isn't that right?" The man pales. Faith's stomach turns.

"It's a take on oysters Rockefeller." His voice is thin with stress. His hand clutches at the towel in front of him. The oyster farmers in the next stall over stop shucking and raise their heads to watch. "It's quite popular," he says. And Faith can tell he isn't sure he's said the right thing.

"Oh, is it? Then I'll take an order."

The man goes white. "Are you sure you want—?"

"What's wrong? I can't have the oysters? They're fucking named after me. They're popular because of me, after all." Geoffrey turns on the man, his voice rising to a loud growl. Two women behind a pile of ice in tall waders also turn to watch.

"Yes, of course you can," he says.

The knife slips, gouging the man in the thigh. He gasps in pain.

"Oh my god!" Faith cries out, reaching her hand to him. "Are you okay?"

"He's fine, aren't you?" Geoffrey says, stepping between them. "Look at the size of that blade, can't be that bad."

"Never mind. Nothing to worry about," the man says, gritting his teeth. He presses a stained white towel to the leg of his jeans. He calls to the boy, "Go ahead and make Geoffrey Clarke some oysters." The boy scowls, but his father gives him a desperate stare and his son prepares the oysters, shucking them expertly and loading them with sauce and breadcrumbs, throwing them onto a wood-fired oven set up in the back of the tent. It's the first time Faith has seen Geoffrey look like he is genuinely enjoying himself. He is the only one. Even his posse of polo-shirted men shuffle uncomfortably behind him as he waits.

"What's everyone so quiet for?" Geoffrey booms. "This is supposed to be fun."

The boy hands over a paper tray with a blossom of oysters inside. "The Crooked Clarke, eh?" Geoffrey says. The air is suffused with tension as he lifts one to his mouth and tosses it back.

"That's damn good," he says, dropping the empty shell onto the ground. Faith feels the whole tent exhale simultaneously. He has chosen mercy this time.

"So glad you like it," says the man, whose hand hangs limply in front of him as a red spot grows on the leg of his pants. Geoffrey ignores the injury, letting out a loud barking laugh.

"It's so good you should make your help here sign an NDA." As he says this he turns to look directly at Faith. His eyes, sharp and calculating, meet hers. She raises her chin and forces a smile back at him. She glances at David to see if he's noticed, but he has turned away and is staring pensively down into his phone. Faith knows that nothing Geoffrey does is by accident. Even as she maintains her smile, a jolt of terrible recognition shoots through her.

He knows.

Part Three

OPHELIA

HENRY

The small blue-and-white police boat has been in the water all morning. Henry watches it move from house to house, two blue-shirted officers on board. It is currently bobbing in the water next to the Clarkes' main dock. The officers, Brody and some young willowy man Henry doesn't recognize, wait with a member of Geoffrey's staff as they confer with another staff member on the dock.

Geoffrey appears, marching down the dock in golf whites. His face shows an expression of exasperation that he has to do this himself. *He has aged badly*, Henry thinks, considering his wealth. His hair is nearly white. His face sags unhappily in the cheeks. At the end of the dock, he stops and stoops slightly, catching his breath with his hands on his knees. There is a bit of back-and-forth between the men. Geoffrey gestures impatiently at the Rock. His mouth moves angrily. Henry can imagine what he is saying though he'd rather not.

The officers get back into the boat and it pulls away from the dock, turning abruptly away from shore and cutting toward the Rock through the bay. Henry stumbles back, knocking over a chair.

He leans forward and focuses on the boat. As it grows closer, he can see the two policemen more clearly. One looks familiar, and he is startled to realize that it must be *Brody*, all grown. Henry knew his father, Hadley Island's former police chief, for decades. He owed him. The other man is tall and thin.

The unexpected company sends his heart racing. He turns away from the window and frantically snatches up the logbooks and stashes them in the cupboard under the sink. Outside, the boat noisily scrapes up against the side of his dock.

The younger man jumps out first, clumsily tying the boat up as Henry steps out onto the deck. Brody jumps up onto the dock and waves a large hand in greeting. Henry cautiously raises his hand in response. He goes to the stairs. Better to meet them down there, away from the house. He's not used to visitors in the best of circumstances. And now, with the girl. They'll have questions. Ones that he won't be able to answer.

"Long time no see, Henry," Brody says when he gets close enough. He looks remarkably like Ed up close; the ruddy cheeks, the sturdy build, even the small patch of thinning hair on top are a carbon copy of his father.

"Hello," Henry coughs out while trying to convey a normal, unsuspicious appearance.

"This is Sam." Brody jerks his thumb at the young man standing behind him. His lip curls back as he looks at Henry. That's how they think of him on Hadley now, as some sort of monster, he realizes with discomfort. That's why they're here again after all these years, isn't it? Another girl missing.

"How is Ed?" Henry asks, attempting to act like a normal person, but his voice goes up into a strange unnatural octave.

Brody's cheeks sag. "Oh, you didn't know? Dad passed about six years ago now. Had a heart attack." *Damn it.* Henry should have remembered that. Had Jean told him? He normally would remember the details of something so important, but he is flustered.

"Oh," he says. "I-I'm sorry to hear it." Brody has the same way of moving that Ed did. The same slow deliberateness that is so often lacking in folks in general but especially in those who carry a gun.

Henry is suddenly very aware of his body, the awkwardness of it, the way his knees lock when he stands and his hands clasp and unclasp. The younger one stares at him, his mouth gaping. His eyes have followed Henry's every move since he got out of the boat like he is some sort of curiosity.

"We're looking for a young girl," Brody says. Henry's heart thuds.

"Sam, give me the picture," Brody calls to the young one, snapping his fingers impatiently.

Henry's body stiffens as young Sam pulls a piece of paper from inside his breast pocket and unfolds it, smoothing it on the roof of the boat. He eyes Henry warily as he thrusts it over to him.

Henry takes it, his stomach twisting sickly at the familiar face looking back at him from the page, so open and youthful.

"I don't know her," Henry says quickly, thrusting it back at them. But his voice comes out panicked, high-pitched. He glances back at the house, where the lens of the telescope catches the sun. Henry has forgotten to move it. If they go up there and look, it will be pointed at the Gallo house.

Brody watches him intently, his face bearing that same inscrutable calmness his father had often worn.

Henry begins to sweat in the direct sun. If they go up there and look through the scope, it will draw more suspicion. Brody follows his gaze.

"You're sure?"

"I said I've never seen her," Henry says. It comes out strangled. "I don't know any of the children on the island anymore." At the last words, he sees Brody flinch and look down. And it hits him, a wallop to the stomach. He'd thought perhaps foolishly that after enough time, he'd have paid his dues. That his self-imposed prison sentence would have been enough for them. But as he sees the face of the other policeman, Henry realizes that he was wrong. The younger man looks at him now with open disgust. He has heard things.

All this time in isolation Henry had thought that maybe he could wait the rumors out, that one day he could make his return to the island. In his most optimistic days, he'd even imagined that one day he could make a friend or two. A few people to talk to quietly and look out at the water with in the evenings. But now he sees he was being naive, a deluded old man who lives alone on an island. One who people believe killed a young girl. No matter how many years pass, the island's residents won't forget. And they won't forgive him. In that way they are alike. Henry won't forgive himself either.

Sam is examining a spot of something on the dock. He beckons Brody, who crouches down to inspect it.

"Henry, do you know what this is?" Henry draws closer to them, warily following the line of Brody's finger down to a dark splatter. "It looks an awful lot like blood."

Henry grimaces. He had known the bandage wouldn't be enough.

"It's Jean's. She cut herself at work, looks like it must have soaked through the bandage," he says carefully.

The younger man gives Henry an openly hostile look and continues down the dock, a swagger in his steps now, searching for more. From his pocket Brody produces a plastic bag and a Swiss army knife that he unfolds. Henry's face grows hot as Brody uses it to pry up a piece of the stained wood. Surely they will just test it and know he is telling the truth, that it is Jean's blood.

Brody starts to stand and stumbles on a jagged piece of the dock. Instinctively Henry reaches out a hand to steady him.

"What is that from?" Brody asks him. He is looking at Henry's wrist. Henry looks down in horror at the tiny white beads.

Henry jerks away, caught out. Sam is standing behind Brody now, listening.

"She came with Jean. It was just the one time. Jean cut her hand and needed help."

"Jean was here with a girl? Gemma?" he asks softly as Henry's chest heaves.

He nods.

"You piece of shit," Sam spits. He moves toward Henry, looming over him. Henry shrinks away, raising his arms above his face to protect himself. But Brody steps forward, cutting Sam off.

"Why didn't you tell me straightaway, Henry?"

Unable to speak, Henry only manages to shrug helplessly. He doesn't know exactly why he lied except that he didn't want to be tied up in all that again. Brody is shaking his head.

"This doesn't look good. There's blood on your dock and this—" Brody holds out his hand for the bracelet. Henry reluctantly pulls it from his wrist and watches as Brody drops it into the plastic bag. "God, Henry. Why did you say you'd never seen her?" Henry looks down at the dock, spattered brown with Jean's blood. It's all more than Henry can bear.

"We'll be back soon. With a warrant," says Sam.

"That all right with you, Henry?" Brody says with a gentleness that Henry wonders if he deserves.

"Why are you asking him? You're giving him time to get away with it—" Sam starts, his fists clenching in frustration. But Brody throws him a severe look, shutting him up.

"Let's go, Sam."

"Yes, yes, of course." Henry bobs his head trying to cooperate though he knows he is too late. His vision is beginning to tunnel. "Come back whenever you like."

As soon as they get back into the boat Henry scrambles up the stairs, desperate to be safely inside, no longer exposed. But the house shudders and creaks around him as leans back against the door.

FAITH

From the dressing room window Faith looks down at the vast lawn, where the final preparations for the Clarkes' Fourth of July party are being made. White-clad waitstaff zip across the grass, smoothing down tablecloths on round cocktail tables and arranging elaborate fans of florals. Servers stock the bar with top-shelf bottles and towers of crystal martini glasses. Faith squints down at a gazebo, erected in the center of the lawn, which looks to be set up as some sort of stage complete with microphones and speakers. Off to the side a man hurries past holding a cello. Faith's stomach clenches.

She turns to the dressing room and pulls her dress off the hanger and slides into it in front of the mirror. She'd saved this dress for tonight. It's the one Elena had insisted she buy when she tried it on in the Bergdorf's dressing room even though the price was astronomical. The print is innocent enough, a deep cerulean blue scattered with yellow flowers. But the fabric is fine silk. It is thin and shimmery, clinging to her hips and waist. The neckline loops down around one shoulder. Back then all she'd wanted was to fit in with the rich islanders, but now she isn't sure she could even if she wanted to. All this time she's been wondering what it would take to make someone like Geoffrey accept her. She suspects more and more that he lives in a constant state of paranoia, never truly accepting anyone, perhaps not even his own son. "Can you help zip me?" Faith calls to David.

He stands behind her, so close she can smell the aftershave she loves. She holds her breath, waiting for his hands to grab at her waist the way he normally would. But he stiffly slides the zipper up without any further contact. Faith's rib cage contracts uncomfortably.

"David?" He looks up into the mirror and their eyes meet.

Faith and David haven't talked about the fight they had at the lighthouse. But Faith can feel the remnants of it in their every interaction. No longer a singular unit, they step carefully around each other now as though careful not to undo the thin tether that unites them.

"Yes?" He gives her a perfunctory close-lipped smile in the mirror before turning away to fasten his cuff links.

"Nothing."

She puts her shoes on, bending to fasten the thin straps around her ankles. She wobbles in them. *Never wear shoes you can't run in*, her mom had often said. What Faith would be running from went without saying: *There are bad men out there. Men who will take advantage. Men who only care about themselves.*

"Are you ready for tonight?" David asks, slipping into his jacket.

"Sure am," Faith says. Her heart flutters nervously. But in her mind Faith has already begun to plot her escape from the Clarkes. She goes over it again, the way she will slink off into the early morning. She's carefully packed a bag already and stashed it under the bed just in case. Though she does so hate to leave all those beautiful clothes behind.

She isn't sure whether she'll stay in New York or try someplace else. Paris maybe. Faith thinks of Gemma and her stomach drops. There has been no sign of her yet.

"Elena should be here soon," she says with forced cheer, putting on a pair of delicate diamond earrings. "I should go look out for her."

"I can't wait to meet her," David says. "Any friend of yours is bound to be amazing."

"You haven't met?"

"No, but you've said so many things about her it feels like I have."

"You must've though. All the parties we've been to together."

"Maybe I've just forgotten." He kisses her neck, and she feels her skin tingle there. She pulls away, trying to disguise her reaction. She would have left sooner were it not for her friend. She'll tell her everything when she arrives.

"Yes, you must have." But inside Faith thinks that Elena would be impossible not to remember.

She finds Elena near the front entrance of the house, gazing up into the stairwell, a rapt look on her face. She's looking impossibly chic holding a stack of garment bags over her arm, her hair already smoothed into a tight updo. Faith is so happy to see her she could nearly cry.

She turns to Faith with a look of absolute awe on her face. It makes Faith feel better somehow.

"You're here!" Faith squeals.

"What's wrong?"

"Nothing, I'm just so happy to see you," she says, squeezing her in a tight hug.

Elena turns to the huge windows facing the water. "These views! Wow, I could get used to a place like this. I can't believe I am actually at David Clarke's mansion."

"I can't believe you're here either," Faith says, feeling surprisingly emotional. Throughout this entire trip, Faith realizes, she's been mostly alone.

"Show me everything!" Elena grabs Faith by the arm.

"It's quite creepy really," she whispers, leading her away from the front entrance and through the house. "After a few days alone here, you start to feel like you're going insane."

A rhythmic humming interrupts them. Elena points through a giant picture window as a helicopter lowers through a space in the clouds, its descent sending giant ripples of wind out across the lawn and flapping the tops of the white tents.

"Looks like Geoffrey Clarke has arrived," she says dryly as Faith watches the staff scramble to save decorations from scattering across the lawn. He'd been gone for the last couple of days, leaving his "boys" the run of the house. Faith had found them lounging around the mansion, their feet up on furniture. They would appraise her, their hooded eyes traveling silently over her body in a way that made her sure what they were after, leaving powdery cigar ashes in their wakes.

"Let's go do your makeup," Elena says quickly, squeezing her hand. "Show me your room."

"The bedroom is this way." Faith leads her up the marble staircase to her and David's suite.

"This place is even bigger than I expected," Elena says, falling into step with Faith, the garment bags dangling from her hand.

They sit across from each other at the long bathroom counter while Elena unpacks her makeup, setting out endless tubes of Dior lipsticks and Armani powders next to a row of brushes like she is preparing for surgery.

"What are we going for tonight? Sweet and serene? Or perhaps something a bit . . . darker."

In the mirror, Faith watches as something passes over her friend's features like a fast-moving storm. Is she jealous? It's gone as fast as it came. Elena takes a brush and swirls it around in a pot of bronzer.

"And what about our little artist, Orla; have you been feeling any better about her?" Faith detects a bitter edge to the words.

"I haven't seen her again," Faith says. *But David has,* she thinks.

"Look up," Elena commands. Faith trains her eyes on the crystal light fixture at the ceiling.

She feels the rough brush of a mascara wand against her lower lashes and tries hard not to blink. When she looks back across at her friend, her face has gone back to normal.

She's missed Elena, missed having a girlfriend around. They gossip about the Clarke family as they get dressed, and Faith calls down for a bottle of champagne to be sent up to the room. It comes on a tray with a bowl of fruit next to it. It's funny how the luxury is starting to feel commonplace. Incredible how quickly your expectations can shift. Amazing what we can get used to.

"What good is money if you can't even talk to your partner?"

"Plenty." Elena laughs, dusting Faith's face with finishing powder. "Blot." She slips a tissue between Faith's lips. "Are you ready for tonight?"

"I'm nervous," she says.

Elena smiles at her a bit wistfully in the mirror. "Don't be. You're absolutely perfect." She squeezes Faith's shoulder with one hand before dabbing a thin brush into a square of iridescent powder. Faith feels it touch the inside of her lash line, the tip of her nose, her cupid's bow. "There," Elena says. "All done. Some of my best work if I do say so myself."

Faith stands and Elena turns her to see herself in the mirror. The woman looking back at her now is sophisticated and lovely. Her hair, done earlier in the day by a woman she'd arranged to come up all the way from New York, is done like a 1930s movie starlet in thick waves. Her cheekbones chiseled; her eyes framed with a smoky black-gold glitter. Her lips are a deep plum red.

Faith is nearly intimidated by her own reflection.

"You're an artist. Truly," Faith says, smiling at her friend in the mirror. She takes in their heart-shaped faces and Elena's smooth brown hair. Elena strokes her hair affectionately. She puts her cheek next to Faith's and smiles. "I know. Look at us. We could be sisters."

HENRY

Despite all that has happened, Henry feels like joining the party, even if it is from afar. It feels proper to mark the occasion. He's taken his time shaving with a fresh razor blade. He goes to the closet and takes out his nicest shirt, the one Margie always said brought out the green of his eyes. As Henry dresses, he allows himself to imagine her standing in front of him. *Now hold still*, she'd have said, her fingers fumbling with the top button. Back then he might have brushed her away and said, *Don't be silly, I can manage on my own.* What he wouldn't do for the warmth of her so close again. He should have appreciated it more. If he had only paid more attention. Maybe then he could have saved her.

Henry touches his wrist, looking for the comforting shape of the bracelet, and finds it missing. The bracelet should be enough to tie him to her. There's been no further sign of the police officers, but Henry suspects it is only a matter of time until they return with a search warrant or possibly even one for his arrest. He has no real alibi, after all, no one to vouch for him. And there was the blood. It won't be a match. But it will take a while for them to verify that. He has been replaying their visit in his mind, lying awake at night staring up into the skylight with worry gnawing at his chest. Henry shouldn't have said the thing about the girls. There are no other suspects, that much was clear to him from the bloodthirsty way the younger cop looked at him. And then what will happen? Jail, he supposes.

Henry knows he should be panicking at the thought of it all, but something has changed inside him these last two weeks. Ever since Orla O'Connor returned and the whole shameful business of fifteen years ago got dredged up again, Henry feels like he's been broken open. He wonders if part of him will be relieved when he is finally hauled off the little island and forced to reckon with everything. Without Margie here things have been unbearable most days anyway. The visit has shaken her loose from his mind as well. He'd been able to conjure her up so clearly before Jean had called him out. He could pretend she was still there. But now she only appears to him in pieces, her memory so transparent he is afraid to blink, or she'll be gone.

His heart can't take it out here alone anymore.

He swallows the lump forming in his throat and goes into the kitchen, where he pulls a dusty bottle of port from the back of one of the cabinets. It is the lone bottle of alcohol he could find in the house, still there from back when Margie was alive and liked to have an occasional tipple after dinner. He pours the rest into a small, chipped juice glass and takes it with him out onto the deck. It is a clear, balmy night. Warmer than normal. The perfect night for a soiree. He brings his telescope outside and positions it, moving across the sound until he finds the edge of the Clarkes' lawn.

Through the telescope Henry watches as the guests begin to arrive at the Clarke estate. He focuses in on the men in their pressed linen suits, groomed within an inch of their lives and the women, their tan limbs peeking through slits and spilling from the tops of sleeveless dresses. They trickle in until the lawn vibrates with color. Rows of cocktail glasses sparkle on the tables waiting to be filled. Waitstaff in fitted black suits crisscross the lawn holding aloft trays with tiny crudites. People greet one another, but their raucous laughs and slaps on the back are all silent to Henry, swallowed up by the expanse between them.

He takes a moment to sip from his drink. The port is bitter, the liquid long gone rancid. He gags a little, disgusted, wishing he'd had the foresight to ask Jean to bring him something better. *Jean.* He hadn't seen her this past week. She'd brought his groceries, anyway, leaving the sagging bags on the end of the dock one morning. Inside were a bunch of his staples. There were no special treats, no ice cream bars or brightly colored packages. He wonders if the police have gone to her yet. She would tell them the blood was hers. She'd back him up, wouldn't she?

At the Clarkes', partygoers begin to shuffle en masse collectively turning their bodies toward the center of the lawn. By the time Henry reaches the white-framed gazebo with his telescope, Geoffrey Clarke has come to stand in the center of it. Henry's throat constricts at the sight of him there—a king observing his subjects.

David Clarke stands next to him, clutching a champagne glass. His shoulders are slightly hunched, a grim smile frozen on his lips. Geoffrey begins to speak. Henry wishes he could hear what he is saying. Whatever it is, the crowd seems enthralled. They lower their drinks from their lips and lean forward, hanging on every word.

Henry pans right, and his telescope lands on a face buried in the crowd. He focuses in on it, taking in the shape of it, the dress, astonished. The glass falls from his hand and shatters, the dark red liquid spilling through the cracks in the deck and dripping into the rocks below.

ORLA

Now Orla is happy to see that David looks miserable up on the gazebo next to his father. She sips her drink, entertained as she watches him shuffle. She had debated all week about coming to the party at all, laying out the pros and cons. She'd planned to leave the island first thing. But this moment makes it worthwhile it for her, watching him being paraded onstage like Geoffrey's little puppet.

A cold breeze ripples across the lawn, unsettling the air. Orla stands awkwardly at the edge of the party. At the bar she orders another gin and tonic. It's her third and she is starting to feel the effects of them, making her limbs feel loose and heavy. Her mind feels clearer than it has all week. She's been sick with anxiety, jumping in fear at every rabbit crossing the lawn, every gust of wind and shifting branch. She hasn't been able to go back upstairs and look at the closet. She'd accomplished this by avoiding the upstairs altogether.

Orla looks behind her at the crowd of rapt faces. She recognizes more than a few of them from her childhood. A couple of them have made uneasy eye contact with her. Her outsider status is enough to keep them to themselves. Even if they hate the Clarkes, which she assumes most of them do, there is enough theater in this whole thing, enough wealth on display, to keep anyone from missing out on it.

The Fourth of July had arrived that summer despite her and Alice's falling-out. Orla had ordered a new dress in shimmery green silk that caught the curves of her body under the right light. She'd hoped it would be intoxicating to David. He'd mentioned once that he liked her green shirt, and she'd read online somewhere that green is the color of commitment. She did her hair long and straight, working for hours taming it with a blow-dryer and round brush to make it smooth. Then she went downstairs to wait for David at the living room window. The house was quiet. Her parents were at dinner. She looked out at the road.

There was a flash of something silver on the street. Orla held her breath and looked out as Alice walked by, watching her through the slit of the curtain. She was wearing a dress covered in silver sequins. It was such a beautiful dress it made Orla instantly feel badly about herself. Alice had the kind of determined expression on her face reserved for when she was enacting a plan. Orla raised her hand to rap at the glass and stopped herself. If she was going to the Clarkes' she'd end up having to invite Alice to come with her, and she couldn't have that. She'd been waiting far too long for a moment alone with David. She watched Alice's lithe body swish down Harbor Street instead.

It took another hour for Orla to finally hear a honk coming from the far side of the house. It was followed by the sound of a boat engine. Orla ran out to the back porch. David had arrived by water in a small skiff. He stood in the bow, bracing against the steering wheel as the boat idled, his fitted jacket catching in the wind.

"You coming?" he shouted over the waves. Orla smiled, letting all her worry about Alice disappear for the moment.

"Yes, be right there." She rushed back inside to grab her clutch and ran out to the dock as he pulled the boat in, swirling up a froth around it. He cut the engine and reached his hand out to her, looking like some sort of absurd billionaire Disney prince.

Orla sat just behind him on a little bench while he steered the boat out into the deeper water.

"I was thinking of taking us somewhere else first," he'd said mischievously, glancing down at her thigh, which looked tan in the fading light. An electric charge shot through her. This was the night.

"Where to?" She smiled back at him, trying to look confident, though the idea of being alone-alone with him filled her with nerves.

David steered them out into the open water, where the Clarkes' giant yacht sat moored in the harbor.

"What do you think? Wanna check it out?" He nodded at the yacht.

"Won't someone see us?" Orla asked.

"Nah. Everyone will be at the party," David said.

"Sure," she said, the rush of being alone with David coursing through her.

He cut the engine again and they glided silently through the black water to the back of the yacht. *Ophelia* was spelled in gold along the back. He took Orla's hand and she stepped up onto the deck.

"This way," David said, leading her up a set of stairs to the next level. She heard music now, muffled laughter.

"I thought you said no one was here." Orla laughed nervously.

"There shouldn't be. It is probably just some of the crew." But he went quietly and they crept around the deck, silently taking the stairs up to the third floor.

"There's a bar in here." Orla followed David down a narrow walkway along the side of the yacht. He was about to open a door when a loud guffaw came from the other side of it. He turned to her and pressed a finger to his lips. He dropped to his knees below a window, pulling her down with him.

Together they slowly raised their eyes to the window. Orla gasped when she saw Alice in her sparkling gown surrounded by a group of older men. Alice narrowed her eyes at one of the men, crossing her bare legs. He moved to the bar and poured a drink. She watched him pick up a clear bottle and pour a lot of liquor into it. It all made Orla feel childish and inconsequential.

"What are they doing?" Orla hissed at David, but he was no longer standing next to her. He was backing away, his face stricken. Orla turned back to the window as the man's shadow fell over Alice. He handed her the drink and she reached for the glass with two hands, tilting it to her lips. As she slurped it down her eyes dulled almost instantly. Orla watched in fascination as her friend's head lolled forward. Off to the side Geoffrey Clarke smoked a cigar, watching it all.

"Come on," David whispered, his breath hot and insistent on Orla's neck. He pulled at her arm.

"But why?" Orla had started to protest, frustration bubbling up inside her. "If Alice is here, why can't we be too?" David's hand clamped over her mouth, startling her. He pulled her down with him to just below the window. They were closer than they'd ever been. His arms out on either side of her pinning her to the deck.

"Orla. Now," David hissed. His fingers found hers, interlacing, and she allowed herself to be pulled up away from the window. They ducked down and ran back across the deck. "This way." She followed him in a low crouch to a set of stairs on the far side of the deck. Downstairs he took Orla into a long dining area with tables and wide benches. Out the wide glass window she watched the lights from the party. The yacht swayed silently under her. She longed to be back on the island suddenly, in the crowd with the music playing or maybe at home in her living room listening to the sounds of her father cooking. She wandered into the kitchen, where David was rummaging through cupboards looking for something.

"What's going on with Alice?" she asked him.

"How should I know?" David said, without turning around.

"Has she been hanging out with your dad?" she asked, incredulous, remembering the Bentley pulling up on their street.

"Forget about her. Let's have a drink," David said, holding up a bottle victoriously.

"Happy Fourth," he said tapping the side of her glass with his own. She raised the glass to her lips as David watched, not caring that it burned her throat. Orla had waited all summer for three years to spend time alone with David. But it didn't feel the way she hoped. When the glass was empty she let David pour her another. She drank it faster this time, the buzz was helping her forget that Alice was there too. She drank until the alcohol erased the image of the thick hand on her friend's knee and the sick feeling that something was happening up there that shouldn't be.

"Can I have your attention, please?" Geoffrey Clarke begins. "I promise you this won't take long. I want to begin by welcoming you to my home. We may not be full-time residents like some of you lot, but Hadley has always been a special place for the Clarke family. When my grandfather built this home, he imagined it being a place of leisure. A place where the great men of the world would come to relax, to put their feet up and look out at the water. Where they could be away from the prying eyes and gossip of Manhattan and spend time like normal people."

Normal people, ha. He means where no one will watch them, Orla thinks. David puts a charming smile on his face, but it is easy for Orla to spot his discomfort. His face is drawn, his eyes darting as if looking for an escape. As if sensing David's reluctance, Geoffrey's hand comes down on his shoulder, pinning his son in place. Geoffrey clears his throat.

"I've been reflecting on that a bit more lately, perhaps because I am going to retire soon. So, I'd like to take this moment to reintroduce my son, David," Geoffrey says. Orla looks at David, confused. "Most of you know him from when he was a boy. But he's grown into quite an adult. He is going to be taking over the business. Oh, whoops, cat's out of the bag! It seemed like as good a place as any, surrounded by our nearest and dearest. Now, instead of me stepping back, I like to think of it as David stepping forward."

He is interrupted by the sudden blast of a boat's horn. People clutch at their chests and laugh, looking out at the water, where the yacht must have let out some sort of congratulatory honk. Geoffrey raises his glass and grins. Orla's skin crawls.

"As I was saying, my son here—my pride and joy—has graciously agreed to take the helm as of next year," Geoffrey says to a burst of obligatory applause. David's eyes find Orla's. They go wide with surprise and then narrow at her as if to say, *What are you doing here?* She raises her glass to him, in fake congratulations. Is that true anger she sees on David's face now? It is gone in a flash as Geoffrey continues.

"Don't worry, I'm not going anywhere. I will still be steering the ship. I'll just be a backseat driver. Though it may be from the *Ophelia II.*"

The yacht's horn toots again as though laughing at his bad joke.

Sycophantic chuckles float around her. David shifts back and forth onstage. Orla can see, even from way down on the lawn, the sweat on his forehead starting. So, he never got out from under his father's thumb like he said he wanted to as a kid. It should make Orla sad for him, but she has a flood of satisfaction wash through her. Like it was all preordained. David was never going to do anything other than what he did, and Orla wasn't ever going to be anything other than a failure. It makes her feel surprisingly calm.

"I'll have another," she calls out to the bartender, drawing a few glares from people around her. He doesn't hear her.

"There is one more announcement before I leave you all to your oysters and champagne. Faith, where is Faith?" Geoffrey shields his eyes theatrically, squinting into the crowd. They begin to look, too, their curiosity piqued.

"Who doesn't love the sound of that name? So innocent and hopeful. Faith: an old-fashioned girl with a heart of gold."

A rush of servers fill the lawn holding trays of champagne glasses.

"Don't mind if I do," Orla says, taking a flute off a tray as it passes.

"Ah! There she is. She's a sneaky one." Geoffrey points to a place just in front and to the left of Orla. Orla swivels her head along with the rest of the crowd, searching. How could she not? She stands on her tiptoes trying to spot her, David's chosen one. Orla's chest drops when she spots Faith in profile—glowing, flawless. Her doe-shaped eyes wide. A stricken look takes over her delicate features and then a moment later is gone.

"Don't be shy, Faith. Come on up here!" Geoffrey commands. He waves his hand impatiently.

Faith makes her way up the stairs. Her gown, a blue silk printed with an explosion of yellow flowers, ripples across her body as she takes her place next to David. They look so uncomfortable up there that Orla almost pities them.

FAITH

The crowd parts for Faith as she makes her way up to the gazebo. She feels their eyes on her as she passes through them like a princess in a fairy tale. Or is she Marie Antoinette, heading to the chopping block?

She stumbles up the steps to the platform, where the two Clarke men stand waiting.

As soon as she reaches the top, David's hand is on her elbow leading her, or she wonders if maybe he's preventing her from leaving.

"Surprise," he whispers in her ear as he guides her to the edge of the gazebo, the vibration of his voice sending a shiver through her.

"Ladies and gentlemen, this is Faith. She has been David's guest here on the island. We hope we haven't scared her off." Geoffrey bares his teeth into a tense smile. He holds his champagne glass aloft. He is daring her to make a move.

The air rushes from Faith's lungs. She looks out at them all. A sea of strangers. But something is off about all of it.

"What's going on?" Faith says under her breath, keeping her smile in place.

"I wanted to surprise you," David whispers back, but a sheen has appeared on his forehead. A strange clench to his jaw.

"Let's get on with it, shall we?" Geoffrey booms, raising his arms out to the partygoers like some sort of circus conductor.

"Get on with what?" Faith's heart lurches.

"Trust me," David says, taking her hand. Faith looks out at the crowd. A shimmer of red hair catches the sunset, glowing like an ember. Orla O'Connor looks straight back at her, unsmiling. A shiver climbs up Faith's neck. *What is she doing here?* Faith doesn't have time to figure it out. There is a collective gasp from the crowd. When she turns to look at David, he is no longer next to her but has dropped to the floor of the gazebo. It takes her a moment to understand that he is on one knee. She stifles a surprised cough as he reaches into his jacket pocket.

No no no.

"Faith, this past year with you has been one of the happiest of my life," he says loud enough for the crowd to hear it. This isn't how she wanted it. She doesn't like the strange clench to David's jaw or the leer of Geoffrey behind him, or the audience watching. Their mouths hang open, rapt, as David holds the little red box up toward her.

"I've been waiting for the right moment. I know neither of us are very public people, but Dad convinced me that this was the perfect time and place. To share my commitment to you with this island. I hope he was right."

Faith knows how it looks: perfect man, down on one knee in front of a turquoise sea, beautiful woman, hands still to her mouth in surprise. David even manages to let out a nervous chuckle. The crowd laughs along with him. All is forgiven. Forgotten.

No, stop, she wants to cry out. *This isn't how it is supposed to go.*

But the ring is there in front of her suddenly, shining up at her.

The sunset shows up right on time. It streams godlike rays of golden light onto the gazebo. As though it was scheduled for this exact moment. As though the Clarkes paid it too.

"Faith? Will you marry me?" David isn't waiting for her reply. He's already begun to pull the ring from its box.

The crowd chants.

Say yes, say yes!

She is nodding, stunned. The ring is heavy on her finger. It almost looks gaudy now, a display of wealth so obscene it is rendered meaningless. An impressed murmur rises from the audience as the facets of the diamond capture the light.

Everything wobbles a bit. And then David is lifting her off the ground, his lips are on hers. Her ears are rushing with blood. *The Clarkes have a way of making things happen*, Jean had said, and Faith wonders if she ever had a choice in the matter.

Faith watches as Geoffrey descends the gazebo steps in front of them. The smile falls from his face the moment he turns away from the crowd. David follows quickly behind him holding Faith by the arm. She nearly trips in her high heels trying to keep up. It is obvious Geoffrey had a hand in David's proposal. Faith wants to know why. They are intercepted at the bottom of the stairs. The man has a wide build and round cheeks ruddy with alcohol.

"Congratulations!" he says, clapping David on the back. His arm nearly hits Faith in the face as he reaches past her to embrace David. "Off the market, buddy. You have no idea the trouble we used to get into," he says too loudly. His breath reeks of beer. His hands clamp onto David's shoulders, edging her out. "Some of that shit wasn't even legal."

She looks past him, her eyes scanning for Elena, but instead she finds a vision of her mother. Yesterday's mascara is caked on her upper cheeks, her bra straps dig indents into the tops of her shoulders. It's the way she always looked on a very bad morning after a very good night out. The cigarette is burned down almost to the end, but she pays it no mind. She points it at Geoffrey, who is moving across the lawn ahead of her, smiling insincerely to his subjects.

"Be careful, sweet pea. I don't like this for you. That man is up to no good. You remember what I told you back when you were just a kid?"

Faith's chest hurts. *If it seems too good to be true, it probably is.*

"That's right, honey bear."

"Look at you two, the perfect couple," a woman is gushing when she turns her attention back to David. "Isn't it a miracle when we find that special person?"

"I'm the lucky one," David says, his teeth locked into an ultrawhite smile. His arm rests too heavily around Faith's shoulders. As though he is trying to keep her from escaping. She glances to where she last saw Geoffrey. He is moving with purpose now, deeper into the crowd, no longer pausing to chitchat. The last remnants of the sunset fade in the sky.

"I'm going to go get a drink," she says, ducking out of David's grasp before he can stop her. She forces herself to kiss him on the cheek, reassuring him. He gives a quick smile, still trapped in conversation. But when she is sure he isn't looking, she moves away from the bar, slipping along the side of the lawn, following Geoffrey. He stops and says something to a bodyguard in a black suit who gives him a quick nod.

Geoffrey Clarke marches away from the party, escorted by the bodyguard. Faith shadows him, stepping to the far side of the lawn, ducking in and out of the crowd as she tries to keep pace. He is on a mission, she realizes; his arms pump as he moves with surprising speed toward the dock. Faith hangs back at the edge of the lawn watching as they bound down the dock toward the white speedboat. Geoffrey doesn't break his stride as he steps aboard. Faith watches helplessly as it pulls away and speeds out toward the *Ophelia II*.

Faith's fists clench as the boat recedes from the bay. She thinks of the pictures she saw inside the drawer. She remembers the young legs with the knobby knees and the reflection in the portal window. Geoffrey standing next to the *Ophelia*. Faith runs down to the beach and ducks under the dock, where a small rowboat is overturned. She kicks her shoes off, digging her feet into the sand as she struggles to flip it. It falls over with a metallic thump. She waits under the dock for a moment, her heart pumping, in case someone heard. But no sound of footsteps or call of voices breaks through from the din of the party. When she is sure she hasn't been caught, she pulls the rowboat the short distance across the sand, shoving it into the waves. She wades out next to it until the bottom of her dress drags across the black surface of the water. Then she takes the hem in her hands and steps carefully aboard.

Using the dock for cover Faith pushes the boat out into the water with an oar, driving it into the sand until finally she scoops the oar down and no longer finds the bottom with it. She dips both of the oars into the water now, cautiously at first, slowly pulling the boat out into the open bay. As she leaves the safety of the dock, the sounds of the party fade into the rush of the water. The boat is surprisingly swift as she gains momentum, cutting through the waves in the path of the moonlight.

ORLA

O rla tilts the rest of her drink into her mouth and drops the empty glass on the tray of a passing waiter. She'll need another. She doesn't know if she is more upset about the engagement, a stunningly public show of commitment from a Clarke, or the fact that David is up there pretending that he doesn't have a care in the world.

She watches the three of them descend from the gazebo in a flurry of handshakes and pats on the back. A white-hot fury crawls its way up her chest at the injustice of it all. Rich daddy's boy gets to move on with his life when she so clearly has not. And won't.

Or maybe he isn't so happy. David has a strange tension in his jaw, like he is trying to keep himself calm. But his forehead looks damp. His eyes dart around the crowd like he's trapped. Orla remembers that look. A group of well-wishers surround the couple, blocking her view. When they finally disperse, she finds David alone and moving toward the bar, his face frozen in an uneasy smile. From the corners of her eyes Orla sees the heads turn toward her as she snakes through the crowd, pushing rudely up to the bar and standing beside him. She raises her hand above the bar, beckoning to the bartender. "Another gin and tonic," she calls out, ignoring the groans of the people she cut in front of. She doesn't have anything to lose anymore.

"Orla," David says. "Wasn't expecting to see you here." He says it louder than he must have intended, and she wonders if he's a little drunk just like she is. Maybe he'd had something before, to get himself through the engagement.

"You invited me, you idiot, when you showed up at my house wasted." She lifts her glass up to his, sloshing some over the side. It falls onto the front of his jacket, turning a patch of it dark. "Fun night, the way it ended wasn't exactly what I'd expected."

He glances anxiously around him. "Orla, please."

"No worries. It'll dry clear," she says flippantly, pretending he is talking about the stain.

He leans in and drops his voice, giving her a warning look. "Orla, can we not?'"

"I don't know what you're talking about. I just wanted to congratulate my old friend on his upcoming nuptials." David looks furtively around the bar. His neck is turning bright red against his white collar.

"You don't have to go through with it, you know," she stage-whispers.

"Not here," he says angrily, pulling away from the bar. "If you have something you need to say, let's go talk somewhere quiet." He grips her by the arm and steers her forcefully toward the dark end of the lawn where it dips down to the beach.

"I don't have long." David glances back at the party. "Faith will be looking for me."

Orla ignores him and looks into her cup. It is nearly empty now, half of it having spilled on the walk down to the beach. "Ah, remember gin and tonics? That summer, before everything went to shit?"

He cuts her off.

"What is it that you want?"

She looks out toward those horrible dark waves, hugging herself. "I've seen her in New York. More than once."

"What are you talking about?" he scoffs. But his features have shifted, and she can see that he is afraid.

"I see her everywhere. But every time I realize I'm wrong. It's not her at all. It's just my guilty conscience. I can't escape what we did. What I did."

David steps away from her, rubbing his neck with his hand and glancing back in the direction of the party. "Is that right? You might want to talk to someone, Orla, that sounds a bit psycho—"

"Looks like Geoffrey's off to celebrate on his yacht," she interrupts him, her voice dripping with meaning. David pales.

"He probably has a meeting out there. You know Dad, always working."

She nearly laughs. "God, you are always protecting him, aren't you. You just can't help it."

"He's my father."

She lowers her voice. "You know what I mean."

"Is that all?" He glances back at the party.

"Off to his new hobby, then?" Orla says. "I don't think you ever meant the boat when you said that, though, did you? You always knew what he was up to with his friends."

"Stop it. That's enough," David snaps. "You don't know what you're talking about. I don't know what you think you saw. We were children."

"Oh, we were old enough, though." Orla presses on. "You knew, didn't you? All along. You knew what was happening to her with those disgusting guys."

"It wasn't like that," he says quietly. "She didn't have any money. She said she needed help."

"Help her by *what*? Bringing her as an offering to Geoffrey?"

"That's not what it was. He was going to hire her on to help her, like a little job working on the yacht."

"You're delusional."

"Dad isn't some pedophile."

"Really? Well, his friends certainly are. Maybe he's just a fucking creepy middleman. But whatever it is, if he weren't Geoffrey Clarke, he would have to pay for what he did to her."

"Fuck you, Orla." David spins back, his eyes flashing.

"Oh, big Clarke man anger coming out there," Orla spits. "Can pretend to be so civilized, but you can't hide from it, can you? Maybe Alice saw you for what you really were. Maybe that's why she wanted to leave."

"I never wanted to be like him. You know that," David says. "I always thought I would do something different. But it wasn't that easy in the end."

She ignores him. "I messed up. In so many ways. We should have helped her. We lied, and I feel like I will pay for it forever." She thinks she sees a little boat out there, tossing around on the waves.

"What is your point?"

"I'm going to tell the police I lied." She'd been turning it over in her mind since the night of David's visit to her house.

"What would be the point of that?" He snorts.

"I can't hurt Henry more than I already have. It's messed up. He's going to take the fall for another girl. But you probably knew that already, didn't you?"

"No." His hand clamps onto her wrist. "You can't do that. I'll ruin you."

"How?" She laughs. "My career is shit. I see a dead girl everywhere." She tugs away from him. "I'll do whatever the fuck I want. Your father already ruined my life. Pathetic how you can't even see that he's ruined yours."

"No, Orla. You won't. You signed an NDA, remember?"

The NDA had arrived the morning after her betrayal. It was delivered personally by a lawyer who stood just inside her front door as she took the pages into her hands. Orla had looked at it queasily. It was a written promise not to divulge any of the details from the night of the party. But what did it matter anymore? Alice was gone. She'd signed it silently and handed it back, watching it disappear with the car down the drive, unsure of what she had done.

"None of it matters, don't you understand?"

"You might not have anything to protect, but I do. I'm not about to let you go and fuck things up for me, you selfish—" His hand drops from her arm.

"What. The. Fuck?" A look of horror has transformed his face, dropping his jaw. David raises his hand and points past her shoulder.

Far past the beach to where the shore curves around. Orla follows the line of his finger down the shoreline. Just past the peak of Orla's own house through a tangle of trees is Alice Gallo's house, a light flickering in the upstairs window.

"What is happening?" He clutches his head with his hands, stunned.

Her heart thumps. Orla squints as it blinks in and out. *Come over. Emergency.* But before Orla can process it, David starts running toward Alice's house.

HENRY

The gall of them to have a party after what happened. He hears Margie's voice behind him. It slips in and out like a breeze. He grimaces into the dark. If he doesn't turn around, he can pretend that the voice is real, that she is still there. He imagines what she'd say next. *You remember last time?*

"Of course. How could I forget?"

That day was frozen in time because it was the last day they ever had that way, the last time Margie and he had taken the boat into Hadley just for fun. They'd spent the afternoon wandering around Port Mary. Had stopped into the Salty Crab for a quick drink and to see Jean. It had been busy, it being the Fourth. Their last stop had been to the little fish store down on the pier, where they'd bought a whole pound of scallops. Back home, Henry had cooked while Margie nursed another glass of wine and watched the sun begin to set. When they finally sat down to dinner, it was nearly dark.

"Aren't you going to look?" she'd asked, a glint in her eyes. She was in an unusually chipper mood.

"I thought you hated my spying," he'd admonished playfully.

"It's not really spying if it's a party, is it? Besides, the whole island was invited. We could have gone if we'd really wanted to, I'm sure."

He'd gone to the telescope. At some point during the time he was watching the Clarkes' party, the *Ophelia* had pushed out into the open water, sitting between the Rock and the shore. It was close enough to see the men who had come on board.

Margie stood behind him. "What's happening?" she asked eagerly.

"Give me that, I want a look." She had playfully bumped Henry aside and lowered her eye to the lens.

"My god. Who are those men?"

"I don't know. I haven't seen them before this weekend. They just showed up yesterday."

"A bunch of them," she said. "Looks like Geoffrey cloned himself."

She stood still for a moment. Henry had watched her mouth drop open. "Oh dear."

She'd stepped away from the eye of the telescope, inviting Henry to look.

Alice Gallo in a dress far too adult for her to be wearing. She was drinking something from a martini glass. One of the older men took her by the arm. Henry had watched her break free from him.

"We have to do something." Margie gripped Henry's sleeve. "I'm not letting those people get away with—I'm going to go out there." She had that stubborn look on her face. "I'm going to climb onto that boat if I have to."

"Margie, no, you're not. And then what?"

"I'm going to ring the police," she said, starting to the phone. Henry worried he'd already wasted too much time.

"Aren't you the one who always says he has the officials in his pockets?"

"Well, I'm not going to just sit there, while they, they—poor—" At this her chin had begun to crumple.

"No, of course not," Henry said quickly, nothing more upsetting to him than his wife's tears. He went back to the telescope to assess the situation.

There were more people on the deck. A different, higher deck than earlier. He had caught sight of the dress. It was easy to see, the way it caught the light like a flare. Alice was arguing with someone. He saw only another set of hands gesticulating wildly as she inched farther and farther back toward the edge of the railing.

There was a flurry of movement, and she was tipping with a sudden violent force over the side of the yacht.

"What's happening, Henry?" Margie cried, her voice shrill with fear.

But Henry was already thudding down the steps and skidding out onto the dock to the tiny boat. He yanked at the motor cord, but it didn't catch. He'd been meaning to fix it, hadn't Margie been on him to fix it? The oars in the bottom of the boat would have to do. He had snatched them up and sank quickly into the seat, pulling with all his might toward the *Ophelia*.

It was all quiet on board. The light from the yacht shone in patchy spots on the water as he rowed toward it. "Hello?" he called out as he drew closer to it. "Is anyone there?"

Henry looked down into the water and saw the flash of something bright. He dropped to his knees in the hull of the boat and leaned over the side, reaching for it. His fingertips touched something in the darkness. He grabbed under the water, searching.

His hand had closed around something. Not human. A piece of fabric, heavy and waterlogged. He thrashed around looking for the girl, but she was gone.

There were confused yells on board. "Where'd she go?"

"Goddamn it! Find her!" A scurry of flashlights.

The light had hit Henry square in the eye, blinding him. When it moved, he could see the outline of someone looking down at him.

"Alice?" A young woman's voice tore through the night. As his eyes adjusted, he realized he was looking up into the face of Orla O'Connor. "Help! Have you seen my friend?"

"Hey! Who's there?" It was the young Clarke boy next to her. "Look, it's that freak! I bet he's got her."

Henry began to row away. He was panicking now. As he retreated toward the Rock he saw another figure join them on the deck. He could barely make out the rumble of Geoffrey Clarke's voice across the waves. "What's going on here? Who was that?"

Henry had rowed as fast as he could away from the yacht, the dress glittering dully like the skin of a fish in the hull of the boat.

Now Henry looks out at the *Ophelia II*. The new Clarke yacht is as still and white as a mausoleum.

A line of movement in his periphery makes Henry move the telescope away from the lawn, skimming the water. A small rowboat is moving toward the yacht. He recognizes the slender back of the woman bowing forward as she rows.

FAITH

Faith pulls herself up onto the sleek edge of the yacht. Geoffrey's skiff had arrived ages ago now, but she sees no sign of life on the bottom deck of the boat. She secures the rowboat off to the side with a rope, hoping that in the shadows no one will notice it there.

She creeps barefoot up the steps to the second-floor deck, passing through a row of empty lounge chairs. She can hear music now, a thin bass line coming from one of the floors above her. Faith tiptoes to the central stairway encased in glass and cautiously follows it up to the third floor. She finds another smaller open deck here. Behind it is a set of closed French doors. The music is louder now. It's electronic and clubby, something that Faith might have heard at a bad tourist-filled nightclub in her early twenties. The low grumble of a man's voice rises up over the beats on the other side of the wall. Geoffrey. She moves toward the door. If she bursts into the room and finds him with Gemma, it will do nothing. He will surely deny it all. She has to catch him in the act. She retreats, moving out around the side of the yacht.

The window to the room is beyond the walkway, the base of it sitting upon on a ledge that narrows aerodynamically toward the front of the ship. A dim light from a window shines out into the dark, and Faith steps toward it. Inching out farther and farther until her fingertips grip at the smooth white wall of the boat. The boat sways and she looks down. A mistake. The waves have gotten rougher since she rowed out here. They pound against the hull, their crests glowing in the light from the yacht.

The vibrato of Geoffrey's voice carries out into the night, sending her stomach into her throat. Faith turns her head and inches forward until she is just beside the window. From this angle she can see the edge of a plush white sofa and across the room a built-in bar. A man stands in front of it, dropping cubes of ice into a glass with a set of silver tongs. Faith recognizes the back of his boxy head. He turns and she sees the phone pressed up to his ear. He sits heavily on a leather banquette, tossing the phone onto the table in front of him.

Faith presses her face to the window looking for Gemma or the men. The boat begins to hum and sway as the motor starts up, and Faith realizes with a jolt of horror that she's miscalculated. There is no missing girl here. There is no one else at all. Geoffrey Clarke is alone.

ORLA

Orla's lungs burn as she follows the flash of David's shoes, keeping her eyes trained on the white bob of his shirt as he tears up Harbor Street toward the Gallos' house. The wind blows up off the water sending the seagrass slicing at her legs. Insects chirp from the sides of the road. A rhythmic pulsing. She hears them as a singular voice. *You lie you lie you lie.*

How David had pleaded with her.

"You can't say anything about Dad," David had instructed her, taking her hand and squeezing it. "Please. You can't ever tell them."

"What should I say then?" Her body was still buzzing from adrenaline, her head fuzzy from the gin.

"Tell them about Henry," he'd replied. It was Orla's flashlight that had discovered him out there in his little boat. His hair and eyes were wild as she caught him in the beam, a stricken look on his face. And there in the hull of the boat the bright sparkle of sequins. She saw them only for a moment, one that she questioned every single day after, but she had thought immediately that the fabric was too flat and empty to contain a body.

"I can't lie," she'd said to David before the official questioning, her legs pressing into the plastic chair in the community center. "*I won't.*"

"But it's not a lie, it's what you saw," David had said, kneeling in front of Orla, begging now. "She fell into the water. That's all we know. You just don't have to say the other part out loud." The other part. She'd looked at him, trying to come to terms with what she'd seen out there. The flailing arms, the gasping face, the tangle of hair. The swirl of waves. All in dim flashes beneath the beam of her flashlight.

"She was so scared." Orla's eyes began to blur.

He'd leaned in and put his forehead to hers. How long she had craved this kind of closeness with him. His voice was filled with regret. "Orla, listen to me. Alice got herself into this."

Just over his shoulder, Orla could see through the doorway to where Henry Wright blinked into the press conference cameras. His face looked pale and scared. A cornered creature. *I came looking for the girl. I was only trying to help.*

"Orla, please. I need you." David had taken her hands, pressing them together between his like in prayer.

"They're ready for you," an officer had said, standing over Orla.

She felt David's eyes on her as she'd stood up there in the bright lights, waiting to see what she'd do. She'd swallowed as she looked out at the townspeople. They already suspected Henry Wright, she didn't need to convince them. She only needed to go along with the narrative.

"What were you doing out there?" Orla had blinked into the bright lights the newspeople had set up, looking for David.

"We went to the yacht to just, you know, hang out during the party." She'd blushed when she said it, knowing how it sounded and feeling suddenly very stupid that her childish crush was being broadcast to the entire island.

"Were you the only ones on the yacht?" the interviewer asked.

Orla finally found David. She could see only the shape of him hanging back next to the doorframe, the broad shoulders and halo of his hair in silhouette.

"No."

She saw Geoffrey Clarke just then, next to David, his arms crossed in front of his chest.

"No, you weren't the only people on the yacht?"

"No, I mean, it was the three of us. Me and David and Alice."

She thought of the way Geoffrey had watched Alice drinking with those men. Was David right? Did Alice lead them on?

"When did you notice Alice was missing?"

"I fell asleep, I think we both did. We'd had a lot to drink," she had explained, looking out at David's unmoving form. "When we woke up, she was gone. And we started looking for her."

"What did you see when you looked down into the water?" the newsperson asked gently.

Ed, the police chief, was on the other side of her suddenly. "You don't have to answer. You can talk to a lawyer if you want," he whispered. But it was too late. The story was already unspooling behind her, too late to change.

"I saw Henry Wright." She began to cry, her shoulders convulsing so hard she could no longer speak. Her lungs burned, unable to fill, as though she were the one drowning. She felt herself being escorted by one of the officers out of the spotlight over to a bench just outside the room, where she put her head down between her knees and was given a glass of water. Through the ringing in her ears she could hear David talking to them again. With his father there he seemed more sure of himself.

"She'd been gone for a while," he'd said to the interviewer. "We were looking for her on the yacht but then thought she might have fallen overboard. I didn't realize that he had come on board while we were sleeping and taken her."

Orla had gasped audibly at the lie. But David's eyes had snapped toward her, daring her to contradict him. She'd choked back tears.

As Geoffrey Clarke led him away, David had turned back to her mouthing, *I'll call you soon.*

But after that she never heard from David Clarke again. And Orla found that the spell was finally broken, because she had already stopped looking for him.

Time passed. Soon it was too much time for a person to survive on their own out in the elements. The more the story was repeated—talked about at the station and whispered in the aisles of Danny's—the more it stuck. Soon the entire island had become convinced. And nobody questioned that it was Henry Wright who had killed Alice.

Geoffrey Clarke made sure his son's story was believed by everyone who mattered. After all, it seemed so plausible that a creepy old man was behind it all, much more plausible than a rich young one, a boy really. But Geoffrey never managed to fully convince the chief of police. Even though she repeated the details of what she saw later that night to the police, shivering in a plastic chair in the station while she could see his broad shoulders hovering outside, making sure his son didn't take the fall.

Interrupting Orla's thoughts, David swerves left now, cutting through her yard. He comes to an abrupt stop next to Alice's house. The flashes of light have stopped. He doubles over and pants for breath, hands on his knees. Alice's house is a series of vague angles in the moonlight.

"The light was probably a reflection. Look. It's gone now," Orla says, comforted by the thought of it.

David's shirt is soaked through on the back. Dark patches of fabric stick to his shoulder blades, rising and falling with each labored breath. He scans the thicket of overgrowth with his phone light. The vines are knitted together, almost completely shut. David pushes through them, kicking and stomping everything down with his dress shoes. Destroying everything until he has made a path. Sharp branches slice at Orla's bare legs, anyway, as she stumbles through the darkness behind him. The light comes on again. One longer flash followed by two short. *Emergency.* She looks to see if David noticed but he is making his way up the sagging front steps to the porch. Orla starts behind him, shining the light from her phone onto the skeletal set of metal chairs and a long bench missing their cushions. She tilts her head up toward the window. Does she see someone there in the dark looking down at her?

"I'm going inside," David says, setting his jaw.

"No! Why?" She reaches for his shoulder to stop him but he ducks away from her grasp and approaches the front door. Orla hopes it is locked, but the knob turns easily in David's hand and the door swings in, letting out a rusty groan. David stops at the threshold, shining his phone into the gloom of the house.

"Are you coming?" David asks impatiently.

Reluctantly she follows him. Of course she does. They step into the hall. In front of them a staircase splits the house, a spacious living room with a fireplace to one side and a dining room to the other. The furniture Orla remembers is still there but it is misshapen from humidity, discolored with mildew. Black mold blooms along the ceiling and across the walls.

That is when she sees the tracks on the dust-coated floor, the unmistakable scuffs of recent footfalls that wind around the house, like someone has been running in circles. The footprints are small and delicate. *A woman's shoe*, she thinks, swallowing.

"David," she calls to his back, her voice thick with fear.

"I see them," he says. His voice wavers. He is afraid too.

Something scurries behind her. Orla can hear the faint scratch of claws on the hardwood floor. She keeps her phone's light trained out in front of her, walking behind David toward the staircase. He steps forward, placing one foot on the bottom stair. It creaks dangerously. Orla swings the light up into the stairwell. The banister is warped, the spindles stretched with a sticky mesh of cobwebs. She glances back at the open front door, the moonlight spilling across the threshold. Through the black mass of vines and brush she can see the water moving in the moonlight. She could turn now and run. She could go back to New York the way she planned. But then what? Could she ever escape Alice?

"You coming?" David calls from the landing. She looks up at his face in the glow of the phone. Her downfall. She could never say no to David. Not when he wants her there. She starts up the stairs behind him.

"Be careful," she gasps as his foot almost goes through a rotten board.

"This place is falling apart," David grumbles. "I don't know why he never tore it down."

"He?" There is a creak far above them. They freeze and look up into the stairwell.

"Shh, do you hear that?" His broad shoulders swivel in both directions.

But Orla already knows where the sound is coming from. A strange terror spreads across her skin as David reaches the landing and turns onto the hall.

"Oh my god," he breathes. When Orla catches up to him, she sees the bright strip of light that shines through the cracks around the door to Alice's room, causing it to appear to float supernaturally at the end of the hallway. They inch toward it, stepping carefully across the rotten floor.

Orla feels like she is in some sort of dream as David reaches his hand to the doorknob. He stops and turns back to her. The look in his eyes is familiar. It's the same kind of helpless fear she saw back when they were teenagers looking through the yacht's window. Orla has the sensation now that she did then, a feeling that things are about to change. That nothing is going to be the same. Not ever again.

Eyes wide, she nods. David turns the knob and pushes the door. It swings in with a horrible groan. The light from inside spills out into the hall. Orla follows him inside blinking until her eyes adjust.

A lone fishing lantern sits on top of the dresser. A single white bulb glows through its metal cage. The walls are black with mold and decay, but Alice's bed is freshly made in the center of the room. A suitcase at its foot is swung open to reveal a pile of neatly folded clothing. Orla's eyes land on a black coat draped over the side of a chair. Its hood sags toward the ground.

"David," Orla breathes, her back prickling. He returns the look, his eyes wide and afraid. "Someone is staying here."

He snatches up the lantern and thrusts it out into the room, illuminating patches of peeling floral wallpaper. A thick fog of spiderwebs obscures the corners, where the room narrows with the eaves. But Orla can feel the presence of someone there with them, holding their breath in the dark, trying not to move.

Another low creak vibrates through the fragile floorboards, this time from behind them. David swings the light toward the sound. Holding the lantern aloft he plunges it into the corner of the room. It takes her a moment to make out the shape of the woman there. Orla lurches back clutching her chest, feeling like her heart might explode. The woman's dress shimmers as she steps out of the corner toward them.

FAITH

Footsteps tap on the deck just below. Faith jerks away from the window and presses her back against the slick outer wall of the yacht. Just over the edge, there is the flash of a white shirt as a deckhand strides past, carrying a stack of fresh linens. When she is sure they've passed, Faith leans carefully back over toward the window. Geoffrey is gone now. The room is completely empty.

As she starts back across the ledge she glances out toward the party. But it is no longer directly across from her. She finds the Clarkes' lawn has slipped behind her and the yacht has started moving. The boat is gliding on the water away from shore into the vast black ocean. The chasm between her and the shore grows. Her foot reaches for the deck.

"Careful. Slippery out there. I'd hate for you to fall." The voice rumbles through the dark behind her. Faith stops. The skin on her neck prickles as she slowly turns around, caught. Geoffrey stands at the far end of the deck. He is holding his drink in one hand. His shirt, unbuttoned on top, shows a gray patch of chest hair.

"Always poking around, aren't you?" he says, smiling a little as she steps fully back onto the deck. "Before you married my son you wanted to know there were no skeletons in the closet?"

She remembers the article she'd read on Geoffrey back when she first met David. One of America's twenty most powerful men. There he is, standing right in front of her. He looks haggard under the overhead lights. His cheeks, scattered with stubble, are hollow in the centers. Not some golden god like they'd have you believe. Just a person.

"Something like that." Her breath is ragged as she watches him, unsure what will come next.

"What did you think you'd find here? A drug ring? Stolen guns?" He raises his brows, amused, and takes a drink. "Underage women, perhaps?" At this Faith takes a step back, coming up against the railing. She's miscalculated.

"I just wanted to make sure. Gemma is missing, and I thought . . ."

"You must think I'm pretty sloppy," Geoffrey says, smirking now.

"No, I—" Faith is caught.

His voice grows louder, angrier. "Funny how you are the one digging for skeletons when your closet is full of them. You have quite the past. *Forgery. Breaking and entering.* I believe those were two separate arrests."

Faith's stomach lurches. "Those were dismissed. I was so young. A child really—"

"They are still findable," he tuts. "You think with this much money I don't have the resources to do a little digging on who my son is dating? Those were only practice, of course. For the big one. I think you know what I'm talking about." He smirks, victorious. "That poor dead woman."

"I had nothing to do with that." Faith feels the blood draining from her head.

"Maybe not. But you were there, weren't you? Lucky they caught the guy and never ran those extra prints or you'd have been in trouble."

"I—" Faith can't find the words to reply to him. She's been trying to uncover his secrets, when all along he's known hers. He must have been saving the information up, waiting to deploy it when it would best serve his needs.

"Why did you let David propose to me, then?" she says. "You wouldn't want a criminal marrying your son."

Geoffrey smiles a bit ruefully at the diamond on her finger. "Oh, the public proposal was my idea. David was having second thoughts, but I convinced him. I like to watch these things play out. I thought a ring might have been enough for you, but it seems like it wasn't."

Faith glances down at it guiltily.

"And I changed my mind somewhere along the way. My son could use a wife. Someone who will keep him reeled in. He needs a bit of control in his life. You are the type who wouldn't just let him walk all over you. No, you'd need to find out what he was up to. You'd have to turn over every single stone." There is tension just below the surface of his skin. It ripples across his face, dragging the corners of his mouth down.

"No, I—" There is a creak below her, and Faith looks down at the water, reeling.

"Your little investigation this time came up dry, though, didn't it? Maybe you're not quite the sleuth you think you are."

"Investigation?"

"Oh, I'm a little bit sharper than you might expect, even for an old man. I have friends in, shall we say, low places. Not that I frequent the Salty Crab myself, mind you."

"Walter? I thought he was friends with Jean."

"That idiot will play any side that pays him well enough." Geoffrey smirks. "So what do you say? Better to keep you close. It's a good deal for you. You get to marry my son. Live a life of comfort. Escape your past."

"In exchange for what?"

"You leaving everything well enough alone," he snaps. His anger drives her back against the railing. "It's a long drive back to Manassas, Oklahoma. Or should we say a long fall?"

Faith looks down at the black water swirling below. Would she make it if she jumped? Could she swim back to shore?

"So, what'll it be, Faith? Maybe it's time to just take your wins and calm down, live your life."

"No."

Geoffrey's expression changes. The volatile smile falls off his face and he steps close to her. His fingers dig into her shoulder. His breath is hot and acrid in her face. "How fucking dare you? You thought you could waltz in here and disrupt everything. Who the fuck are you? Some little nobody from nowhere. Do you know who I am?" Spit gathers in the corners of his mouth as he releases his full Clarke anger on her. "Look at that ring. It's worth more than anything you've ever owned in your life. But it's still not enough for you, is it? Women." He waves his hand, disgusted.

"No. I don't want it," Faith says with sudden clarity. "Not anymore. Not like this."

"Well then, you may as well be dead to me." His hands are on her shoulders in an instant, shoving her with surprising force against the rail. Faith squirms beneath his grasp. He is red-faced, winded. She feels her feet leave the ground. She is tipping back when a small voice breaks through the sound of the waves, barely audible.

"Faith!" The voice makes Geoffrey draw back, surprised. Faith looks over his shoulder as a young woman runs barefoot across the deck, clutching the hem of her long, fitted dress.

"Gemma!" Faith yells to her.

"What are you doing out here?" Geoffrey barks. He spins back toward Gemma, unpinning Faith from the railing. "Who let you out?"

Two very large men have appeared at the top of the glass staircase. There to do Geoffrey's bidding. *The Clarkes have a way of getting out of things.* "Run Gemma!" Faith yells, her feet grip the deck as they run toward the back of the ship. The men follow them, efficiently moving their huge bodies in pursuit. They reach a deck that juts out over the water. The waves rush below, white crests on black.

"I didn't understand what it all meant," Gemma cries. "I thought they were going to help me. I just wanted my future to be better." Faith understands her completely then. She understands the way someone could tie their future to a terrible man. Faith had done it herself.

"We have to jump," Faith whispers, helping Gemma up over the railing as the men close in on them.

"Will we be okay?" Gemma asks, her teeth already chattering. But Faith doesn't answer. There is no time, and she doesn't know. She steps off the ledge, Gemma's hand in hers, and they plummet toward the inky water.

HENRY

Their dresses trail through the night sky like banners until they hit the water with barely perceptible splashes.

Henry steps away from the telescope and dashes outside skidding down the old staircase with panic rising in his throat. He freezes at the threshold of the dock, where he stops and stands, trembling. He can't just leave, can he? What about Margie? He looks up at the windows as though Margie is still inside and he needs to care for her, to keep her safe.

But it was never really safe, was it? Her voice is at his back. It is kind and nurturing.

No, it wasn't, Henry thinks, blinking back tears.

You must go now, Henry.

This will change everything.

Yes.

What about you? But there's no answer.

Margie's sickness had advanced almost without him even noticing. First, she'd spent more time in bed. Then they'd stopped taking meals at the table. It was slow, over the course of months. He should have paid closer attention. He hadn't had time to prepare.

"Bury me here," she'd instructed him near the end. She knew her time was coming, of course she did. But Henry still couldn't imagine it. He shook his head, unwilling to hear her. "Here on the island," she'd repeated.

"Do you want a piece of toast? Some tea?" he asked instead, trying to push away the panic that had gripped his throat.

Her fingers were weak on his arm. She was insistent. "Hush, Henry. Enough, now listen. I don't want to leave this place. Keep me here."

"Stop, Margie, I don't want to hear it," he choked.

"There's a place on the leeward side. The stones are loose. It'll work nicely." She'd said it with enough conviction to send dread coursing through his veins.

"Margie," he had moaned. The horror of it was upon him now. She was telling him the truth.

"I don't want you to leave," Henry admitted.

"I won't leave." She patted his hand. "I will be right here with you, always."

His vision blurred then and he had to look away, to the wood paneling on the walls, slowly going in and out of focus.

"Promise me you'll do what I ask." He had only been able to give her a short nod before leaving her there on the bed. He wanted to shut it out. He'd felt like a curse had been cast as he backed quickly out of the room. As though her saying it out loud was willing it all into existence.

He doesn't have any more time to think. He runs to the boat and drops into the hull. It's been so long since his feet have left the Rock, they feel uncertain in the bottom of the boat. His chest is floating as he pushes off from the dock. Henry pulls at the starter of the small motor with all his might. It sputters at first and then roars to life, drowning out everything else.

FAITH

Up. Faith chokes on the salt water as she thrashes in the surf looking for Gemma. She'd been there only a moment ago. But she'd lost hold of Gemma's hand in that dark water. Now there is no sign of her. Struggling to stay afloat she turns her neck up at the yacht. She catches a glimpse of Geoffrey then. He's been standing at the back of the yacht watching them struggle. As the yacht moves away, his broad shoulders and square head turn from the railing and disappear into the cabin. Satisfied that she and Gemma are done for.

Faith tries to scream. A wave obscures her view, crashing over her head. *Down.* Water rushes into her mouth as she descends. It burns her throat. She kicks, kicks. She is getting tired now.

Up. She looks longingly at the shoreline, where the Clarkes' party glitters in the distance. A song carries lightly across the waves. Something her mom used to play on the jukebox at their local dive bar.

Down. Her limbs are getting heavy. They move in slow motion against the waves, fighting, fighting.

Up. This will surely be the last time. Faith barely hits the surface, tilting her head back only to release a scream from her raw throat for the last time. She looks up at the sky, the deep gray film of clouds moving across the field of stars.

Down down down. Below the surface everything is smooth and black. Faith shouldn't have risked it. It was reckless. What was any of it worth now? She sees her mother's face, disappointed. Her mouth twists in pain. "You know I did my best."

I know, Faith says to her. *I'm sorry too.* A hand reaches hers in the darkness, fingers interlacing with her own. But it is too late. She can't stay awake anymore.

HENRY

Henry finds Gemma first. She is holding Faith's head above the water as best she can, bobbing and coughing as the two of them are bounced around by the swells. He cuts the engine and reaches into the waves, bracing himself against the thin metal as the boat tilts precariously. With all his might he pulls Faith from the water onto the floor of the little boat.

As he takes Gemma's hands and helps her up over the side he glances up, halfway expecting a beam of light to expose him just like it did last time. But the yacht is far away from them now, speeding away from shore as though trying to escape what its inhabitants have done.

Faith coughs violently in the hull of the boat. The force of the cold air and rocking boat assaults her at once. Turning to the side, she throws up violently onto the hard metal hull of the boat. Her eyes fly open. They go wide with fear when she sees him above her. He can imagine what he looks like. Pale, slack-jawed, his wild hair catching the light. She lets out a guttural scream and thrashes violently, kicking her bare feet out at him. Henry dodges them, rocking onto his heels.

"It's okay," Gemma says from just behind him. "He helped us, Faith."

"Are you all right? Are you hurt?" Henry's voice is hoarse.

Faith looks down at herself and nods. She shakily pulls herself up on her arms in the bottom of the boat. The soaking fabric of her party dress wraps around her, curling at her feet.

They sway there, quietly. Henry watches as she assesses the situation, the tiny boat, surrounded by dark waves, and finally him, the strange man across from her.

"You're Henry Wright, aren't you?" Faith says. Her voice, wobbly and thin, startles him. When he turns to her, she is looking at him with curiosity.

He nods in affirmation.

"David told me about you."

Henry clears his throat, feeling a hot buzz of shame travel through his body. "Don't believe everything you hear," he says quietly. He begins to row again, heading into the shore.

"I would never. Not from that family." Faith wraps her arms tighter around herself.

As though just now remembering what happened, her fingers grasp the side of the boat, and she turns herself frantically looking out over the water. "Where is it?"

"The yacht? It left." He shakes his head.

"They meant to just let us drown out there," Gemma says, shivering.

Henry squints at the shore. The lights from the harbor blur in front of him. "Margie, my wife, never trusted Geoffrey."

"That vile man." Faith looks down at the ring on her finger, her mouth twisting in disgust.

"I'm afraid that even if you did expose him, a man like Geoffrey would find a way to worm himself out of any sort of punishment," Henry says bitterly.

"He nearly got away with it again," Faith says. "He would have killed Gemma just like Alice."

He looks at her in surprise. "Geoffrey Clarke didn't kill Alice."

"What do you mean?" Faith asks, staring at him with open surprise on her face. "Who did?"

But Henry's jaw has dropped open. He is looking across the water at the Gallo house. The door on the front porch is flung wide open. And above, in the upstairs window, a light flickers, illuminating the waifish shape of a woman in a sparkling dress.

ORLA

There was never a body. That was always the problem. With no body there could be no closure. Not for Orla, anyway. Not ever again. There was always Alice. She was everywhere Orla went. In the halls at school. Every time a car passed her house at night, sending its headlights though Orla's curtains. And most of all in the water, her legs and arms moving below the swells, her hair tangled up with the seaweed.

Orla thought she could escape her by moving away to New York. But she saw Alice there too. Waiting on subway platforms as Orla's train sped by, eyeing her on the periphery of parties, drink in hand. Sometimes Orla would approach, cautiously, only to realize that it wasn't her. It was someone else. Someone who really didn't look anything like her at all.

After a while Alice's presence almost became a normal part of Orla's existence. Her friend's ghostly appearances reminding her of her guilt. It was part of the reason Orla could never let go, never fully relax. At night her heart would pump with fear. *She's dead*, she would remind herself then.

But now Alice is standing right in front of Orla. So stunningly beautiful and alive that Orla feels like she is dreaming. She is wearing a dress that looks almost exactly like the one she wore that last night. The sequins shimmer like liquid as she steps out of the corner toward them.

"I can't believe you're real. How are you real?" Orla starts toward Alice, her body flooding with relief. This is her chance to fix everything. She can still make things right. Her eyes sting with tears. "All this time I've lived with you inside my head, praying there was some way that you made it, that you were okay. And look at you here, alive." Tears are spilling down her cheeks as she reaches out to embrace her best friend.

But Alice's face doesn't soften at her remorse. Her body stiffens and she looks Orla dead in the eye.

"Are you sure of that, Orla? Or do you want to make sure *you're* okay? You want me to tell you I forgive you? I don't." Orla draws back, stunned. "And David, of course. Lucky little rich boy almost got away with murder, huh?" Alice says now, walking toward them across her rotting bedroom.

"Alice—" David starts, putting a hand up as though to stop her from continuing. But she merely looks at him, amused.

"You had plenty of chances to come clean about that night. You could have told the reporters the truth. Wouldn't it have been better for you to face the consequences? Maybe you could have saved yourself then, disconnected yourself from your father, David. But the both of you were so selfish. It took me so long to trust anyone again. To find another friend."

"You have to help me," Alice said when Orla came to, a throbbing pain behind her eyes as she took stock of where she was. Still on the yacht, lying down on one of the long sofas the men had been hanging out on. She looked to the floor, where the nearly empty bottle of gin was tipped on its side.

"I need to get out of here," Alice said, sounding far away. Orla's eyelids were still so heavy. She forced herself to look in the direction of her friend's voice. Alice stood in the doorway at the far end of the room in her sparkly dress. It was torn at the bottom, Orla noticed, a jagged rip that went up one side and exposed her leg. It was then Orla realized that Alice wasn't talking to her. She was talking to David who stood just in front of her, his arm stretched across the doorway blocking her path.

"He's Dad's friend. You can't just leave."

Alice had lowered her voice then. It shook with fear. "No, David. He is messed up. Please."

"What did you think was going to happen?" David sneered. "You said you wanted this. You were flirting with them all night."

Orla shoved herself up onto her elbows. Her head hurt like it had been split in two as she tried to focus on them. *Wanted what?*

"No, I—I thought they were going to help me. They said they were going to take me to New York, take my art around to some galleries. I thought it was just drinks. A party. I didn't realize." Her voice was growing desperate.

"Alice?" Orla's voice stuck in her throat. They didn't hear her. Her body was slow and heavy as she pulled herself to stand. The gentle movement of the boat sent her careening into the wall. She moved along the side toward the doorway. David was still blocking Alice's path.

"These guys are sick," Alice said, starting to cry. "They say I owe them."

"This was your choice," David repeated, unmoved. Orla hadn't ever heard him sound that way, like all the emotion had been drained from him. Later she told herself that he was drunk, too, that this might just have been his way of responding to too much alcohol.

"If you don't help me get out of here, I am going to tell everyone that your dad did this to me. He can't get away with this."

"No, you're fucking not," David murmured. His voice had become disturbingly calm. Now Orla was running with shaky footsteps toward them.

Alice registered Orla there, and a look of relief spread across her face just as David's hand came down on her shoulders.

"What are you doing?" Orla cried as David drove Alice back into the guardrail.

"Don't you ever fucking threaten me." His newly broad shoulders flexed menacingly.

"David! Stop!" But it was too late. Alice was falling over the side. There was barely a splash as she hit the water. By the time the two of them got to the edge, there was no sign she'd ever been there at all.

"Alice," Orla called out, filled with instant, horrified regret.

"What do we do?" she'd cried to David. "We have to go find her."

"She fell," David had said, not moving.

"What are you talking about, David?" Orla looked at him uncertainly. "Alice," she screamed then, panicking. "We have to find her." She'd shoved David in the chest. Why was he not moving, not reacting? "What are you doing?"

He was frozen, looking out at the water.

"Alice?" Orla had screamed. She'd pointed the flashlight down into the water, and that's when she saw Henry Wright in his little boat. He was holding her friend's dress. At first she thought it was Alice. But then he turned his face up toward her, white as a ghost in the beam of the light, and Orla could see that all he had was a scrap of empty fabric. It shone from his hands.

Geoffrey had boomed out at them, "David? What are you doing here?"

"She fell," David said, the lie so smooth and confident it had knocked the wind out of her.

Geoffrey's mouth twitched as he did some mental calculus. Orla felt as though she could see him planning, projecting all the possible outcomes in front of him, and his face settled into something of a satisfied smile as he lifted his phone to his ear and stormed from the deck.

"Oh, David didn't kill me," Alice says now to Orla. "But you thought he did. And you covered for him."

"I thought we paid you to stay far away." David is sweating now, his face turned down in an angry scowl.

Orla spins toward him, sputtering in disbelief. "You knew? All this time you knew she was alive?"

"Dad's men found her. She'd somehow made it to shore. They helped her start over," he says, staring at Alice and ignoring Orla. In the light of the fishing lamp, Orla can see the sweat gathering on his forehead. "They helped her mother, too, in agreement that they leave it alone, and that they never *come back*."

"Helped is a strong word for what you did," Alice says. "You helped yourselves. You paid us all off."

"You've been here all along, haven't you?" Orla thinks of the paint inside the crawl space and the flashing lights she was sure she was hallucinating.

Alice smiles in admission.

"You signed an agreement," David says, his voice rising into a whine. "It's legally binding."

"I planned to keep to my NDA. I really did. I'd just come up here to lurk from afar. But my plan changed when Faith told me about Gemma going missing. Then I knew I had to intervene. I couldn't let you get away with it a second time."

"You're crazy. Totally fucking crazy. I should never have helped you." David is holding his phone to his ear. "Pick up, pick up," he mutters angrily.

"Where are you going?" Orla cries, pulling the phone away from his ear.

"I have to find my dad." He shoves her off him and she falls hard into the corner, cracking her head on the low eave.

"No one wants to end up in prison for grooming children. No money can protect you there. But you don't think you can go to prison, do you? Not David Clarke," Alice says.

Orla pulls herself up from the floor in time to see Alice give him a rueful smile. "Oh, Geoffrey is long gone. Ran off on his yacht. See for yourself."

Orla glances through the open door to the rounded hall window. It would have once framed a view of the mooring but is now completely empty, the waves illuminated by a crescent moon. David looks like he might be sick.

"Left you to take the fall, didn't he? I guess Daddy doesn't want to get caught doing something naughty." Alice taps her chin. "It all feels familiar somehow, doesn't it?"

"You shut up," David roars, pointing his finger in her face. Alice blinks but seems unfazed by this outburst. Orla can tell that Alice is relishing this moment. Orla always knew her friend was talented and kind, but she realizes now that Alice is also so incredibly brave.

"What are you going to do? Warn him that I am here? And that I know what he's done with little Gemma?"

"David? Is all this true?" A new voice comes from the doorway.

"Faith?" David calls out to her. "Are you okay? God, why are you soaking wet? What happened?" He says it in a tone that implies he thinks he might still be able to salvage this situation for himself. "We should go back to the house, get you cleaned up."

Orla looks on in disbelief as he reaches his hand toward Faith.

But Faith is staring at David as though they've never met. "Henry Wright brought me here. Turns out he's not the villain in all this. But you know that already, don't you? That poor man. All this time I thought you were protecting your father but you're in on it all too. How many girls have you recruited for him? Was it just Gemma and Alice or were there more?"

"You have to give me a chance to explain. Because what you are suggesting is just wrong." David's voice rises sharply. He takes a step toward her. The floor creaks dangerously. "The girl, Gemma, she needed help. Please, I need you to believe me."

"You're right, she did need help." Faith's lip quivers. She stands there a moment looking between them all, trying to decide what to do. Her shoulders finally drop and she stretches her hand toward him.

"Thank you," he breathes. "I promise I can explain everything."

But as David starts toward her, Faith moves to the side of him and it becomes clear it isn't his hand she is reaching for. Alice steps around David and her fingers entwine with Faith's.

"Elena," Faith breathes, pulling her into an embrace. "I was so worried."

Orla watches from the corner of the room, stunned. "You two are friends?"

"Best friends," Alice says, giving her a sly smile. Orla draws back, wounded. How could those words hurt her still? Like she was fifteen again.

David's lips part at Faith in outrage. "You little traitorous bitch. After all I did for you," he sputters, turning to Alice. "And *you*, you didn't even know how good you had it. I'm going to bury you for good this time."

David begins to stomp toward the door. He has almost reached Orla when a violent crack rattles the floor. He wobbles for a moment, his face contorting in a spectrum of shock and disbelief as the floor begins to splinter below him. David looks at Orla and his mouth opens in surprise. Everything has always gone his way until now. There was nothing his father couldn't fix. Except this.

A scream rips from Orla's throat as the floor gives way, crumbling below them. There is a deafening crack followed by a burst of dust as the center of the house collapses and swallows them up.

FAITH

Faith shines the light from her phone into the empty space where only seconds before David and Orla had stood, but it can't penetrate the tangle of debris and boards below.

"David? Orla?" Elena calls out into the chasm. There is no reply, only the creaks and moans of the house settling.

"I'm Alice Gallo," Elena had admitted to Faith finally, the week before the engagement. She had told her the whole story the moment she'd found out about Gemma's disappearance, explaining how Geoffrey's men had searched until they found Alice, alone in the dark treading water. "I think they wished I had died. It would have been so much less messy. So much cheaper."

They took her back to the yacht, where Geoffrey had held her against her will until Alice signed the NDA. The payment would be enough to keep her very comfortable in the city she'd always wanted to live in. Her only stipulation was that her mother be able to come too. "She'd been through so much with my dad, I could never have let her think I was dead."

After a respectable amount of time had passed, her mother followed her to the city, and the two of them severed all ties to the island. "But I could never fully move on. Of course I couldn't. You can never truly escape the place you came from. Especially when your new friend starts dating the son of your kidnapper."

"Why didn't you tell me about David?" Faith had said, hurt.

"I signed an NDA, remember? What if you had lived happily ever after? I couldn't risk blowing up my entire life. And my mother's." She paused. "And I was curious, I suppose. I wanted David to have grown up, to have changed."

"It would seem he didn't," Faith said bitterly, still processing the information.

"No. He is still his father's son. He never changed like he wanted to."

Faith had begun to panic once she heard what he was capable of.

"I'm all alone here. And Geoffrey knows that I know something. I'm sure of it. He's been dropping hints."

There had been a long pause on the other side. "You're not alone. I'm here. I thought if I could keep a close enough eye on you—" She'd broken off. "I've been staying in the house."

Faith was stunned. "The abandoned one? You've been there all alone?"

"I wanted to be close, in case something happened. But listen to me, Faith. You should leave now. Go back to New York on the next ferry. You can forget this whole thing ever happened. I'm sorry. I didn't want you involved in all this. It wasn't fair of me."

"No," Faith had said, surprising herself. "I need to stay and find Gemma. I could never forgive myself if something happened to her now after everything I know."

"I'll help you," Elena had said right away, and they'd spent the next hours carefully devising a plan.

"What if David sees you, or Geoffrey?" Faith had asked right before they hung up. Elena, now Alice, had snorted derisively. "I might be the only person on the planet who is not afraid of Geoffrey Clarke."

*   *   *

There is a clatter as loose flooring falls now through the hole in front of them.

"It's not safe up here," Elena says, pulling Faith back from the edge. They inch their way down the hall, Faith's hand on Elena's shoulder, carefully taking the stairs to the first floor. The house shifts and groans around them.

On the way through the living room Faith's flashlight catches on a chair printed with moldy red flowers. Her mom is perched on the edge of it. Her hair is wet. Her face, free of makeup, looks dignified, beautiful. She smiles, a real smile.

"You dodged a bullet with that one, baby girl."

"Sure did."

"Look at you. I'm so proud of you."

Elena's voice echoes through the dark. "Faith, over here. I found them."

Faith follows Elena's voice though the living room to the place where the upstairs floor had given way. They shine their flashlights into the pile of rotted boards. A ring of debris surrounds the space where David and Orla fell. Their lights catch the dust, refracting in a halo of particles falling gently around them like snow. As it settles, Faith can finally see the shape of them, there in the middle. David's limbs are twisted, bent at unnatural angles over a pile of broken floorboards. His mouth and eyes are still open in shock. His chest is still. David has broken Orla's fall. She landed artfully on the center of his body, her arms stretched out as though she is still trying to embrace him, covering him with a veil of fine red hair.

THE SALTY CRAB

Y ou can't live trying to avoid all the bad things in the world. There's no place you can safely hide and not enough money that will truly protect you. That's what Faith's mother had told her back at their local dive bar, and it's what Faith and Henry mused about later after everything had finally settled down, when fall came and reclaimed the island for the locals. Henry had been a fool to try and hide from what happened fifteen years ago. But there is still a chance for a fresh start. And for the first time he feels a lightness in his step as he makes his way through town toward the Crab.

Henry gets the occasional look from a local as he walks through town or helps Jean in the bar. Some of them, especially those who are drunk enough, will ask him questions about that night or the other more recent one, the night when he redeemed himself—or so the gossip went—by saving two girls from drowning. Though Henry never saw it that way. He didn't need redemption. He will answer them honestly and quickly, moving along to change over a keg or ring someone through at the till. Most people say nothing. He can only see the curiosity in their eyes when they look at him a beat longer than normal. But he'll take it. You can't please everyone. Any place can be hell, even paradise.

He does the books for Jean these days, taking stock of kegs of beer and frozen bags of french fries, of payrolls and the quarters inside the pool table. It's fulfilling in its own way. He likes the rhythm of it, the regularity with which he sees people. They all tell him their business now, freely. The novelty of saying hi to local passersby hasn't yet dulled. He's even had a few dinners out and has been relieved to find his table manners intact.

Though he misses it sometimes, his old view of the houses lit from within like a Christmas village lined up on a mantelpiece, Henry has been surprised at the relief he feels in being away from the Rock. If not for the events of last summer, he might never have left. The house is falling down now, the stilts sagging and bent. Henry is getting ready to tear it down. The island will be Margie's memorial.

"Hi, Henry," Faith says, sliding into a stool in front of him. "Good to see you."

Henry was surprised that she'd stayed on with Alice after the Fourth, sharing a rental in town. Alice had some things to take care of, and Faith hadn't seen any reason to leave. She wanted to support her friend. And there was the matter of Geoffrey's impending trial. In the wake of David's death, he'd tried to pin it all on his son, but his influence had begun to crumble the moment Gemma spoke into the camera the following morning. She has a flair for the dramatic, it turns out. And a face for television, according to Faith.

"How's Orla lately?" Jean asks, tucking a bar towel into her apron.

"She's doing fine. Expected to make a full recovery," Alice, who has seated herself beside Faith, assures Jean and Henry. "We'll see if our relationship does too. Doubtful."

"I still feel awful about what happened," Faith admits. "God, I just wanted to get away from that family. I never wanted him to *die*. David never really had a chance at a normal life."

"He had plenty of chances," Alice reminds her. "All his life."

Jean slides a drink toward them.

"Is that . . . ?" Henry starts, a laugh beginning in his throat.

"Disgusting." Alice shudders. "The smell, I can't."

"We don't judge here," Jean says, looking down the bar at Walter. "Not even people who fraternize with the enemy."

Henry has stopped with the logbooks. He no longer feels compelled to keep them. Perhaps he needed them once to keep himself from fading. To prove he was still here. He doesn't need that anymore. The village does it for him. There were more than a few apologies when Henry returned to the island. "We always knew you weren't to blame," a few of them said. *Did they?* Maybe not. But Henry doesn't have the time or energy to be cynical. Who knows what he would have thought if he'd been in their shoes? For now, he takes in their goodwill gladly, letting it heal him.

He knows that there are two sides to living someplace so small. The downsides are obvious—the isolation, the tedium, the relentless gossip. But there are invisible benefits to everyone around you knowing your business. It means that there are always people you can call for help, people who know you well enough they can tell your stories for you long after you are gone.

ACKNOWLEDGMENTS

There were many times when I didn't know if I would be able to finish this book. I wrote most of it at the end of my pregnancy and then picked it back up again in the haze of postpartum. It was so important for me to come back to writing and to myself, but I found that looked so different than it had before. I had less time, of course, and also less focus. So I eked out hours here and there while the baby slept or while my mom played with him. I appreciate the help and support I had during that time. Writing is a different kind of job without a strict schedule, and I am so grateful I was able to work when it is always easier not to.

I am as always grateful to my agent, Alexandra, for steering me through sometimes rough waters and to Maudee and Falon for being so good at what you do. Thanks to Lara for her guidance and to Kate for her leadership.

Thank you to my husband, Tim, for reading more versions of this than anyone should have to, and to my mom for providing a sounding board about plot and character.

Thank you to the people of Jamestown, my island home, for being so supportive of my career and coming out to celebrate my books each year. This book is closer to home than the other two, and I hope you enjoy it!